CRAZY
TO
LEAVE YOU

ALSO BY MARILYN SIMON ROTHSTEIN

Lift and Separate

Husbands and Other Sharp Objects

CRAZY TO LEAVE YOU

A Novel

MARILYN SIMON ROTHSTEIN

LAKE UNION
PUBLISHING

Published by Lake Union Publishing, Seattle

www.apub.com

Amazon, the Amazon logo, and Lake Union Publishing are trademarks of Amazon.com, Inc., or its affiliates.

ISBN-13: 9781542034487
ISBN-10: 1542034485

Cover design by David Drummond

Printed in the United States of America

In loving memory of my parents.
And for Alan.

Chapter 1

Diets consumed me. I was either on my way up or on my way down the scale. I called my family with news of my engagement and launched my prewedding diet plan. It was a Saturday. I had never kicked off a diet on any day but a Monday. I had never started one in the middle of a day. Early that morning, Eric David Farkas had gotten down on his khaki-clad knee and asked me to marry him. At the time, we were floating—buoyant in a red-and-white hot-air balloon. He said he would have brought the ring, but he had taken it to be reset. I couldn't have cared less about a ring. Only Eric was of interest to me. We sipped champagne from real crystal glasses. We ate strawberries dipped in white chocolate. We marveled at the world below. Everything that happened in the hot-air balloon was more romantic than I had dared to dream. And I had done a lot of dreaming. I held a record among my friends I could have done without—I was the last to marry.

Upon descent, I was flabbergasted to find Eric's parents, Myrna and Short Stanley, on the ground, gunning to take over, specifically with the wedding. My future mother-in-law was a retired event planner. No one mentioned she was a dictator. I had ideas, expressed and repressed, about the big day—the venue, the music, the menu, the time of year. However, Eric acquiesced to his mother, whose idea of an unpretentious, small, informal gathering was the annual fashion gala attended by A-list celebrities at the Metropolitan Museum of Art.

The wedding had to happen at Temple Sons of Abraham, their longtime place of worship, scene of Eric's over-the-top bar mitzvah and his parents' wedding during the Reagan years. Myrna had contacted the synagogue already. There had been a cancellation. We could hold our wedding on a Sunday in March, dreariest month of the year. The best I could hope for was black ice. The worst? A snowstorm that made it impossible for anyone to attend. Forget the month, Lauren, and the venue. Get married and start living your life.

From then on, I dieted, surviving on four organic egg whites for breakfast, green salad—no dressing—for lunch. Dinnertime, I grilled a six-ounce fillet of salmon—illegally on my tiny terrace overlooking a schoolyard in Manhattan. I searched five states for six months looking for the perfect wedding gown. I was so full of pride to finally fit into a size 12, I would've worn the tag down the aisle instead of the actual dress.

On my wedding day, I waited, breathless, in the bridal quarters at Temple Sons of Abraham. The suite was elaborate, the square footage of a studio co-op in the city or a living room anywhere else. An uneasy bottle-blond waitress in a tuxedo delivered smoked-salmon cucumber bites, tuna tartare cones, brie-pear-pecan lollipops, Perrier, and Prosecco to me, personally, as two hundred black-tie-optional guests were welcomed at a spirited, booze-infused gathering in the rotunda of the synagogue.

I was euphoric, buzzing in my dazzling wedding gown, white satin and lace, a backless A-line with long, tapered sleeves. I am five eight and chose silver high heels, making me the height of my intended. I preferred a natural look—a touch of makeup on my fair skin, neutral shadow, and a bit of mascara on my dark-brown eyes; beach waves of long chestnut hair; a sheer, floor-length veil. The bridal bouquet was a cascading cluster of white roses, peonies, hydrangea.

My best friends were with me—in teal. Teal was the color of the season. Everything was teal. We had ordered the strapless dresses—similar but not identical—from Francesca Dare's Bridal. Although a sign in the fitting room said tailoring was included, Francesca attempted to charge us for alterations. Weddings are one con after another. My longtime hairstylist tacked on a day-of-the-wedding surcharge. I should have lied, told Angel I was the keynote speaker at an advertising conference that afternoon.

Kate Kaufman, my best friend from summer camp, handed me a gift box with "Lauren" written in big letters as though she might forget it was for me. It was the five-speed Ultra-Deluxe Fem Discreet G-Spot Vibrator. On the slim carton was a cover girl, maybe sixteen in real life. She was ecstatic in a see-through negligee. Also, there were directions—with arrows: how to use a vibrator. I think I knew that already.

I hugged my gift. "Well, it's something blue. Now I have to hope it's not borrowed."

"Just preused," Joanna said in jest.

Joanna Wells and I were in the advertising business. We worked together at Steinbach Kraus. I was in account management. Joanna was a media maven specializing in television commercials. She bought time . . . literally.

"I love it," I said, regarding the vibrator. "How did you know, Kate? I'm sure it will fit perfectly. And every time I use it, I will think of you."

"Lauren, please don't."

"I swear you haven't changed since sleepaway camp."

Back when we were cocounselors, caring for third graders, Kate had given me a rubber plant—a potted rhododendron blooming with condoms. In fact, camp was where I had first met Eric. I had even made out with him behind Bunk 8 when we were thirteen. We didn't date until I was thirty-nine years old and bumped into him at the annual reunion. I had no desire to attend the event, but I had been persuaded by Kate, relentless Kate. At the opening reception, in the great barn converted to a recreation hall, I was happy to spot Eric, more handsome than I remembered.

Eric had approached with an impish grin. He asked whether I would enjoy a drink. I said no, because I didn't want him to veer to the bar on the far side of the congested room and be hijacked by another single woman who also noticed Eric had become attractive with age.

"Do you remember me?" he asked, as though I should.

Yes, I thought. *How could I forget? You were my first kiss. I was thirteen. I raced back to my bunk to tell Kate all about it.*

"Bunk 8," he said.

Historic Bunk 8.

"Did you say 9?" I said, toying with him.

He smiled mischievously. Then he confessed, "That was my first kiss."

"Your first kiss. My first kiss. Kismet."

We grinned at each other. I liked grinning at him, enjoyed flirting with him.

When Eric was thirty, he had invented an innovative way to scan groceries. He sold the patent to a supermarket conglomerate, spending a portion of his nest egg to launch Eric's Famous—his small-batch mayonnaise company. "We are artisanal," he liked to say.

Before rediscovering Eric, I never thought about mayonnaise—except when chopping Bumble Bee Tuna, for which I opened Hellmann's, which was what my mother used, but only for my father, because my mother thought mayonnaise was the work of the devil and ate her tuna dry. Eric loved mayonnaise. On our third date, we toured his headquarters, an old loft he said he was fortunate to buy for less than a song, a hum, because the neighborhood was turning over. A couple, faded jeans, white T-shirts, the husband in a baseball cap, the wife with shiny, swinging hair, passed us on the street, their twins asleep in a double stroller. Mom sipped iced tea. Dad commandeered the stroller.

Eric said, "Lauren, tell me. Would you push the kids or would I?"

Who asks that on a third date? A third-date question would be "Travel much?"

That night, I called Kate in Chicago. "I'm going to marry Eric." "Is he aware of this?" Kate said.

Weeks later, Eric and I laughed our way through Friday-afternoon traffic on our drive to Cape Cod. We lingered five nights at the Crusty Crustacean, a romantic inn, a stroll to Nauset Beach. We fired up the stone fireplace. We soaked in the hot tub on the deck. We walked to town. We biked the Cape Cod Rail Trail. We read at the beach. We dozed by the pool. Evenings, the innkeeper served warm cookies gooey with chocolate chips as well as wine and brandy in the parlor. We drank a lot. We fantasized about living at the Crusty Crustacean forever.

Back in New York, we stayed at his one-bedroom or mine. I imagined planning our wedding, then having a baby. I visualized our young son in Little League telling us "batter" was his favorite position; years later, Eric and me imploring our teen prodigy to finish his college essay—*write why you want to help people*. Eric loved my plan. And I loved Eric.

My youngest sister, Stephanie, appeared at the door of the bridal quarters. Stephanie was my person of honor and my mother's favorite daughter.

My eldest sister, Margo, an actress who lived in Santa Monica, was not in attendance. Her birth name was Madeline, but she switched it, mostly to annoy my mother. Also, she swapped out our surname, which was Leo, to Lamour. Margo Lamour.

Family celebrations were not Margo's thing. Actually, our family was not her thing. My mother ignited my sister. She had done it forever, and she could do it without a match. Nevertheless, I was wounded Margo had said "not a chance" to my bridal party and "no" to the wedding, devastated she wouldn't grin and bear it for me, the sister she liked. Certainly, I had stood plenty of ground for her.

I waved my newest accessory, the vibrator, in Stephanie's direction. "Look at this thoughtful wedding gift. Kate, you should have bought two, we could fence."

Stephanie had seductive green eyes like my mother. Her hair was blunt, to the point, chestnut, like mine, but with strategic highlights. She wore a sleeveless dress—also teal—a cinched silver belt with a bow, teal sequins accentuating her waist. I had never worn a bow—even in my hair. A bow called too much attention to my hips. Tell me, please: Does this body make me look fat?

Stephanie barged in, speaking rapid-fire, pointing her teacher finger. "There's a change. Rabbi Millstein would like Kate and Joanna in the chapel now. I'll wait here with the beautiful bride." No one ever questioned Stephanie. My girlfriends filed out, glancing back to beam at me.

"Right behind you," I said, tingling with eagerness and excitement.

Kate replied, "Wahoo. Go get him, Lauren."

I could still see Kate's back when Stephanie took my arms. I was ready for her to say something endearing or give me a special gift.

Instead, her face lost color, and she said, "I received a strange message from Eric."

"What? Why?"

"He said he was backing out. He was backing out of the wedding."

My brain couldn't process what she was saying. I took a breath, another breath. Had my heart stopped?

"He called? On the phone?"

"He texted."

"Eric texted to tell you he is not marrying me?"

Who does that? No one does that, I thought. *That can't possibly be.*

Stephanie was crying. Her tears scared me.

"He texted?" I repeated like I believed all she had said except for the part about the texting. I felt chills through my neck, a cold creep that moved into my head. I began to shiver.

"It's freezing in here. Turn up the heat," I said.

"It's on," Stephanie said.

"Where's the text?" I said, fumbling with her phone, dropping it, then scrambling to pick it up.

My eyes stung at Eric's sentence: "Please tell Lauren I am too young (emotionally) to get married."

Who used parentheses in a text?

In a panic, I rushed to the vanity, snatched my iPhone, and hit number 1. Eric was 1. He had been 1 for two years. Eric's cell rang. And rang. And rang. Of course he wasn't going to answer. Not if he was the runaway groom.

But he wasn't. It was too ridiculous. We weren't kids. We were forty-one years old. Eric would never do this to me. He loved me. I loved him. We were planning a family. I had been off the birth-control pills for a year, attempting a jump start. I yearned for two kids—at least. Eric, an only child, preferred one. I believed Eric would change his mind, have a second child when he realized how amazing it was to parent. We talked about visiting our kid at our camp. How we would know all the songs.

"He's not picking up," I said to Stephanie. "He won't pick up."

"Leave a message."

"And say what?"

"He's supposed to be here," she declared, as though I were ignorant of the situation.

"I think he knows that."

I sweated as my disbelief became panic. My last-ditch hope of a wonderful family, swirling down the drain. I disconnected. I counted to ten and tried again.

"What do you want to do?" Stephanie said.

"What the . . . ?" I hollered, freaked out.

"Listen, I am sorry to be the one he texted. I am sorry he texted! Did you have a hint of what he was thinking?"

Did I? About a month before, I had noticed he was seeing his psychologist more often. Three times a week? However, I didn't have a clue Eric was "too young," parenthesis, "emotionally," end parenthesis. I felt I might collapse. My phone rang in my hand, startling me.

"Lauren?" Eric said, whispering, his quiet voice alarming.

"What is going on?" I cried before he could say another word. Maybe something dreadful had happened.

"I'm okay," he said. But he sounded like he wasn't.

"What does that mean?"

"I can't do it. I-I'm not ready to do it," he stammered.

"What? What are you saying?"

"It's not my time. I'm not ready—emotionally."

"Emotionally" again? I had never heard him say this word before.

I could fix this. Sweetly, I said, "Eric, my Pooh Bear, you're anxious. All grooms are anxious."

"I need to back out."

"Well, Eric. I am in my wedding gown waiting to walk down the aisle. Do you think you could have thought of this sooner?"

"I did."

"What?" He hadn't mentioned it sooner.

"I've been thinking about bailing since the moment my pop signed the contract with the synagogue. I knew something was off when I allowed my parents to get involved, to take over the show, the entire event, even though I knew it wasn't what you wanted."

I wanted to scream until my head popped off, but if I remained composed, even-keeled, maybe Eric would understand how off the roof and out of his mind he was. "It doesn't matter. The synagogue is fine."

Ignoring me, he continued. "And then once we started—with guests I swear my parents plucked from a faded phone book, the invitations with the typo, that ridiculous tasting where my mom insisted gluten-free was just a hoax and your father said kale would leave him on the pot for the rest of the night. I'm not ready to get married. Dr. Breen-Donnelly says I have to find my own way."

"He meant your own way away from your parents."

"No. He meant my own way."

"No. Wrong. Incorrect. The shrink meant your own way away from your parents." I spoke as though providing careful instructions, specifications that would save my life.

Eric didn't require a psychiatric workup. He was a sheltered only child, a late-in-life surprise. His parents were as annoying as vaginitis. His father called me Laurie or Laura, never Lauren. His mother was certain everyone was out to get her. But if you spent an afternoon with her, you didn't want to get her—you wanted to run in the opposite direction.

"We will be married, and we will find our own way," I said.

"I'm not ready to be married. I am not. And do you know when I accepted that? Truly accepted it?"

I shuddered, terrified to guess.

"At my bachelor party."

Someone pick my heart up from the floor. "You flew to New Orleans for a weeklong celebration with an entourage of friends. You swigged Hurricanes on the street, listened to jazz, binged on the beignets, ate elaborate brunches, and slept with a blow-up doll."

"How do you know about the blow-up doll?"

"Calvin told Glenn. Glenn told Kate. Kate told me."

"I loved New Orleans. I didn't want to come home. I looked for an apartment near Bourbon Street. New Orleans is less expensive than New York. I could live like a king in a place with a historic marker."

"Eric, you already live very nicely." *He is lost,* I thought. *He's panicking. Stay calm, Lauren. Be the grown-up. Everything will be all right.* "Eric, tell me where you are, and I'll come there."

"In a Starbucks."

Did he actually say Starbucks? "You're breaking up with me over coffee? Tell me you don't have a coffee. Or worse, a cappuccino you waited for."

"I had to use the bathroom. There's only one, and there's a line."

I took in Stephanie, on the couch with two round pillows on her teal lap. She sighed, "Oh, Lauren," as she shook her head repeatedly left to right, right to left, and back again.

Then I heard Eric say, "28357."

"Are you speaking to me?" I said, infuriated that he might be chatting with a stranger in Starbucks.

"No."

"Then what are those numbers?"

"The combination for the restroom."

How could this be happening? I was a good person. I didn't deserve this.

"Don't do it, Eric. Don't give out numbers while I'm dying here." "Dying" was probably an understatement.

"He really had to go," Eric said.

"Eric, I'll come to Starbucks, and we'll talk."

"No," he said. "It's done. It's over."

"Please stop this," I said, my despair mounting.

"Lauren, listen to me. I want you to have everything. Keep the presents. Keep the gift cards. And you can keep the ring. Well, maybe not the ring. The diamond belonged to my mother's great-great-aunt, and she did bring the stone, sewn into a winter coat, all the way on the boat from Hungary—actually, England—and my mother will want it back."

I dropped the cell. It would have been less painful to hold molten lava.

I considered how much water I had been drinking a day on the diet. Enough to cry buckets for months. I wiped my nose with my hand.

"Breathe," Stephanie said as she stood next to me.

"I feel nauseous."

Stephanie held my waist and helped me to a chair. I had aged—maybe ten years in the moments since the phone call.

"I'm sorry, Lauren," she said, brows so furrowed, the two almost touched.

"I can't believe this is happening. Eric running off. Leaving me. I'm forty-one years old. What if I never have kids? If I never have children with Eric, I will never have children."

"Maybe he'll come back."

"I was fine on my own. My career. My friends. But now I want Eric, a husband to come home to, a child to take care of. I want a reason to leave work. I want to utilize the twelve weeks of paid parental leave I fought for at Steinbach Kraus."

"I thought you did that to advance the rights of women at your firm," Stephanie said.

"I'm a woman. I did it for me."

"You have plenty of time," Stephanie said. "Women give birth late in life now. You'll be all right. You'll get back in the saddle."

"Do you not understand I love Eric? He is the one. Besides, to get back in the saddle, you need a horse—and a saddle." I seethed as I grabbed a Kleenex from the tissue box. I dabbed my eyes, burning from brown-black mascara. It was supposed to be waterproof. Nothing was working. Not the mascara. Not the groom. Nothing.

"There are plenty of horses, Lauren."

Easy for her to say. She was married to the prince of personal finance—Robert Jeffrey Levine, JD, CPA, CFP, PM, as in Perfect Man. She lived in a show house in Connecticut, where she was teacher of the year. She had two children, my nieces, Olivia and Liza, hands down my favorite relatives. Her life was a dream. If something wretched had ever happened to Stephanie, no one told me about it.

Why hadn't I noticed Eric was troubled? I should have realized how he felt. I was naive. Yakking about the wedding. Wedding this, wedding that—while my fiancé was plotting the great escape.

"Don't do it," Stephanie said.

"What?"

"Blame yourself. You always blame yourself."

"I'm not blaming myself."

"Okay. What were you thinking?"

"That maybe this is all my fault. That I should have been aware." She stared me down. "Like I said."

"How did this happen?" I wailed to Stephanie, who was checking her Cartier watch.

She glanced away, then back at her wrist, intent on each passing minute.

"Stop clocking the time, Stephanie."

She planted herself in front of me, held me still, focusing on my eyes. There was no escaping her. "The wedding is supposed to begin. What do you want to do?"

I didn't know. Consult *Brides* magazine?

"You stay here," she said. "I'll go find Dad. We need Dad."

"No way. Dad will bring Mom."

"Okay, then. I'll find the rabbi."

"Rabbi Millstein? Or Joey, as Eric's mom calls him? He's Eric's rabbi." I had no idea that when Myrna and Stanley offered to cover the cost of the wedding, it was so they could have everything from clergy to cocktails their way. "I want my own rabbi."

"You don't have a rabbi," Stephanie said.

Suddenly I felt my backbone become a steel rod—one foot thick. So I was left at the station. That didn't mean I had to take it like a chump.

"I will make the announcement. I want to tell everyone," I said to my sister.

"No, you don't."

"Yes, I do," I insisted.

Stephanie shook a finger. "No, you really don't." She was afraid for me. "You'll get yourself upset."

I laughed uncontrollably. "Now, getting myself upset, that would be awful."

"Lauren, this is not a good decision. You are brokenhearted. You might regret what you say for the rest of your life, relive it slumped in a wheelchair, drooling in a nursing home."

"I have no intention of sneaking out of here. I will not slink. I do not slink." I slammed my bouquet multiple times on the vanity.

"You could wait here, in this room, until everyone leaves," she suggested.

"Stephanie, shut up. You always act like you're the older one, but I'm the older one."

Stephanie was silent, resigning herself to my tyranny. What's the point of a good-hearted sister like Stephanie if you can't take everything out on her?

I glanced in the mirror. My face was a Stephen King story.

"Let me fix your makeup," Stephanie said. "You don't want to walk in there like this."

I sat, a wreck, tapping my French manicure on the table.

When she finished, I mustered my strength. "I will walk into the chapel holding my bouquet. I will hold my head high, and without a tear, I will explain."

"All right, Lauren. I'm with you. I am not leaving your side."

Thank heaven someone wasn't leaving. I grabbed my phone from the vanity, my rolling bag from the closet. "Please take my suitcase," I instructed Stephanie.

"You're going into the chapel with your suitcase?"

"Pretend you're a friend, not a sister. Stop asking questions."

We proceeded down the passage to the chapel—biblical tapestries on the wall. The entrance was elaborate—stained glass panes depicting the Burning Bush. The bush loomed in front of me on double doors. I took a breath from my nose to my toes.

Stephanie whispered, "Are you ready?"

I could hear my heart. "Don't rush me. I have to think."

"I'm not rushing. It's okay to change your mind," she said, as though speaking to a young child.

"I'm not changing my mind."

For a moment, I imagined I could see through the doors, down the aisle, to the white wedding canopy blossoming with flowers, to the ark, to the Torah, to the Eternal Light.

"I'll be right back," I said to Stephanie.

"Where are you going?" she said.

I turned from my sister.

And I ran.

Chapter 2

I stood outside, beneath the awning of the synagogue. There was a sign: WEDDING OF LAUREN LEO AND ERIC DAVID FARKAS. I preferred keeping my last name, Leo, but I had decided to take his because I believed it would be easier for the future teachers of our unborn children. I'd prayed no middle school bully would call my kid Fark Ass. I wept, dabbing my eyes, my nose, with the tapered sleeve of my gown. March rain pounded the awning. I ran down the steps to the street. Wildly, I waved for a cab. There was something in my hand. An appendage. I stared at my bouquet like I had no idea what it was. I had caught bouquets—aimed directly, purposefully at me—at the last three weddings I had attended. A lot of good it had done. I pitched my bouquet as far and hard as I could. It landed in the middle of the four-lane road. A garbage truck, Dainty Rubbish, ran over it. The sky crackled with lightning.

There was a diner, Eva and Louie's, on the corner, across the avenue. I had been there with Eric and his parents the day we chose the linen colors. A sign blinked in the window, OPEN 24 HOURS. I could go to Eva and Louie's and never leave, never have to decide what to do with my life. Years later, I'd be hunched over in a booth wearing my dilapidated wedding dress. Miss Havisham for the millennial set.

Before the light flashed red, I dashed across the boulevard, hoisting the train of my gown. I no longer cared about the gown—I just didn't want to trip. I had to get out of the rain and into the diner before anyone discovered me. I needed to vanish. Poof.

As I reached the curb, I lost my balance, tipping forward. I extended my hands to break the fall, but I fell anyway. My face hit the pavement. I was roadkill. I tried to stand, but my heels were trapped in my gown. I kicked free, shredding the train. Before, I had no desire to be seen. Not now. Now I prayed someone, anyone would save me. Not a soul passed by. I crawled to a US post office box, struggling to stand. At last, a waitress inside the diner noticed me. She waved, ran out, yanked me up. One swoop and I collapsed in her arms.

"Sit down, sit down." She helped me to the first booth—beyond the cash register.

"I fell," I blurted, placing my aching hands in front of me. I was at my lowest. I might as well have been hit by a train.

"I'll grab some wipes. We need to clean your face."

The waitress returned. There were streaks of purple in her blond hair. She wore a waffle-stitch T-shirt and an apron over jeans. Gently, she dabbed my face with a wipe. I had been crying but now I was weeping, bordering on hysteria.

"I don't think you busted anything."

"How do you know?" I sobbed.

"Believe me. You'd be in a lot more pain."

"Are you a nurse?"

"Nurse's daughter."

"What's your name?" I asked.

"Margo," she said.

"My older sister is named Margo."

"Do you want me to call her?"

"No."

She pointed across the street. "Is your sister at the wedding?"

"Why would Margo be at the wedding? Even the groom isn't at the wedding." I leaned into the booth, sickened by my own words—"the groom isn't at the wedding."

The diner was deserted. The fluorescent lights were too bright. The booths were drab, olive with red piping. The place was sadder than me. Looking out, I could see Temple Sons of Abraham through the window.

"I guess you've had some day," the waitress said when she returned with water in a glass that said Coca-Cola. "Would you like a menu?"

"Carbs." I was done dieting. I had reached my goal. A lot of good it did me.

"You deserve carbs."

"Hamburger with onion rings and fries, a side of spaghetti, cheesecake. Wait. And a giant black-and-white cookie. Also, a chocolate shake."

I turned the knob on the jukebox, watching the old hits flip on faded cards. I spotted "Breaking Up Is Hard to Do." I burst into tears once again. I pressed A3 without depositing money and miraculously, the song came on. I listened to the lyrics: "I beg of you. Don't say goodbye."

I thought of the day a year before when Eric and I lollygagged through the Ninth Avenue street fair and I said I wanted to live with him, my place or his, and he said he had to keep his own apartment. I was hurt, but I didn't push. "Look, there's a booth for corn," I said. As I sprinkled Parmesan cheese on my cob, we agreed to wait and hunt for our new home after the wedding.

Through the window, I scrutinized guests departing the synagogue—down the few steps under the awning, under umbrellas, onto the wet street. Eric's family set forth first. His aunts carried out the gifts they had brought for us. Now that was quick thinking. I slouched in a corner of my booth, staring out the window in a stupor, mortified and in shock, watching everyone leave. How could this be real?

I saw Kate and Glenn and the twins huddled under the synagogue canopy. They were flying back to Chicago in the morning. I touched my stretched fingers to the window. I wondered what Kate had told her toddlers, my ring bearers—"you'll do it next time"? I thought of my flower girls, Olivia and Liza, practicing—prancing up and down the "aisle" in Stephanie's family room, clutching imaginary flowers. I had let children down.

The waitress brought the chocolate shake. "I understand it's not the same, but my guy broke up with me. He said he was too young to see one person."

"Well, if it makes you feel better, mine is too infantile to marry a person."

"How old is he?" she asked.

"Forty-one."

"That's pretty old."

Not to me, because I felt like ninety.

"Well, maybe he has cold feet but he still wants to marry you. Like my cousin. Her fiancé deserted her at the church, but they eloped the next day."

"How did that work out?"

"They're separated."

"No more stories, okay?" I turned to survey the guests leaving the wedding. "Do you see that slight woman in the magenta coat, standing next to the heavy man in the black trench?"

Margo the waitress nodded.

"My parents. I'm concerned they are worried about me."

She touched my shoulder.

"Can you do me a favor?"

"Of course," she said.

"Can you let my parents know I'm here? I'd call, but my mother can't find her phone—especially when she's holding it—and my father never picks up."

The waitress grabbed a slicker from the coatrack. She crossed the boulevard, waving at my parents. My dad raised a hand, indicating my mother stay put. He hurried down the synagogue steps under an umbrella.

Dad conferred with the waitress. He motioned to my mother. The waitress pointed to Eva and Louie's.

"Oh no," my mother cried upon entering the diner, spotting me in the first booth. "Don't tell me he beat you."

"I tripped—in the street," I said without expression. "Besides, I haven't seen him. He sent a text to Stephanie."

"We know." My dad shook his head, closed his eyes.

"Who leaves a text?" my mother said.

"Eric," I replied.

"How could you disappear like that? You vanished. How could you do that to us?" Mom asked.

Why had I sent for my parents? "You're kidding, right? How could I do this to you?"

"Stop, Ellen. Give her a moment." Dad could barely get a word in when Mom was on a roll.

My parents settled across from me in the booth, pain on their faces. Mom was sixty-nine years old, younger than my father. Dad liked to say he robbed the high school, which always made people cringe. I wished Dad would come up with a new joke.

The waitress delivered my hamburger with fries and onion rings, a side plate of spaghetti in marinara.

"Are you expecting guests?" Mom said.

"This is a size-twelve gown. Size twelve! My whole life I wanted to be a size twelve, and I am a size twelve, and now I'm going to eat whatever I want."

My father loosened his bow tie. "You do that, honey. Eat whatever you want."

My mother gave him an eyeful.

"What, Ellen? What did I say?"

"Stop," I said, my face in my food.

"Let me test that burger to be sure it is safe for you to eat," my father said. A standing jest when he wanted a bite.

I handed it to him.

"Did you put ketchup on the burger?" he said.

"No," I said. "I'm a purist."

Dad snagged a few crinkle-cut fries from my plate.

"How's the shake?"

"Try it, Dad."

"Listen to me," Mom said as my father and I gorged. "If this marriage wasn't meant to be, it wasn't meant to be. Better now than after a child. You're fortunate he didn't leave you with a baby to raise by yourself. And if it was a boy? What do you know about boys? Of course, we would have helped."

I whimpered, attempting not to bawl. I would have loved a baby.

She patted the table. "I promise. You can do better than Eric." She had been pleasant to Eric. She had told him to call her Mom, but he called her Ellen.

"Mom, why didn't you warn me?" My mother had no difficulty voicing her opinions. The woman threw grenades. If there was something you didn't want to know, my mother would be happy to tell it to you.

"If I told you, you would have resented me and married him anyway. Time would not heal. Years later, you won't let me watch the baby. I don't know my own grandchild. I'm not invited to the bar mitzvah. Besides, we were relieved."

"Relieved? Relieved about what?"

"You were forty-one," my dad said, "and we were lucky he was Jewish."

My parents—in a nutshell.

"Maybe it was my mistake. I wanted to get married. I was unwise."

Dad shook his head. "Don't blame yourself. When Eric asked for your hand, I should have said no."

"Dad, he didn't ask you for my hand. I told him if he did, I wouldn't marry him."

Dad appeared confused. "Come home with us tonight. We don't want you to be alone."

"But I am alone, and I'll probably be alone for the rest of my life."

"You'll meet someone else," Mom said. "Just go back on the diet—and freeze your eggs."

Helpful as ever, Mom. I was in my forties, a single woman in Manhattan. My eggs were frozen. Probably had frostbite from all those years in the freezer. Break glass for emergency use only. I dreamed of a partner. I was a relic. I wanted my children to have a father and a mother.

"Not to worry. You can do anything today. You can be a lesbian today." She turned to my father. "Am I right, Phil?"

Dad popped a fry.

It wasn't as though my mother shocked me with her commentary. After all, to know her was to want to wire her mouth shut. I couldn't be concerned about her anyway. I had to concentrate on what would enable me to place one foot in front of the other. Then it occurred to me—work. I knew if I went to work, I had a chance of survival.

"I'm going to my apartment tonight and to my office tomorrow."

Mom droned on. "I still don't understand who delays a honeymoon and rushes to work the day after a wedding."

"That was our plan. The cruise is in May."

"What if you break down at work?" she said, always betting on the upside.

21

"I won't cry at the office. That's why I can go. Besides, Joanna will be there. What do you want me to do? All I have now is my career."

"Come home with us," my father said. "You'll be in your room."

My room. Sunflower yellow. With the twin beds, the posters. My mother had never changed a thing in the space I shared with Margo. She had converted Stephanie's room into a cave for my father after Stephanie married. Did she expect me to come back—out of necessity—but not Stephanie, her golden girl?

"You'll check up on me by phone. You'll call," I said, appeasing my parents. I didn't want them to call. I didn't want anyone to call. Except Eric.

The waitress brought the black-and-white cookie and the cheesecake.

"What would you do if you were me?" I asked.

My mother pointed to my desserts. "I wouldn't eat myself sick."

I called the limousine service that had brought Kate and Joanna and me from my building, the Max, on the West Side of Manhattan to the synagogue. I had been in the center seat, surrounded by love.

"I have confidence in you," my father said. "You met Eric. You'll meet someone else. He'll be a real person, a mensch. Don't worry. When one door closes, another opens."

When one door closes, I thought, another slams in your face.

"Exactly, Phil," my mother chimed in.

I saw the white stretch. I was relieved to leave off the discussion with my parents. Optimism, heartfelt or otherwise, would not do the trick. "My car has arrived."

"You're going home from your wedding with a stranger?" my mother said.

"Not my first choice."

The chauffeur, round-shouldered in a suit and string tie, welcomed me. *Please don't talk,* I thought as I leaned on the headrest, shutting my eyes, remembering the first time I was with Eric at sleepaway camp.

My camp meant a lot to me. I had invited a dozen friends from camp—actually, six women and their husbands—to the wedding. On Friday evenings when we were kids, we wore white T-shirts featuring the camp logo, forest green with a pine tree, and gathered in the recreation hall, a great barn of a room. In retrospect, religious services were abbreviated, but for kids they seemed longer than forty years wandering the desert. To welcome the Sabbath, we turned completely around, then back to the altar, colorful and handcrafted, which held the Torah. We sang a variety of Hebrew songs, the Israeli national anthem—as well as Bob Dylan. I was thirty when I realized "Blowin' in the Wind" was not of Hebrew origin.

Afterward, there was a shindig. The camp rock band—Three Jakes and a Josh—performed all summer and dispersed when August was over. The popular kids huddled in a corner, paired up, taking off in twos, reminiscent of Noah's ark. The rest of us hoped the event would be over—the sooner the better.

The summer we turned thirteen, Eric had become a man—at his bar mitzvah in June. I wasn't invited, but I heard there was a stop-at-nothing adult soiree as well as a party for kids. The latter featured a disc jockey, a photo booth, video machines, and a team of fire swallowers. What's a bar mitzvah without fire swallowers?

At the first social of the summer, a friend, Rochelle, and I huddled behind the long tables with chocolate chip cookies and yellow-and-red coolers filled with diluted lemonade referred to as bug juice. Rochelle and I were worse than wallflowers. We were wall weeds. Where was Kate? Kate was as popular as Katy Perry speaking at a middle school graduation.

Rochelle and I had been lamenting our positions on the social step stool when Eric approached. That's when I learned something that I have carried with me to this day. It only takes one boy to make you popular. Eric spoke to me as though we had never laid eyes on each other, despite the fact we had been at the same summer camp for five years. He asked where I went to school and about the lanyard around my neck. It was red and pink, a box stitch, the easiest to make. I was nervous but excited Eric had approached me. No boy had come up to me before. I couldn't wait to write this in my diary, which I hid under lock and key in my denim laundry bag. Little did I know diaries would soon be called journals.

"Seems everyone is leaving," Eric said as the in crowd filed out.

Was he asking me to leave? Dear Diary, I think he asked me to leave.

"Do you want to leave?" he said meekly.

Dear Diary, he did ask me to leave.

"I don't want to get in trouble." I disliked getting in trouble—as well as any confrontation and rocking the boat. Not much had changed.

"Lauren, you won't. We won't."

Dear Diary, what if my parents find out I was with a boy?

Eric took my arm with his hand. He tugged me lightly. I considered this very twelfth grade for someone who was going into high school in the fall. I followed him without a word. We fumbled around behind Cabin 8 because the other bunks were taken. We kissed with our tongues, and I was positive I would soon be pregnant. Dear Diary, what if I'm pregnant?

As we necked, I imagined scenarios in which I was in my parents' house at the kitchen table explaining my pregnancy to my mom, pleading salvation. I imagined shrieking at Mom, making it clear I had never been with a boy before and I would never be with one again. Then she'd say the words I feared: "Wait until your father gets home. Explain this to him."

We continued kissing, Eric licking my lips, while I decided I would tell my parents about my pregnancy in front of my sister Margo. She would prevent them from killing me. And if Margo couldn't save me, there would at least be a witness to my execution.

As soon as I returned to my bunk, I dragged Kate to the porch, where an air force of mosquitoes and fireflies swirled around the ceiling light. Kate was striking then and now. She was medium in height as compared to my five eight, with a reedy appearance that boys loved. She had straight hair down her back. A girl who looked like that had many opportunities at camp. I really didn't know how she'd gotten back to the bunk on a Friday night before me.

"So you and Eric," she said, before I could get a word out.

"What do I do?" I begged. "What if I'm pregnant? My life is ruined."

"Lauren, what do you mean? Do you like him?"

"Yes," I said.

"So meet him next Friday night."

"That's it? That's your advice?"

Was she going to help me or not?

"Kate, we were kissing!" I explained, moving my tongue in and out of my mouth.

She wiggled her tongue in response. "Lauren Leo. No longer a virgin."

The next summer, Eric and I made out in the back of the dining hall. That was it. We were kids. We never spoke again. Decades later, I went to a camp reunion. Then voilà, I'm forty-one, a jilted bride.

In my apartment, I tore off my wedding gown and dropped it on the floor—in a heap. I opened a window for air and tossed out my veil. I watched as it landed on the roof of a parked van. I looked around the room at all the photos on the walls. There were a few of Eric and me.

My tuxedo cat, Tuesday, sniffed the gown. She let out a harsh meow, unusual as Tuesday was the world's most silent feline. I kicked the wedding gown, then dragged it around with my foot. I stared at it and waited for a response as though the dress were alive and would growl or fight back.

Standing in the lingerie I'd received as a shower gift, I realized that even after my gorge in the diner, I had to eat more. I needed to chew, to swallow, to digest. I craved my favorites. I pulled on a T-shirt and pajama pants, grabbed a jacket from the closet. I walked to the bodega several doors down. I bought my old friend, the Good Humor Strawberry Shortcake ice cream, which I'd loved since I was a child. Back then, I chased the white truck down the block, fearful I couldn't catch up and the driver wouldn't stop. In the store, I unwrapped the ice cream before I paid for it. I grabbed a pint of Ben & Jerry's, some Oreos. I was about to add Cape Cod chips, but I remembered Cape Cod was where Eric and I had first made love. I chose Wise brand instead—onion and sour cream.

When I returned to my apartment, Kate in her teal dress was on my sofa. At once, I knew she was the assigned representative of all those concerned about me. I was relieved I was not met by a committee. I put the groceries down. She hugged me. I tried not to be limp.

"How did you get in?" I said to Kate.

"Stephanie gave me her key."

"Where are your kids?"

"At the hotel. With Glenn. I couldn't go back to Chicago without seeing you."

I wiped my eyes. "I'm fine."

"Naturally you are. You've never been better. Can I tell you a secret? I have no plans to wear teal again."

"What happened in the chapel?" I wanted to know, but I also didn't want to know.

"Stephanie walked calmly to the podium. She nodded to the rabbi. He stepped aside. She said the wedding was postponed."

"Stephanie? Did she give a reason?"

"No. People were murmuring. The murmurs became louder. Then radio silence. Everyone stood still, in shock, for a while. Eric's mom became hysterical. She was wailing. People were staring at her. And Eric's father said, 'Myrna, shut the hell up.'"

I wondered about Myrna's nuclear reaction. Was it due to shock, to disbelief? Was she overwhelmed with despair, disappointment in her only son?

Or was it that she had paid for the wedding?

"Where were you?" Kate said.

"Across the street in a diner watching everyone leave, the loneliest, lowest moment of my life."

Thus far. Who knew what was ahead?

"I have a flight to Chicago in the morning, but if you would like, I can send the boys back with Glenn; he won't mind if I stay a few days."

I said that wasn't necessary, but I was thinking, *How about a few years?*

Kate and I downed wine as I ate my snacks. When the ice cream was gone, I blacked out in my armchair. Abruptly, I awoke. Kate told me I had been in a daze for half an hour. She tucked me into my bed, surrounded by my painted bookshelves, my personal paraphernalia on top. I reached for a tissue. Kate handed me the box. "I'll be on the couch," she said. I shook my head. I tapped the space next to me, and she lay down beside me on the bed.

∽

In the morning, Kate was gone, gone to Chicago. I was in a fog and had the headache from hell. I knew it was a weekday—I heard kids at play in the schoolyard across the street. The area included a playground—swings, slides, a sandbox, seesaws—reminding me every day when I looked out how much I wanted to marry and have a child.

I was petrified that if I didn't go to the advertising agency, I would become depressed and despondent. I would lie in my bed surrounded by candy wrappers, unread books, Hulu or Amazon Prime on nothing, plates piled up. I would binge until I gained the weight I had lost for the wedding. The New York Fire Department would send men with axes to widen my front door, creating room to hoist me out of my apartment and into the hall. I'd trend on Twitter. I'd loop on CNN.

The phone. Stephanie.

"How are you?" she asked.

Great. Fabulous. Can't wipe the smile off my face.

"I never saw Eric as immature," I said. "Do you think he's immature?"

Silence.

"You never liked him," I said, turning on her, even knowing full well she had been my savior the day before.

"I," she started, then stopped.

"Don't lie to me, Stephanie."

"I liked him fine."

"You thought he was immature."

"Yes, but I must have been wrong. Because texting me to say he doesn't want to marry you is way, way grown-up."

This statement would have hurt me, but I was already in too much pain.

After Stephanie, half a dozen messages.

A call from my mother as she blew her nose.

"I will come to the city and keep you company," she offered.

I was definitely going to the agency.

Eric and I had delayed our honeymoon, a cruise in Europe, until May, hoping for good weather. We'd planned two days off right after the wedding, but now I had no reason to delay. For me, work worked. At the agency, I would think less about what had happened, whether Eric was going to call, apologize, and implore me to forgive him, even

28

beg me to take him back. All so I could make him squirm, then say, "Go to hell."

In addition to Joanna and my boss, Corey Steinbach, I had invited my assistant, Mallory, to the wedding. Joanna was as tight-lipped as a bottle of baby aspirin. Mallory was in her twenties, as lively as she was efficient, with a gaggle of agency friends. If Mallory mentioned my misfortune to one coworker, my great humiliation would be a sack of feathers released in the wind.

Who was I kidding? Mallory or no Mallory, they would all know soon enough.

I was nervous to walk in, but I did have a strategy. I wouldn't broach what happened, but if any of my peers asked straight-out, I would be honest. Brutally honest.

I would say Eric had died. Suddenly.

Chapter 3

I arrived later than usual. Coworkers whispered hello as though it were a national day of mourning and flags were at half-staff. (Would anyone ever forget where they were the moment Lauren Leo returned to the office after being left at the altar?) Reticent, soft-spoken women asked if I wanted tea. Oh yes, a cup of Earl Grey—and a noose—will make this all better.

Stop being an asshole, Lauren. Your friends, your coworkers are being nice. After today, this humiliation will be over. By tomorrow, the people in the office will forget you were jilted.

No, they wouldn't. Who was I kidding? I envisioned the whispers years hence. "That's the head of accounts. She was left at the altar. Never married after that. She lives on the West Side with a dozen cats."

What if I did live with a dozen cats? Damn lucky cats. I was smart. Educated. Successful. I would thrive on my own.

The environment at Steinbach Kraus was ultramodern. Weathered gray rafters. Lanterns dangling from cords. A wide-plank floor. Air hockey. Ping-Pong. Our vending machines? Vegan and gluten-free.

I started at Steinbach Kraus after college and had been there eighteen years. It blew my mind to think eighteen was almost half of forty, which meant I had been at the agency for half my life. The only thing I had done longer was placate my mother. I was one of the few employees with an actual office—four walls. I earned those walls by working. Head down. Hard. Long hours. My billables were legend. That's it. That's my secret to success. Add some luck. I had hoped to one day be a partner, but then I met Eric and let that ambition waver. Now I was back. And I was bucking. If I couldn't be a mother, I was going to be a partner.

I tucked my bag in a cabinet, collapsed behind my wooden sawhorse desk. My head back, I stretched my neck. My office was on the top floor of the complex. I stared up at the skylight. *Let the light come in,* I thought. *You can do this. Breathe.*

I checked my cell phone. Many voice mails, more text messages than there would be if it were the morning I had been nominated for an Oscar. I scrolled. Yet another letdown. Eric had not called. I wondered whether I would ever speak to Eric again. If he called, would I pick up? I would not. I was never conversing with that Fark Ass again. Well, maybe. No. Never. Never.

I was at work on my laptop when Marguerite, my boss's long-legged assistant, peeked in my office and said Steinbach wanted to see me. I was anxious. Steinbach would ask about the wedding. Not what happened in detail but how I was feeling now.

Corey Steinbach had been good to me. He was sixty-nine with gray streaks through white hair, silver bifocals low on his nose. He was sturdy for his age, built like a man who had played football in college. He went to the gym every morning. He had attended Yale, and he acted like he went to Yale—as though anyone would be glad to have him around. I wish I had been Ivy League. You could get straight Cs. It didn't matter. People assumed you were Einstein as soon as you dropped "I went to Yale."

I didn't go to Yale. I went to Boston University. No one thought you were a genius if you said you went to BU. They just thought you wanted to spend four years in Boston, which I did.

At the time I was hired, Steinbach was sleeping with two clients. He met one client at lunch and one before he went home to his wife. To my knowledge, he had never harassed or had an affair with an employee. In any case, a philandering advertising guy was not exactly an endangered species at the time.

When I entered his office, Steinbach was on his couch thumbing through e-mails on his Mac. He greeted me by placing his laptop on his mosaic end table. I stood in front of him, wilting with sadness.

"Are you okay?" he said.

I mustered strength to smile. I didn't want Steinbach to feel sorry for me. I didn't want to feel sorry for me. When I had seen Steinbach before the wedding, he had given me my wedding bonus—a whopper of a check. The cash was great, but more important, it was wonderful to know Steinbach valued me. He had been my mentor, and I knew it was because of him I was the first woman vice president of the agency.

"I'm surprised you're here today."

"I was left at the altar. Well, actually, before the altar."

I started to cry. My mother was right. Damn Eric.

"I heard. I'm sorry, Lauren."

Steinbach stood and walked over to me. He hugged me, a salve on my bitter wound, and I choked up.

"He didn't want to get married. He wasn't ready."

Eric was forty-one. Would "emotionally too young" make him thirty or ten?

Steinbach responded softly. "I wish my nephew's wedding had been any other night; then I would have been there."

"What could you do?" I said, actually glad he didn't attend. It would have been even more humiliating. If that was possible.

"Now, listen to me, Lauren. I met Eric at our holiday party."

"I know."

"The guy is a kid, a baby. You need an older man."

I was surprised at his words, and I wondered—was he suggesting himself?

Steinbach patted my hand. Something about the pat made me close my eyes. I had been lonely before I started seeing Eric. It had been a while between boyfriends; my girlfriends were married, and most had children.

"Poor Lauren." Steinbach rubbed my back above my bra. I desired his tenderness, any tenderness. I needed a man to be gentle, kindhearted to me. Suddenly I didn't care that he was my boss. That he wasn't older, he was just old. That he was married. That his petite, blond, blue-eyed wife belonged to the same health club as I did, that I went to his son's three-day bar mitzvah on a Celebrity cruise, his daughter's birthday bash at Chelsea Piers.

I approached Steinbach.

I took a step. I leaned in.

I unbuttoned my shirt.

Our offices were on the twentieth floor, and Steinbach couldn't have been more shocked if I leaped out the window. Maybe I *was* attempting suicide. Starting with Steinbach was suicide. And I knew it. But I needed someone to touch me, to make me feel wanted and worthwhile.

Steinbach backed up. He faked a cough. Another cough.

I held my hand to my neck. I buttoned up.

Steinbach shook his head slightly. "Not going to happen."

I couldn't believe it. Even Steinbach was backing out. Steinbach, a man who never saw a skirt he didn't wish was shorter.

"You're going through posttraumatic syndrome. You know that, right?" He smiled at me warmly, like a father. I didn't need a father. I already had one.

"Not just that. You must know how much I respect you, Lauren. You're the last woman here I would start up with."

Well, thanks.

He noticed the shame on my face and explained, "I didn't mean it that way."

I couldn't have been more embarrassed. "I know and I'm sorry. It's been less than twenty-four hours."

"I understand."

How many hours, days, months, and years would it take to get over this?

"You are going to meet someone else," Steinbach said.

Everyone kept saying that. It was the equivalent of well-meaning friends telling a dying woman she'd get well soon. Sure, all I had to do was get over Eric, who still had not reached out to me in any way, which made everything worse. Okay, so I fell in love with the wrong guy. I made a mistake. I wanted to get married, so I'd chosen not to notice what Steinbach saw clearly. Could I trust my judgment ever again?

Steinbach went to his desk for a tissue. He strutted back with purpose. I dabbed at my eyes. I should have been happy he turned me down, that he had respect for me, that he chose not to mine my pathetic situation. But all I felt was mortification.

"Come over to my desk," he said.

In a trance, I walked to the bucket chair facing his desk, overloaded with personal paraphernalia, including miniature replicas of endangered species—Bengal tiger, greenhorn frog, howler monkey. There were rocks and gems. It wasn't a place to work. It was the museum of natural history. He settled in his high leather chair. Then he used my father's line.

"When one door closes, another one opens," he said, swiveling to face me directly.

A penny saved is a penny earned. Please stop with the proverbs, Ben Franklin.

"You miss one bus, you catch the next," he offered.

Steinbach had never waited for a bus. He had a Bentley. And a few drivers.

"You need something to take your mind off this," he said. "What about a little business trip? To be honest, George Moore is prickly lately, so I decided to hand deliver the annual report. Take tomorrow off, a day of rest, and see George on Wednesday—instead of me? George knows you are my protégé. He likes that."

"Protégé. I have to wonder. What would you call my relationship with my biggest client if I were a man?"

"You're right. Pardon me. My generation must have been speaking. Go to Massachusetts. It will be good for you. What's better than a client who is glad to see you?"

"Okay," I said, because I knew it was the right answer. But the account was in Far Acres, a small town in northwestern Massachusetts, a substantial drive, particularly in my current state of mind, and I wasn't looking forward to the trip. I didn't enjoy driving. In high school, I had taken the driving test three times before I passed. Then I caused an accident on my first time out with my father's Oldsmobile. I noticed a boy I liked at the wheel of the driver's education car, an instructor next to him. I glanced too long and sideswiped the car. When the instructor asked for my license and where I had gone to driving school, I pointed to the sign on the hood of his Chevy.

"Sure you're up to it?" Steinbach said.

I nodded as I thought, *Of course not.*

"Start out early—that way you won't hit traffic leaving the city. Driving will clear your head. I'm looking out for you, Lauren. Rent a nice car. Upgrade."

I stared out of Steinbach's window to the skyscraper on 50th Street. It was one of the tallest buildings in New York. It had a triangular green roof. The roof reminded me of a hat. I was looking at the only tower in Manhattan that wore a hat. I needed a hat, a huge one to hide under. Maybe then no one could see my shame.

Upon leaving Steinbach's office, I bumped into Joanna. She had sent texts I had not answered. But then, I hadn't answered anyone. What was there to say? She dragged me into a corner near a storage room.

"I can't believe you came in," she said, mystified.

"I didn't sleep all night, but I was afraid if I stayed home, I would never go out again."

Her concern was written on her face. "I would've come over with Kate, but we decided it would be better if there wasn't a parade."

"Thank you, and thanks for the messages," I said.

"How are you?"

"I unbuttoned my top in Steinbach's office."

Joanna squinted as though trying to avoid seeing something awful. "Oh no, no—what happened?"

I rolled my eyes. "He sent me to Massachusetts."

"Today?"

I knew she was aghast at the idea of me driving in my current state.

"Wednesday. I'm taking tomorrow off."

"That's good," she said.

I burst into tears.

"I don't think you should drive to Massachusetts. You're too upset."

"I'll go early and drive slowly," I said through sobs.

⟋⟍

I arrived home, grabbed a diet soda from the fridge, and fell onto the couch. I checked my phone. Nothing from Eric. There were messages—from Kate and Stephanie—as well as seven calls from my mother. She would have called eight times, but seven was her lucky number. I swallowed Tylenol. The bottle recommended two. I took four, crawled into my queen-size bed beneath my down comforter, smooshed my aching head into a pile of pillows, and fell asleep.

Chapter 4

The next morning, the day I was supposed to rest, recover, relax, I woke to the sound of my doorbell. I figured it was my neighbor Allie checking up on me, since she had been at the wedding.

Allie Strum was pregnant with her first child, and her baby shower was imminent. I said I would be there, but now, what could be more depressing? Trouble was, I wasn't certain how to tell Allie I wasn't attending: "I'm happy for you, Allie, but since I may never have a baby, it would be too painful to attend a shower." I didn't have it in me to admit to Allie, years younger than I was, the best neighbor ever, that I was too fragile to revel in her happiness.

But it wasn't Allie at the door anyway. It was my mother and father, Stephanie, and Rob—in that order.

"Surprise! We're here," my mother said.

"How did you know I would be home?"

"Joanna," Stephanie said. "You didn't return my calls, so I texted her."

I wouldn't have invited them. It would have been too much to consider, but I was glad to see them. After all, they had "schlepped in" from Connecticut, as my dad said whenever he came to the city—even when the trip in was easy.

I took their coats. My father and mother looked like the husband and wife in a sitcom. Dad was handsome and hefty with a belly that grew bulkier at night. His jowls were due to decades of losing and gaining weight. He'd pack on fifty pounds, knock off sixty, gain it all again, then return to a black coffee, grapefruit, and steak diet, which my mother was happy to provide. My father did his bingeing outside the house.

Mom was small, a slender woman, delighted to wear size 4, shop exclusively in her hometown boutique—Four—for people who never ate. When I was a kid, I'd accompanied her to Four. As soon as we entered, I felt enormous. Even if the only other person in the store was the saleswoman, I believed a million eyes were glued on me. I fled to a chair in the left corner where a curtain led to a stockroom. I buried my curly hair in a magazine, eyes cast down until it was time to leave. On occasion, my mother would exit a dressing room, model in front of the three-way mirror on a pedestal, and ask me if I liked the dress she was trying on. The saleswoman acted as though I were invisible. I knew exactly what she was thinking: *that girl is too big for this store.* Years later, when I was a businessperson myself, I thought of what an image problem it was for the saleswoman to have me in the shop. Even if I was hiding in a corner.

Mom wanted her girls to be thin, which was an easy assignment for Stephanie, who had inherited not only our mother's green eyes but her metabolism and body type. It was tougher for Margo later in life, but as a child, teenager, and young adult, her weight was not a problem because she ran around so much and rode a bike to get away from our house.

Then, of course, there was me. I enjoyed going to school, playing board games, going to the movies, and reading fiction about other families. I avoided anything that required a ball as though life-threatening.

Marilyn Simon Rothstein

Each season, Mom insisted I choose one sport. To get her off my back, I'd pick one. She'd purchase equipment and the team uniform with my name on it. After that, I'd quit.

I was the middle sister, so I tended to be in the center in portraits, Margo on one side, Stephanie on the other, a volleyball between two hockey sticks. Later on, I would position myself behind my thin sisters—ensuring I was unseen except for my head. One day, Stephanie asked why I stood in the back. I told her the truth, and she said, "That's ridiculous." There was no way she could understand. Stephanie with the dream body, the dream husband and children.

"You think it's ridiculous because you're thin," I said to Stephanie.

"You're not fat," she said.

"Right," I answered sullenly.

"You're only as heavy as you think you are."

Okay, I will never think again.

In my apartment, my mother was wearing black pants and a long-sleeve orange top. She reminded me of Halloween. On her shoulder, she carried her midsize brown Coach bag with the link chain. My father was in corduroy trousers. Stephanie wore her signature look—a cashmere dress, a cardigan tied at her neck. *Vogue* would term the color "cinnamon." Robert was in an ivy polo shirt. Green was popular in Connecticut but had no business in New York.

Stephanie spoke first. "I didn't think you would be thrilled with this entourage. But we had to see you, to be sure you were all right."

"I'm glad you're here. Thanks for coming."

Maybe family would be a distraction from dwelling on Eric. Why he had not come by, called, or texted. The man was a beast, tearing me to pieces.

"How about I run to the bodega and bring back a bite?" Rob said cheerfully, as though this were just another happy day in our lives.

I appreciated the fact that he was trying. My mother was correct: Rob was perfect. Blond with blue-green eyes. Six feet tall. All-American good-looking. He was a jock in high school, on the football team. He went to business college, majoring in accounting. Once, I asked Rob why he'd chosen accounting. He said all the other guys in high school thought it was difficult. He found it easy. During college, Stephanie temped for two days at a financial service company and boom—that's where she met Rob. He joined the firm's New York office. My sister went on to become a teacher, fulfilling her dream of wagging her teacher finger, saying "zip the lip" and "sharing is caring."

I was grateful for Rob's suggestion. There was something about my mother that made me want to eat. I didn't have to see her in person: I could pass her photograph in the hall and begin a binge.

Mom did me in at camp one summer. I had weighed six pounds over average on my precamp visit to the pediatrician, who on that day refused to give me a lollipop. Mom contacted the camp about my "obesity." The nutritionist, who weighed ten pounds holding a ten-pound weight, came into the dining room to tell me to be careful about what I ate, to "enjoy" smaller portions, to refuse desserts—and to avoid the canteen where snacks were sold. She said it loud and clear, in front of all my bunkmates and so that campers at other tables could hear.

"Rob, while you're there, can you pick up a package of tampons?" Stephanie said.

"You're sending him for a sanitary product?" Mom said. "Who sends a man? To a little grocery, no less?"

"Mom, he's not a man. He's my husband."

"He's still a man," my mother insisted.

Rob was laughing.

"Are you a man, Robert?" Mom asked, like it was a serious question.

He looked down at his crotch. "Last time I checked, Ellen."

I chuckled. It felt good.

"We would have brought bagels, lox, cream cheese, but we decided to come at the last minute," Dad said.

"Also, who needs so much food?" my mother chimed in.

"I'll be right back." Rob slipped out of the apartment.

"Where are the girls?" I asked Stephanie.

"In school, of course."

"I would've loved to see the kids," I said wistfully.

My mother replied with her two cents. "They were crushed they didn't get to be flower girls."

"Ellen!" My father gave Mom a stern look.

"Well, Phil, they were. They wanted to walk down the aisle."

Who didn't?

"Let's not talk about the wedding," I said.

Stephanie concurred.

"What are you going to do about the gifts?" my father said.

"Dad!" Stephanie said.

"I think she should keep everything," Dad said.

"Except from his side. The presents from the groom's side she should burn," my mother said. "I'm happy to start the fire."

Stephanie and I stared at each other. My eyes said, "Save me."

"We have big news. Rob was named the number one financial planner in Rhode Island."

"That's wonderful." My father reached down to pet Tuesday.

My mother swatted his hand. "Stop with the cat, Phil."

I was confused. "Why in Rhode Island? He lives and works in Connecticut. Does he have an office in Rhode Island?"

Stephanie explained. "Now he does. The competition was intense in Connecticut—all those firms on the Gold Coast. Rob rented a satellite office in Providence, applied for planner of the year there."

"Lauren, you should invest more with Robert. It's important to have a nest egg," my mother said, like I had nothing to think about but where to stash my cash. But I knew what she was thinking. I could see inside her mind. After all these years, she still didn't understand I earned what she considered a man-size living.

My parents had been married since the Nixon administration. My father, a philosophy major, joined his uncle's shoe business, Mad Murray's. His slogan: "If the shoe fits, buy it already." Dad met Mom when he sold her a pair of platform shoes. A red pair. She still had them. Mom taught first grade in a private school until Margo was born. She didn't understand I could support myself. All she could see was that I had lost my chance to marry Eric. My mother's opinion: Rob, a man, could look out for me. He could be a financial angel, in case I wound up a spinster.

"I already have cash with Rob. And by the way, Rob's firm no longer services clients with less than one million to invest."

"That's true," Stephanie said.

"But we're relatives," Mom said proudly.

"Family is family," my dad said. "Everyone else is a stranger."

Especially when you were a xenophobe.

"I want to keep you abreast of what's going on," my mother said intently.

"What's going on?" I said, expecting dire news about a relative.

"We are considering a reverse mortgage."

"Why? You paid off your house." My parents were solvent.

"Rob suggested it. He's so smart. Rob said why let all that good money sit idle in the house. Put it to work."

"A reverse mortgage is a financially astute move," Dad said. "Right, Stephanie?"

Stephanie nodded. "If that's what Rob thinks." No way Stephanie was up on finance, but everyone always assumed she was because she was married to Rob. Like if she was married to a neurosurgeon, she could operate on your brain.

Dad continued. "Rob said to apply for a reverse mortgage and invest the funds with him. He guarantees a high rate of return on the kind of investments he handles now."

"What investments?" I asked.

"What difference does it make?" Mom asked, annoyed. "Rob said to do it. And we can get our money back at any time."

"Are you sure about this? I never heard of a reverse mortgage."

"That's because you don't watch late-night TV," my mother said. "You're free to ask Rob what we are doing. After all, our money will be your money—to share with Stephanie and Margo. I don't play favorites. I love my girls equally."

I didn't think she loved her girls equally. But I didn't say that. I said, "Mom, you're only sixty-nine. Sixty-nine is the new fifty."

"No," she said. "Don't forget. My own mother passed at fifty. Anyway, ask Rob."

"What's the point? He's the financial guru. I'm sure he has some scheme that will turn your money into more money." I imagined bags of money giving birth to money.

"Maybe you should get a reverse mortgage?"

"Mom, I don't own my apartment."

"If only you had met a Rob," my mother said.

I had thought Eric was a Rob.

"What's that rumpled sack on the floor near the radiator?" Mom craned her neck as though the radiator were miles down the road.

"It's Lauren's wedding gown," Stephanie said.

"I'll pick it up," my mother said.

"Mom, you touch that gown and I will move every penny I have invested with Rob right now."

My mother sat back, but not until she gave my father the eye.

I turned to Stephanie. "I wish the girls were here too."

"I understand. We'll set something up for a weekend."

I relished the chance to be alone with my nieces. On their last visit, we had what we called "ladies' lunch" at Sweet Lily's, a Victorian restaurant with Christmas lights and decorations year-round. At the Children's Museum, we posed at a replica of the president's desk with the US presidential seal. Olivia pretended she was the first woman

44

president of the United States. Often, Eric stopped by my apartment with a stuffed animal for each girl.

Stuff Eric. Why did every memory lead back to him?

My mother continued. "Yesterday, at the nail salon, I met a woman who had a baby late in life. Guess how old she was?"

"The woman or the baby?" I said, and we all laughed.

~

Rob returned with groceries. He was generous, and I knew his generosity was one of the thousand things Mom liked about him. Stephanie helped Rob unpack, then she placed a cloth on my table, big for a single person's place in New York. With a leaf, it sat eight. I opened the table when Eric and I invited a few couples at a time for dinner. We tended to invite his friends one night and mine another. Maybe that should have told me something.

Stephanie brewed and served coffee. I preferred ceramic mugs with messages, a function of being in advertising. If I hadn't been into account service, I would have become a copywriter and created the ads. My sister passed me the mug that said, "Don't worry. Be happy." She pointed to the words. Happy about what?

Rob set out a bowl of fresh fruit, a platter of brownies.

"Those look good," Stephanie said.

"So why haven't you called us?" my dad asked, securing a wedge of melon.

"I guess I needed time to myself," I said, which was the truth.

"No concern for other people," my mother opined.

"Mom, give it a rest." Stephanie glanced in my direction.

I changed the subject. "Your hair looks nice, Mom." The truth was, her hair always looked the same, gray, short, cropped, stylish, as though she were the patient spouse of an aging politician from Arizona. Her green eyes grabbed all the attention; her hair hardly mattered.

"Do you know how long I have been going to Sylvia?" Mom said.

"I don't know how many years exactly," Stephanie said, "but no one has been named Sylvia in at least five decades."

"Please pass the brownies," I said. I wanted. Coveted. Needed a brownie.

Mom touched her cheek like I had told her I was considering prostitution as a career path. "Are you sure?"

"Yes, I'm sure."

My mother leaned back. "But there's fruit."

Stick the fruit up your ass.

"Besides, I can see those brownies are not so good."

Mom had told me food was "not so good" since I was old enough to realize my sister's skirt was half the width of mine.

"I'll have one too," my sister said in support of me. Nice, but her comment was irrelevant. My mother didn't care if Stephanie had a brownie. Stephanie was thin—and married.

"Mom?" I said.

"Yes?"

"Pass the brownies. Or die, Mom."

Chapter 5

We clocked a two-hour visit. Then I accompanied my family to the elevator, where I planned to say goodbye. One of the elevators opened, but no one stepped out, and the door closed again as the elevator headed up. For a moment I suspected it was Eric. Perhaps he was here to apologize, to explain (if that was possible), so I didn't have to wonder the rest of my life what had set him off, so I could tell him what I thought of him for informing Stephanie he didn't want to marry me, and how he had socked me in my reproductive organs.

It made sense: Eric was hiding in the elevator because he wouldn't want to see my family. I scanned the numbers above the door. The elevator lingered on eight for an unreasonable time. He was stalling. I crawled with anxiety and anticipation.

The other elevator arrived—going down. Stephanie zipped her coat. Rob gave me an encouraging thumbs-up. But my father, last in the elevator, stalled the door with one hand. *Go.*

"You'll be all right," Dad said as Mom nodded and I studied the buttons over the other elevator—heading down, heading toward me.

"Of course she'll be all right," Mom chimed in. "She'll meet someone."

What would make her leave? "Well, Mom, I can't meet someone loitering in front of the elevator."

She turned to my father. "Press 'Lobby,' Phil."

I decided to remain at the elevators. Then I changed my mind. I slipped back into my place and waited.

The bell rang. Once. Eric was a multi-bell ringer; sometimes he rang a tune such as "Jingle Bells" or "London Bridge," but this was the new Eric, the one who had left me at the altar. I took a breath. I walked back, forward a few steps so it wouldn't appear I was waiting at the door. "One minute, please." I straightened my top, ran fingers through my hair.

I opened the door.

Standing in the hall was my eldest sister—Margo.

Margo Who Didn't Attend the Wedding.

I was astonished to see her. I hadn't seen Margo in several years, and I guessed she had gained seventy-five pounds—but I wasn't saying a word about it.

Her face—she was beautiful—was round now, and her blue eyes seemed smaller. Her sun-streaked hair was parted in the middle and fell to her bosom, which always seemed to arrive before she did. It was those ample, often unnecessarily displayed breasts that had earned her a reputation for being a slut in junior high. She went to school with a cardigan over a camisole—so my mother wouldn't notice—then removed the sweater in homeroom. Boys christened her Mount Margo. I told her she needed to cover up, but she wouldn't. She liked her girls—and the boys.

She was wearing a loose, plunging V-neck dress, a tangerine her-ringbone pattern to her calves. Her tights were hunter green. Her slouchy boots were red pleather. She could stock a booth at a flea market with the beaded jewelry around her neck. She held a huge plum tapestry handbag. I don't know how to explain this, but somehow it all seemed fashion-forward.

"You're huffing," I said as a greeting, the kind you could only give a sister.

"From the elevator."

"You're huffing from riding an elevator?"

"I had to walk into it, didn't I?" She threw me a theatrical look that said, "Let me in." Margo was dramatic because Margo was an actress. She had scored every female lead in high school, performed in regional theaters and Summer Stock, escaped to LA, hoping to work in TV.

I didn't have the heart left to be welcoming, understanding. Worst of all, she was not Eric. "You didn't come to my wedding."

"The groom didn't come to your wedding."

She had a point. But still.

"You're my favorite sister," Margo said.

"I'm the sister you speak to," I said.

Margo made herself at home. She wheeled two suitcases into the center of the room, plopped on the purple couch, and kicked off her pleather boots.

I dallied in the kitchen and poured myself a Dr. Brown's diet cream soda. Why had she shown up? Why couldn't she be Eric? The gang that couldn't shoot straight had left me minutes before. I didn't need more company. If she wanted to see me, she should have been at the synagogue in the bridal quarters.

"You know why I didn't come to your wedding," she yelled—as though she were across the street, not in the next room.

"Don't blame it on Mom." My sister had spent a lifetime deflecting her own poor decisions on my mother.

For example, Margo claimed it was Mom's fault she couldn't finish a two-year college. "You have to take math and science," she had told me when I was in high school. We were in the basement smoking weed. "At the community college," Margo said, "there are required courses—such as algebra. At a liberal arts school, you select your classes. If Mom shelled for Skidmore, I could take mostly theater and graduate Some Come Louder."

I asked, "Did you apply to Skidmore?"

"Don't be ridiculous. I can't get into Skidmore. But it would have been nice in Saratoga Springs."

A few years later, without money or a degree of any kind, Margo relocated to pursue an acting career. On my college spring break, my parents sent me to Santa Monica to check up on her, and when I saw where she was living, I phoned home for heavy artillery. My parents paid her rent on a decent apartment share for one year. She landed a talent agent and her first role—in a TV commercial for detergent. Soon she went from detergent to soap opera. Margo died twice as Mirabella on *As the Hospital Turns*, once in a helicopter crash—it turned out she had walked away from the accident—and then due to leukemia, which she was only pretending to have. Currently, she was on her third life. It occurred to me that I hadn't watched *As the Hospital Turns* in a while and that maybe Margo was off the show, because it was daytime TV and Mirabella couldn't be fat—unless that was the way the writers planned to bring her down next.

"I can't be in a room with Mom," she said.

"Even for a few hours? Even for me?"

"You? If you were smart, you wouldn't be in a room with her either. You spend way too much time looking the other way."

"So what? It works." Mom frayed Margo's nerves, but she could still show some respect.

"For whom?"

"For everyone."

"Except you." She pointed, putting me over the edge.

"Family means the world to me." *Except right now with you in my face.*

She shut up long enough to stare as though she had never seen something as unusual as me before. I couldn't imagine what the narcissist would say next.

"You mean the world to me."

Yeah, right. "I haven't seen you in years."

"That doesn't mean I don't miss you," she said, pursing her lips, creating a kissing sound. "I'd appreciate a drink, something cold."

"I have arsenic," I said, upset with her. "Diet or regular?"

"Well, maybe I didn't come to your wedding, but I'm here now, now when you need me. And I don't see anyone else here."

"The whole family was here. That's why you didn't get off the elevator."

"You need me," she said, fanning herself in March in New York City.

What the heck was she talking about? *I didn't come to your wedding, but I'm here now to share your misery.* Last time I checked, that was not what sisters were for.

"You need me because I speak the truth."

"Mom speaks the truth."

"That's the problem," she said. "I heard Eric left the wedding."

"Where did you hear this?"

"I read it on Facebook."

Would it be overreacting to stab myself?

"When I didn't see pictures of the wedding on social media, I went to Eric's page. He changed his status to available."

It wasn't enough to leave me at the altar—he had to change his status too?

"You only liked him because he was mini-Rob."

"He was not mini-Rob."

"Well educated. Successful. Knew a bagel from a bialy. Called his mother. Most likely to purchase a top-end crib. Did you know Rob visited me when he was in California? When I read Eric was available, I called Rob, and he told me what happened. That Eric was such a coward, he texted Stephanie. And Stephanie had to tell you. I wouldn't want Stephanie to tell me my skirt was stuck in my thong before I walked onstage to accept an Emmy. I hopped the next flight. Well, not the next flight—the next flight available for twelve thousand points. It's so tight in coach. The woman next to me had a baby on her lap. Can't people leave children home when they fly?"

Margo wasn't big on children or pets or flowers or anything alive that needed care. She wouldn't play "house" with us. All the caring genes had gone to Stephanie and me. Another reason it was a wonder Margo had shown up.

"Does Stephanie know you called Rob?" I asked. It was hard to believe Stephanie never mentioned Margo had phoned. I could hear her in my mind: "Your sister called." She always referred to Margo as "your" sister when she was complaining about her to me. Of late, her biggest complaint about Margo was that she was useless forever because she lived far away and even if she was on the East Coast, she was not someone whom we could depend on to help Mom and Dad. When I replied that our parents were fine, she asked what that had to do with it, adding, of course, all she did on a daily basis because she lived around the corner from them. In this way, her shot at Margo was also a shot at me.

"I told Rob not to say," Margo said assuredly.

"Like Rob would keep a secret from Stephanie."

"You'd be surprised."

"What does that mean?"

"What it means. Can I please have a drink? I'm parched."

I took a can of Diet Coke from the fridge—no way she was getting a Dr. Brown's Diet Cream—returned to the living room, and handed it to her.

"Can you open it?"

I glared at her.

She popped the top. "You look fabulous. I've never seen you this thin. How did you do it?"

"I ate everything I wanted and stopped exercising," I said sardonically. I didn't want a compliment from her.

She laughed. "I tried that, but as you can see, it didn't work. It's really warm in here. Can you turn on the air-conditioning?"

"It's not warm."

"It's warm. I'm sweating." She started to remove jewelry one piece at a time. It could take months for her to discard it all.

I turned on the air-conditioning, sixty-eight degrees.

"Don't be stingy." She fanned herself with one hand and felt her forehead with the other.

I lowered the thermostat two degrees. Two degrees was all she was getting from me. I had not just asked her to the wedding. I had asked her to be in the wedding party with Stephanie, Kate, and Joanna. She said no. She didn't believe in bridesmaids. I could still feel the sting of it.

I sank into the sky-blue-and-white armchair across from the purple couch. "You really came because you thought I needed you?"

"Well, how are you doing?" She was sweating like an air-conditioning unit in a dead-end motel on the turnpike and still removing necklaces, piling them next to her.

I looked at her as though to say, "What do you think?"

"Come on, Lauren. Don't be angry. Punish me. Don't invite me the next time."

If there was a next time . . . who knew? And what if I was jilted again? Had anyone ever been left at the altar two times?

"How's Dad?" she asked to change the subject.

"Married to Mom," I said flatly.

I looked at her behemoth luggage. I could ask her where she was staying, but I knew she was planning to camp on my couch. Already, she appeared too comfortable, her head relaxed on the rolled arms.

"Where are you staying?" I asked anyway.

"The Plaza Hotel. In the residences. I bought a condo," she joked.

"No, really."

"Here, I hope." She guzzled the Diet Coke. "Can I have another? I can't stop drinking."

I pointed to the kitchen, but she remained seated. A crane couldn't move her.

"Margo, I can't have you here now. I'm going through a lot. I need to be alone. It would be better if you went to Connecticut and stayed at Stephanie's house. You can camp here the next time you come east."

"I am here for you. I am not going to Stephanie's to listen to her commentary on my lifestyle. More to the point, it's a secret that I am in town. Please don't tell Stephanie, because she will tell our mother."

"You're not informing the family you're here?"

She shook her head vigorously.

I was not in the mood to argue.

She picked up my *New York* magazine and began fanning herself. "Do you have *The New Yorker*?"

"Since when do you read *The New Yorker*?"

"I don't read *The New Yorker*. But I could use another fan."

I laughed. Big mistake.

She laughed—happy she had gotten through to me.

We smiled at each other. And suddenly we were at a stalemate, the way sisters are when one covets a precious sweater the other one owns and prefers not to lend.

"I came to see you," she said, as though she had slain lions in my defense.

I shrugged. I knew her well. Surely there were other, more compelling reasons.

I went to plug in my phone. When I returned to the living room, my sister was curled up on the couch. Both of her knees were bent to the side so that she reminded me of a baby in utero.

Margo was asleep. Or she was pretending to be.

I was stuck with her.

Chapter 6

In the morning, I tiptoed past Margo splayed on the couch like a woman in a French painting. I was off to New England Can, world's largest designer and distributor of porta potties.

It was windy, bitter cold, and I stopped in a corner store for a hot drink. The paper cup featured the Acropolis: "We are happy to serve you." I rented a humdrum midsize Toyota, crossing Manhattan while it was dark outside. Once the sun rose enough to glare in my eyes, I was out of the city, beyond the commuter suburbs. I chose pleasant country roads in an attempt to remain calm.

Eric and I would have been married for four days—Sunday, Monday, Tuesday, and Wednesday. Paper was the gift for a first-year anniversary. What was appropriate for four days of not being married? Heartache. And a well-deserved sojourn to my idea of nirvana—a bakery.

Best Bakery Ever had a wooden plaque dangling on a post, but the sign was an electronic billboard to me. I had been bingeing my brains out there for years. I parked the white Toyota on an angle in the lot. I needed another coffee. Badly. Or so I told myself. Upon entering, I was overwhelmed by the intoxicating combination of aromas—flour, chocolate, cinnamon, jelly. I stood still for several minutes enjoying the wonderful whiff. Surely this was what was suggested by "heaven scent."

Directly ahead of me was a backdrop of baked confections on aluminum racks, an area with old-fashioned glass coffeepots on burners. Above the clinking black cash register with antique brass keys was a framed sign featuring employee of the month Erin Matthews and newspaper clippings about the shop. The counter closest to me was taken up by a cluster of senior citizens.

"How's the stock market?" asked a man with whiskers and a beard. I watched him bite into a chocolate donut, surprised when icing didn't frost his facial hair.

"I don't know. Buy a *Journal*," said a man in overalls, sitting a few seats down.

"You're the one with a rich son-in-law. You buy the newspaper," the first man said.

The room broke up with laughter, which made me gloomy, and I felt lonely. Eric and I could look in a store window, point to something, and chuckle about it.

I sensed that these men, hale and white and wrinkled, retired or working part-time, were there every morning, sipping coffee from white funnel cups in old-fashioned plastic holders, harassing the waitress in a short denim skirt and checked top, wearing a name tag that said "Erin."

"How about some more coffee, Erin?"

"How 'bout some Erin, Erin?"

I waited in the takeout line, relieved I was not Erin. In other places, these men could be accused of sexual harassment, but Erin ignored them. She should have been employee of the decade.

The donuts looked amazing. The fruit-filled varieties—apple, blueberry, custard, and jelly—were plump and happy.

Then I saw it.

My demise.

The Blueberry Mother Lode—a six-inch crater of deep-fried dough chock-full of fresh blueberries, glazed, then frosted on top. A dieter's suicide note.

I wanted it. But I wanted more than one. Two would be a start. When Erin turned toward me, I blurted, "My friends at the office would go insane over that blueberry fritter."

Erin held up an empty carton. It was white with "Best Bakery Ever" written inside a cartoon of a donut. She said, "This holds five Mother Lodes—or a lucky dozen donuts, big chocolate chip cookies, or brownies, which is thirteen. The Mother Lode is famous, featured in *Yankee*. And I met the beautiful star chef Thelma—from the program on the Food Channel. Do you watch? Thelma came here with a crew. She mentioned me on her show. She is really nice. Oh, and the *Boston Herald* said our fritter was the best in Western Massachusetts, should have been all of Massachusetts."

It was love at first sight. I had to have the Mother Lode. But I was embarrassed to order too many. "I wonder whether the guys at the office would prefer donuts or fritters?" I said, as though thinking aloud.

"Oh, get both," Erin said as a customer at the counter summoned her for a refill. She reached for a coffeepot, scurried to fill his cup.

When she returned, I had made my decision. "A lucky box of donuts and five blueberry fritters. We have a lot of freelancers coming in today."

"What business are you in?" Erin asked.

"Advertising."

"That must be exciting."

"Yes, it is. My favorite part is introducing new products."

"For example?"

"We launched a bird feeder that won't attract squirrels."

"Why not?"

"It comes with a bear."

Erin laughed. "How did you know you wanted to be in advertising?"

I looked back to see if customers were lining up behind me. None. I answered Erin's question. "When I was a kid, I would stay in front of the TV during the commercials and run into the kitchen for my snack when the actual show came back on. Also, I would go from ad to ad in magazines."

I wanted a fritter badly, but the employee of the month was taking her time, about to ask me another question. I felt moments away from circumventing Erin, grabbing a fritter.

"I enjoy chatting, Erin, but I need to get going," I said.

I had two twenty-dollar bills in my hand. I was dying to eat. I couldn't wait.

I handed her the money. "Keep the change."

In the Toyota, I stacked the boxes next to me on the front seat, keyed the ignition, steered with my left hand. With my right arm, I mauled the top box, reached in, and broke off a chunk of fritter. While licking the frosting, I almost missed the red light. I stopped short, bouncing back. I imagined my shameful obituary. "Jilted advertising executive Lauren Leo, 41, dies in crash while bingeing in car."

Would Eric be sorry to hear the news? Certainly he wouldn't have been surprised that I was eating. He was well aware of my obsession but never called me on it. In fact, Eric liked to make me happy by bringing me delicious treats. And I was happy—until I finished swallowing and beat myself up. When I commenced the dead-serious food plan before the wedding, he discontinued the enabling. He understood. I had become a woman on a mission. Size 12 or bust.

For safety, I pulled into the drive-up window at Bank of America, which was closed for business. With the box of Mother Lodes on my lap, I downed one, then another. The fuller I felt, the more I ate, ramming all thoughts, all emotion down. I closed the box. I set it on the seat next to me. I cruised on—toward New England Can.

I reached into the box again, tasted the fritter, closed my eyes in delight—then remembered I was driving. My right hand was sticky from the pastry. The steering wheel was gunky, crumbs on me, around me.

By the next town line, population 2,313, I felt sick. Why did I do it? Why did I need to buy a box? I could have bought one. I could have had coffee only. But no. My mouth felt gross, decrepit from the sugar—like a needling rash had spread on my tongue and gums.

How was I going to move forward with my life—drunk on donuts? In no time, I would gain back the weight I had lost for the wedding. I would be worse than rejected. I'd be overweight again. The endless cycle, round and round. How I envied women who didn't have my problem. Women like Stephanie. When we were kids, Stephanie would leave over half of her cereal in the morning. I would pretend I was removing bowls so I could scarf down the rest of her Cheerios while no one could see me because I was facing the sink. Even as a child, minutes later, I was overcome with self-disgust.

New England Can was headquartered in an industrial universe, miles behind a three-story Sheraton. Founded by the Moore clan, the firm was now spearheaded by George Moore, as good as a land baron in two states, Massachusetts and Maine. George called his summer home, near Bar Harbor, "the compound." I'd seen the photos: a sprawling Elizabethan-style mansion, three coordinated guest cottages on a picturesque cliff, overlooking the Atlantic. Each house had a name. If my summer place had a name, it would be "In Your Dreams."

Customarily, I interfaced with Arthur, vice president of marketing. Sadly, he was in hospice, pancreatic cancer. I missed Arthur. He was smart and fun. When I called on a bad day for him, he said New England Can was a shit show. He knew I was getting married, but I had no idea whether he'd told George. I didn't want to talk about it, so I hoped Arthur had not put George in the loop. I wouldn't say a word unless George mentioned it. Unless George said, "How's the bride?" *Lonely and empty—she ate her way here.*

I dusted myself off and strode into headquarters, a burgundy brief-case swinging from my shoulder, a box of donuts in my hand. Steinbach was correct about traveling; it was a respite, a test of strength to act as though everything was normal, better than normal.

George Moore, CEO, was in the freshly renovated main lobby, talking with several eager college-age interns. George was a big man with a full head of brown hair, a well-trimmed beard, brown eyes, a booming voice, a hearty laugh, a large personality. I was fond of George, and he was warm to me. As usual, he dressed casually, pleated gray kha-kis with cuffs, a long-sleeve L.L.Bean chamois shirt, funky red socks, and brown boat shoes—Sperry Top-Siders.

"Lauren Leo!" George bellowed hello.

"George Moore!" I shouted back.

His face lit up. He enjoyed it when I gave him the big hello he gave everyone else.

"Look, Lauren brought donuts," an intern in a crewneck sweater said as soon as he saw what I was holding.

"From Best Bakery Ever," I announced, so stuffed, I wished I had never stopped at the place.

George said, "Know what we appreciate around here? A visitor with a stash from Best Bakery Ever."

I broke the tape. The interns reached in.

"Aren't you going to have one?" George said to me.

I shook my head. I waved the donuts away.

"Oh, come on, Lauren. Be a sport. You bring donuts, you have a donut."

Blueberry Mother Lode rose in my throat to do battle.

⌒᳁

George and I adjourned to the largest conference room, which was on the third floor. There was a black wood table with steel legs, eight chairs, a wall of awards—all framed in silver—that New England Can had won for design and quality, as well as our campaigns. At the far end of the room was the Luxor, the glitziest, largest, most expensive outdoor potty in the world. A billionaire had rented the Luxor for an outdoor festivity. He paid only three-quarters of the bill from New England Can. George Moore would never do business with him again.

"How have you been, Lauren?"

I debated what to say. I didn't want to tell George about the wedding. But I would be lying if I said I was fine.

"I'm good."

I was about to ask him the same question when he said, "Aren't you getting married soon? I recall Arthur mentioning your fiancé had hit a home run in his first business and was dabbling in mayonnaise now."

It would have been pleasant not to discuss my personal life at this time.

"Yes, I was supposed to get married," I said offhandedly, as though I were talking about taking a trip. "But I decided I'm not ready."

"I'm married forty years and I'm still not ready."

I forced a smile at his joke. "Oh, come on. You have a beautiful family."

He pointed to a picture of his grandchildren, four boys and a girl, all in T-shirts that said "Team Grandpa."

Even at work, I had to see children.

"Let's get started. I've been looking forward to that annual report."

"Here you go," I said, handing it to him.

George studied the cover—a tall, gold porta potty set on a scarlet background. He flipped through the slick pages, nodding his approval.

"Looks like you knocked this one out of the park. You know, Steinbach and I go way back. We went to prep school together. Right here in Massachusetts."

I knew that, but I let him tell his tale. Never interrupt a client's story.

"I was captain of the football team. Steinbach nicknamed me King George. Should have known then and there he would go into the advertising business."

I nodded.

"What about you?"

"Always wanted a career in advertising. I was an intern, then a paid assistant in college, working every semester at a small agency owned by a dynamic woman who had made her name as an award-winning art director. It was a once-in-a-lifetime chance to do a little bit of everything. However, when I graduated from Boston University, I wanted to go to Manhattan, experience the big league. Steinbach was taking off, known throughout the country, hired me straight out of college."

"What made you apply to Steinbach specifically?"

I kept up my game face. "Oh, I heard New England Can was a major account."

George laughed.

"What do you enjoy most about the agency?"

"Success, of course. Take your company. Sales figures jumped thirty percent in the past two years."

"Let's break donuts. I'm on my second. Go ahead—you choose first."

I wasn't hungry, but I stuck to my scheme: easing all pain with an obscene amount of food. I preferred a goopy jelly-filled donut, but I didn't want the confectioners' sugar to dust the conference table. I chose a French cruller. Amazingly, a French cruller was 230 calories. Less than a bagel. What's more—with a bagel, I had to add cream cheese to the count.

"We have news," George announced. "We made the cover of *Plumb Press*."

I clapped.

He held up the issue. "New England Can. Number One College John!"

"I wonder who told them that?"

It was usually public relations, not advertising territory, but I had. I called the editor-in-chief, Beth Collins, and asked if she knew who had the most potties on college campuses. She said she needed to research that. I said she should let me know. Next thing, New England Can is on the cover of *Plumb Press*.

"I have a feeling you had a hand in it."

I lit up. "College Bowl Champion."

Even in my depressed state, I could spout puns forever, a reason I enjoyed New England Can. Puns aside—I liked how George was always looking for new ideas. He had marketed the first upscale portable sinks and portable kitchens for movie sets.

"Well, it's great news." I stood, shook George's free hand—the one that didn't have a donut in it. "Where's the closest campus with a New England can?"

"We got into UMass."

"I'm stopping in Amherst the next time I visit you. And even if I don't have to pee, I will be sitting on a New England can." *Too graphic?*

"I like your spirit," he said. "You're a team player."

What was it with men and sports clichés?

I was pleased I had maintained composure. Returning to work was the right choice for me. As George would probably say, my decision "was a slam dunk."

"I can't wait to show you the Wedding Wonder."

The word before "Wonder" unrelated to my situation made me queasy.

"The prototype arrived yesterday."

The new product was my idea, inspired by my engagement. So many couples leased potties for outdoor ceremonies that I had suggested one designed for weddings.

George and I proceeded to the warehouse, expanded over the years and now the length of a mall. We chatted as we passed potties. We reached the prototype of the Wedding Wonder, which was large and celebratory.

"Forever together" was etched at eye level. At my suggestion, a frilly blue garter encircled the middle of the door near the handle, depressing me. I hadn't worn a garter to my wedding because I thought it was juvenile, more appropriate for a bride in her twenties. Screw garters.

"Would you like to try it?"

"Of course." I believed strongly in utilizing my clients' products. *Here comes the ex-bride,* I thought as I entered the stall. The bride without a groom. My life was down the toilet. I unhooked the garter, entered the porta potty. As I sat on the plush seat, I was surprised to see caricatures of married celebrities on the walls. Caricatures were not in the original design. I wondered who had developed the idea. George? Arthur? I didn't want to criticize the work of a dying man.

I stared at the sketch of Arnold Schwarzenegger and Maria Shriver. Wait. Arnold and Maria. Didn't he have a kid with the housekeeper? Didn't they break up? Angelina Jolie and Brad Pitt? Custody battle. Bill and Melinda Gates! Money was the number one problem in most marriages.

I lingered on the comfortable seat, getting the feel of it. I tried the sink, dried off with the something-blue paper towels. Kate had given me "something blue" in the bridal suite. I wiped my eyes, on the verge of tears. *Get to work, Lauren. This is business.* I checked my reflection in the mirror above the sink.

I stepped out grinning. I believed it was best to offer criticism of a project only after complimenting what I did like. Positives first. Always.

"Well?" George said brightly.

"Wonderful, I feel like a bride," I said, pushing out a smile as I battled back tears. No way my pain, sparked by a can I invented when I became engaged, would interfere with getting my job done.

"One problem," I said.

"You don't like the seat."

"Are you kidding? I wish I had that seat at home. Hand me a good thick book and I could camp on it forever. There's a problem with the caricatures. A few of the couples are divorced."

"Which couples are divorced?"

"All of them."

The divorce rate was fifty-fifty, higher for those who lived together, but Eric and I had maintained our places. Eric kept a few things in my apartment and vice versa. Would he return my stuff? I sure wasn't calling to ask.

"I don't remember the caricatures being part of the plan," I said.

"The design firm suggested the idea. We winged it."

"I see. Well, if you're going in that direction, you will have to picture couples who are married. Then the dilemma is, how do you know they are going to stay married?"

"You're right," George said. "Damn. We dropped the ball."

"I'd stay simple inside. No whistles. Stick to bells. Wedding bells."

George rubbed his hands together. But I wasn't done.

"And may I make another recommendation?"

"That's what you're here for."

With a lip so stiff it might have been frozen, I suggested a finishing touch I had noticed in the bridal suite at Temple Sons of Abraham. "A pretty white bud vase by the sink—for flowers."

And maybe a sign: "Hope the groom shows up."

Chapter 7

For three days, I had been checking my phone for a call from Eric, and before my trip home, I did the same. Each time, I felt the bitter bite of resentment and wondered whether he would ever get in touch at all. At minimum, I deserved an apology. *You're one great judge of character, Lauren Leo.*

The drive back to New York via the highway was longer than I remembered. My stomach ached. I was drowsy, drained, and miserable. Who returns to work right after being left at the altar? *I do.* It was tedious to smile, to keep up pretenses, to toss answers like fastballs, but I knew I had done the spot-on thing for me.

Two hours into the trip, my eyelids weighed on me, heavy as anchors, and I felt as though I was going to fall asleep. *Pull over,* I thought. *Pull over.* But I steered on, thinking about Eric and how he had wrecked my plan, my life. And no small thing—how he had mortified me. The Great Humiliation.

In my head, I relived the camp reunion at which I was reacquainted with Eric. Kate was married to Glenn and still living in New York at the time. She had the two tiny ones and was slogging in product development for Estée Lauder. Yeah! Free cosmetics. Naturally, Kate was burning to attend the annual reunion. She said she wanted "me" time, but women who look like Kate Kaufman want to go everywhere. Kate could pack for a trip around the world by tossing a pair of size-6 skinny jeans, a T-shirt, and a sweater into her designer knapsack. Not me—I required a steamer trunk for my underwire bras.

I had begged off with the excuse that I was too occupied with work, but the truth was I was up a size again—and I didn't want to wear a swimsuit. For me, a bathing suit was an instrument of torture. First was the shopping. Was that a three-way mirror in the two-foot fitting room with a curtain or did I just look three times my size? I had stopped shopping in stores. I ordered online from Sun 'n' Swim. I wanted sun. I wanted to swim. I didn't want to sun and swim in front of other human beings. I left the swimsuit in the carton for a week, distressed my one-piece was delivered in a box—not a flat manila envelope. Was it that big?

I knew from years of experience that my fellow former campers would gather at the junior Olympic pool or the pine-scented, crystal-clear lake. They would loll in the sun or swim, toss one another in the water, jump out of rowboats. I would be there—miserable in my all-black, size-too-big-to-mention swimsuit, as attractive as an old woman in an advertisement for reducing cellulite, noticeably heavier than the summer before. I wasn't torturing myself enough, so I reflected on all the summers as a kid I kept my T-shirt on over my suit, claiming I couldn't take it off because I would be too cold.

The Monday before the reunion, Kate reached out again.

"Now you have to go," she insisted.

"Why is that?" I asked.

"Jillian was going to be my roommate, but she has to cancel. She can't get a refund and said you could go in her place. I'm staying in the main house, so if you don't attend, I'll have a stranger in my room."

"Kate, it's not as though they are putting a stranger in your bed. Besides, you like strangers."

"At happy hours, not when I turn over and wake up."

"Why is Jillian canceling? I hope she's not sick."

"She has to fly to Los Angeles on business."

"Business? She's a psychotherapist."

"Someone is suicidal, and he's waiting for her to get there."

"Honestly, I don't want to go, Kate."

"It will be fun. You'll catch up with the news and see the girls. Did you hear that Gwen Buehler adopted a baby and moved to Israel?"

If she moved to Israel, she wouldn't be at the reunion. She'd be in Tel Aviv, eating falafel. I thought back to attending Gwen's wedding. The invitation was plus one. At the time, I had no one to invite. She assigned me to the singles' table. It was in front of the band. I danced with her cousins who were in college. Kate was at the married couples' table with the rest of my camp friends. Talk about painful.

"And you might meet someone. Then you get hitched at camp under a canopy with a thousand stars in the sky."

"I have already met everyone from camp."

"Remember Josh?"

"Which Josh?" Every boy was Josh. Or David.

"Josh Greenstone."

"The kid who was always selling the snacks his parents sent him?"

"Yes, but he has moved up. Now he sells pharmaceuticals for Eli Lilly."

Maybe I should go to the reunion. After all, I hadn't dated anyone in months. My longest relationship was during college with my first boyfriend ever. Ryan, from Teaneck, New Jersey, was a boy I had noted around campus and befriended, but he was seeing a girl in my dorm. Whenever I saw them together, I wished I was with him. One day I heard they had broken up. Purposefully, I bumped into him in the student union, where he frequented the Drone Club on Tuesdays at one p.m. I asked him what courses he was taking fall semester. He mentioned Literature for Engineers. I dropped Advanced Shakespeare: The Tragedies. I enrolled in his class. Our relationship began at the start of junior year, ended before graduation, when he decided to delay his graduate studies, teach in a remote part of China. I was relocating to the City That Never Sleeps, planning to live there with Kate and start my advertising career.

He reconnected when he returned. But the magic was way over.

In my late twenties, I met Jerry Zeinfeld. He lived in New York, had lots of friends I got to know well, and taught math at Columbia. But he drank too much. Also, I didn't want to spend my life explaining that I wasn't married to Jerry Seinfeld, that I was married to Jerry Zeinfeld with a *Z*. Turned out I didn't have to worry about the alphabet. Jerry Zeinfeld came to my apartment and informed me he had gotten a woman pregnant. She was having twins. It was painful to think he had cheated on me but more upsetting to realize someone else was having my baby.

And, of course, I had tried the internet. My most recent disappointment had been on the match site J-Fig. Bruce was handsome, thirty-eight, had a boat and a good sense of humor. Also, he claimed to be a doctor. With those vital statistics, I wondered why Bruce was still trolling J-Fig. Sketchy. Maybe he was a doctor, but until I saw his medical school diploma, I certainly wouldn't allow him to treat my nieces.

After we agreed that we both loved New York City and that it was the only place in the world to live, we discussed how terrific it was to stroll on Sundays after a lavish brunch. During our fourth communication, he asked me to meet him for a cup of coffee.

"Sure," I typed back. Then I mentioned that I lived on the Upper West Side.

"Well, I know a great Starbucks."

He knew a great Starbucks. This Starbucks was the best, better than any coffee place on the planet.

"What's so great about it?" I wrote.

"It's next to my apartment building."

"Where is that?"

"Lower East Side. You can hop a train."

"Can't we meet halfway? Let's say Midtown?"

"I never go to Midtown," he said.

"Never?"

"I don't go above 14th Street."

So, what? It would be a long-distance romance? I shut my laptop, and the love affair was over.

Kate wasn't done convincing me to take Jillian's place.

"What's the weather going to be like?" I asked her.

"Honestly, that's the rub. The prediction is rain."

"Just Saturday?"

"All weekend long. A downpour. Lightning and thunder."

The forecast was ideal for someone who didn't want to be seen in a swimsuit.

"Are you in?" Kate said. No one could accuse her of ever giving up.

"Does the day of the week end in *y*?"

"Reunion here we come," Kate said.

And it was that reunion that had led to this. Brokenhearted me, half-asleep behind the wheel of a car. I had not slept the night before, unhappy about Margo's arrival, wondering when she would depart. She was a great taker, not much of a giver. What's more, she was the queen of hidden agendas. Unlike Stephanie, I had a soft spot for Margo. I was able to look away, laugh in recognition when she duped me. Stephanie had a scorecard.

Flour and sugar from the Best Bakery Ever swam in my head. Gripping the wheel, I willed myself to stay awake. I shot up, stretched my spine, rotated my neck, searched for a place to cut the ignition—a shoulder on the road. A shoulder to cry on. I fluttered my eyes, blinking to remain vigilant. Pull over, Lauren. Stop the car. Now. Do not wait for a ramp. The next exit is miles away.

Suddenly, I knew nothing. Blackout. I felt the car tumbling.

This woke me—abruptly. Terrified, I grabbed the steering wheel, a lifeboat, my hands shaking. The car was turning, rotating in air. Was this it? Was I to be maimed? Was I to die? I didn't want to die a melancholy, broken woman. But most of all, I didn't want to die alone. I wouldn't die alone. I howled—an animal noise.

Then as swiftly as the Toyota cartwheeled, it landed with a thud, a bang, slamming to the ground as I shuddered.

Shocked, I wasn't sure I was alive or whether anything around me was real. I stared ahead. Could I move? Should I move? Was I bleeding? I raised my left hand past the airbag to the steering wheel to touch it and ascertain I was in the car. In fact, I was right side up. I checked the rearview mirror for blood on my face. Nothing alarming. If my face was okay, was I okay? My arm hurt from elbow to wrist. I drummed my fingers on the steering wheel, but I stopped short because the motion was painful. I held my arm up to look at it. What bruises were out of my sight? How mangled was I? I stared ahead. I was in a ditch on high, wheat-colored grass abutting the highway. Cars and trucks up on the road were swooshing by. I couldn't see them, but I could hear them. My cell had fallen on the floor. If I had broken anything, could reaching for it make things worse? Did I have a concussion? How long would it take for someone to find me? How far was I from a hospital?

A man appeared unexpectedly at the passenger-side window. I was fearful, taken aback. My eyes bulged at the sudden sight of him. Who was he and now what—hadn't I been through enough?

The man smiled as he tapped at the window. On second look, he reminded me of my brother-in-law, Rob, a suburban father type, someone who had an expensive ride-on mower as a toy. He removed his sunglasses. He stared into the car. He waved. I didn't move. If my arm hurt, what else had I broken?

The man forced the passenger door. I didn't know who he was, but I worshipped him. He was going to save me. And I needed to be saved. Saved from my car, saved from the loss of Eric, the sadness, the loneliness, the humiliation. Now I had sunk to my lowest point, literally in a ditch. I didn't deserve any of this.

My hero struggled with the door, positioned himself in the seat next to me.

"What's your name?" he said, as though it were a test.

"Lauren."

"And your last name?"

"Farkas. I mean, Leo."

"Which is it?"

"Leo, but it was supposed to be Farkas."

"Are you mixed up?"

"No. I was jilted."

"By Farkas or by Leo?"

"My name is Lauren Leo," I said with a sob, then a whimper. And even if I meet a good man and we marry, which I am sure will never happen, I am not changing it. If someone is going to change a name, he can take mine.

"I'm Sam. I was behind you. I'm a doctor—an internist, a family doctor. I called for an ambulance. Should be here very soon. How are you doing?"

"Am I bleeding?" I asked. He checked me out, and although I was disoriented, I couldn't help noticing how well-built he was. Even his smile had muscles.

"You're a bit scratched. No big deal. Does anything hurt?"

"My left arm. I bruised it in a fall a few days ago."

"Maybe this added insult to injury." He waved toward himself as though to say, "Let me see it." "No bone peeking through skin. That's good. But I don't know about the rest of you. Stay still. I'll wait here until the ambulance shows up. What were you listening to?" he said, attempting to distract me.

"I don't remember. Mostly I was thinking." About Eric. Eric had totaled me again.

"Were you drinking?"

I shook my head. No. But I had been bingeing all day. Eating was going to kill me one way or another. I worried I was bleeding internally.

"How's my face?"

"You have a nice face," he said.

I couldn't smile, although I wanted to out of gratitude.

"Where's the hospital?" *Please make it nearby.* I couldn't stomach the thought of a lengthy drive to a hospital alone in an ambulance.

"Right down the road. Next exit. Is there someone you want me to call?" he asked, holding up his cell in a cover that had a picture of two small children. Both were fair-skinned and fair-haired like their father.

I was bawling, trembling, wiping my eyes, my nose with my right hand repeatedly. I was afraid to move my left hand.

I hadn't been hit by another driver. I had myself to blame. I imagined the talk at the office: "Of course she had a car accident. How could she focus after she was left at the altar?" Which was better than them saying: "I heard it was because of all the donuts."

Sam noticed my phone on the floor. He picked it up. "How about if I call your number one?"

My heart stopped. "No, no, no," I said, hysterical.

He must have thought my hysteria was general, not specific, because he hit the number.

I resigned myself. I would never call Eric, but I wasn't stopping Sam from doing it.

Eric's phone rang. Would he pick up? Would he come? What would he say?

I conjured how it would go down. Eric would show up at the hospital out of a sense of duty but then realize how much he loved me, needed me, what a miscalculation he had made. He would beg me to forgive him. I would ask him to get in the hospital bed with me. I would kick him where it hurt.

Eric's away message now said, "Still single. And happy to call you back."

I felt as though my chest would split open, as though my cerebrum was about to explode.

"Do you want me to try number two?"

I shook my head maniacally. Stephanie would rush to the hospital. But what was the point of her leaving the girls? And what could she do? Margo was useless. Joanna didn't have a car. My parents? I would see what the damage was before I rang alarms.

I heard sirens.

Sam promised to follow the ambulance to the hospital.

～⌒～

When I awoke, I was on a gurney in an emergency room. The drapes were closed. I stared at the ceiling, blubbering. I wasn't crying due to the accident. I was upset about my life.

A hand moved the curtain. "How are you feeling?" Sam said. "I would have knocked, but no door."

I stared as though he were an apparition. He had the nicest, kindest face. *Please put your arms around me.*

And that's when it occurred to me. Here he was. Sam. The revenge. Less than a week after I'm left at the altar, I have an unfortunate auto accident. A handsome doctor stops his car to rescue me. He follows the ambulance to the hospital. Waits to see how I am.

He asks me to marry him.

"I do," I responded to Sam's question. "I mean I'm fine. I'll be all right."

I liked the way he looked in his Red Sox T-shirt (that showed how loyal a person he was right there) and his jeans that appeared as though he had had them forever, not as though he had bought them that way like some faker. I liked that he wasn't wearing a wedding ring, only a rubber wristband for Cancer Awareness.

I met his gray eyes. I had never dated a man with gray eyes.

He smiled.

"Thank you. You're my hero." *Take me away from all this. I won't interrupt you when you are on your ride-on mower. I promise to care for the kids pictured on your phone. I don't care if you have a wife. Suddenly I believe in polygamy.*

"No need to thank me. I would have done this for anyone."

But you did it for me. The story of how we met will be told by our descendants for generations.

"Well, I've got to go." Then, wagging his finger, he said, "No more shut-eye on the road."

Sam left. I covered my face with a pillow, my dream of revenge shattered.

The hospitalist, Dr. Angela Chen, was about five feet, long hair, warm smile. No scrubs for her. She wore a navy suit with a belted jacket. I wondered if she had stopped to see me on her way out of the hospital. I hoped she wasn't in a hurry. I needed attention. Not for my wound but for my psyche.

Dr. Chen examined my hand. When she touched my wrist, I squeezed my eyes, clenched my teeth, shook my head because it was painful. She ordered X-rays. The news was I had fractured my wrist. Not a bad break but a break, nevertheless. I thought about tripping in my wedding gown. My hand hurt in the diner. I must have damaged it then, finished it off in the accident, gripping the steering wheel.

Dr. Chen said, "Considering you rolled your car, you're a fortunate woman."

She should only know.

I assumed I would be given the kind of fiberglass cast my niece Olivia received when she broke her arm. It was raspberry, and I had signed it. Instead, my hand was immobilized with a short black wrist wrap, a support I could remove when I bathed. Dr. Chen advised moving my fingers to prevent stiffening. She suggested an X-ray in four weeks.

I didn't want to go home. I wanted attention. Margo was at the apartment, but she had blared the television and downed hot tea my mother bought specifically for me when I was sick with chicken pox as a kid. I wanted to chill out in the hospital where medical professionals would tend to me. I craved green Jell-O, red Jell-O, a mound of watery cottage cheese with a discolored cherry on top, one slice of rubber roast beef, potatoes drowned in gravy, canned peaches for dessert, bad coffee in a white Styrofoam cup. What's more, if I remained hospitalized, I would lose weight. Back when I was in Mount Sinai for pneumonia, I had dropped six pounds.

I asked Dr. Chen if, by any chance, she was a cardiologist. When she asked why, I explained my heart hurt. A technician wheeled an electrocardiogram machine into my room, placed stickers on my chest, shoulders, arms, and legs. Sick as it was, I savored the attention. The doctor told me my heart was fine, but she was wrong.

When it was clear I would be released, I reached out to Steinbach. Someone at the office would deal with the rental. Steinbach would send a driver to fetch me, some nice stranger I wouldn't have to talk to. I didn't want to converse with anyone—ever again.

I was taken by wheelchair to the emergency exit, packed with patients in coats and scarves waiting to be seen. I was the only one alone. A tall man came in the door, all bent over. His wife, in a velvet jogging suit, was holding his hand. She kept saying, "Take it easy, Johnson." Johnson had her, and she had Johnson.

What seemed a century later, I noticed a guy about my age in a navy Yankees cap. He approached the receptionist. She directed him to me.

He wore a black down jacket, a T-shirt, basketball shorts, and high-top sneakers. Whatever. As long as he knew how to drive.

"You must be Lauren," he said.

"I am," I said. "And you must be my ride."

He extended his hand. "Rudy. Rudy Cohen."

I worked up a smile and told him my name.

"Corey Steinbach told me to pick up a beautiful girl with long chestnut hair who looked like she had been injured. And you are— injured and beautiful."

I didn't need a charmer. I needed a ride.

"I'm sorry about the shorts. I was playing ball, at P.S. 9 in Brooklyn, when Steinbach texted me to see if I could pick you up. That was good because we were losing the game."

I nodded. "Thanks for coming," I said. "It's a long trip."

"Came as fast as I could. What were you doing in this neck of the woods?"

"On my way back from a client." I prayed he wouldn't ask me anything else. I had no energy left for conversing.

"How long will you have to wear the cast?" He adjusted the cap on his wavy dark hair.

"Four weeks."

"You got off easy. What kind of car? Was the other guy bigger?"

"There was no other guy. I ate too many donuts, drove off the road, and landed in a ditch."

"Never drive under the influence of a donut," he said. "I know that because I like donuts too."

I shuffled out of the wheelchair, hoping to move things along. The driver stood by me protectively. "I'm okay," I said.

Once in the Escalade, I leaned against the window. I noticed bottles of Evian, dried fruits, and nuts. The driver said something cheerful I didn't hear. I wished he wouldn't talk at all.

He pointed toward a pasture, a group of cows grazing beyond a fence near the side of the road. "The cows are having a meeting."

I shut my eyes. Sometimes you've had enough for one day. And this was one of those times.

⌇

Arriving home, I heard water running in the bathroom, which was off the bedroom. Margo was in the shower. I knocked on the door. Because I was injured, it felt good to know I wasn't alone.

"Margo, it's me. I had a car accident."

She peeked out from the side of the curtain, which I had bought at a convention. It was white with classic newspaper advertisements, a good match for the subway tile on the bathroom floor.

"Where? When? Hand me my terry."

I gave her the robe, which she had hung on a hook. She stepped out from behind the curtain, her hair wet, beads of water on her face.

"Oh my, look at you. What's with your hand?" she said.

"My face is scratched, and I have to wear this cast for four weeks."

"Oh. By the way, the water doesn't get hot enough. You should call maintenance. Also, the disposal is broken."

Anything else, Your Highness? What did I expect from the sister who drank the tea my mother had bought for me?

"Margo, I don't care about the disposal. I was in an accident."

"What happened?"

"I fell asleep at the wheel."

"Did you hit someone else?"

"No. But I might have totaled the rental car. My boss is taking care of it."

"Can I do something?" Margo said.

"I can't think of anything you could accomplish while lounging on my couch." No charge for sarcasm.

"Very funny. Also very true."

"I need to get into bed," I said, wiped out.

"Don't you want to change your clothes?"

"I have no energy. I'm done. I can't."

"I'll help." Her tone clued me in. She was hoping I would say no.

"Okay."

She upped an eyebrow, surprised. "Did you say okay?"

Oh no. Now she had to do something. And the place wasn't even on fire.

"Where are the pajamas?" Margo looked around the room as though lost in a corn maze.

"In the dresser."

"Which one?"

I had two dressers. Only two. Ugh. Argh. "The dresser with the TV on it."

"Which drawer?"

"Margo, forget it." I scoffed, crawling into bed, greedy to wrap myself in my comforter.

Margo shut the light on her way to the living room. I was glad she was gone. *Stay out there.*

Minutes later, she returned—with a party-size bag of M&M's.

"Move over. Make room for me."

"Are you kidding, Margo?"

She plumped a pillow, squished next to me. "You don't deserve this."

"Tell that to Eric."

"Screw Eric."

"That's right. Screw him," I said.

"Maybe someone is screwing him," she said.

It takes a sister to verbalize a cutting thought like that. But I knew it wasn't true. "I don't think so. I believe he didn't want to get married."

"Do you want my advice?" she said as she searched for the brown M&M's.

"No," I said flatly.

She popped one in her mouth, dropped two on the bed. "My advice is move on."

I handed her the two M&M's, certain I was overpaying for her tired suggestions. "How?"

"First, eliminate him."

I shot up in bed. "Kill him? You want me to kill him?"

"No. Block his number from your phone."

I reclined again. "I can't do that. What if he calls?"

"What if he doesn't?" she said. "M&M?"

I shook my head. "Margo, I want him to get in touch."

"You wanted him to walk down the aisle."

"Thanks, Margo."

"Oh, come on. He was crazy to leave you."

Maybe she did love me. Also, maybe she was right. How long was I going to check my phone and be upset every time there was no message? If he wanted to reach me, there were plenty of ways to get in touch.

Now she was searching for blue M&M's. Did she plan to go through the entire bag one color at a time?

"Do you have to eat those in bed?"

"Melts in your mouth. Not on your sheets."

"Okay, okay. I'll eliminate him. My phone is in the kitchen."

"So?"

I wasn't Mahatma Gandhi. I was losing patience. "Can you get it?"

She took a big breath.

"Margo, you asked if there was anything you could do."

She handed me the bag. "Don't touch the red ones."

Chapter 8

I blocked Eric for twenty-four hours, then reinstated him. Had he called in the past day? What if he had? I don't know why I listened to Margo. Whatever. There were plenty of other ways for him to reach me. As he had well proven. On our wedding day.

The morning of Allie's shower, I begged Margo to accompany me. She said if I had a brain, I wouldn't go at all. Her litany of comments included it was good I always wore black because it would match my mood when I returned from the shower. I warned her—one more snarky comment and I would inform Mom that her eldest daughter was in town. The last thing she wanted was for Mom—or any person with matching DNA—to know she was around. Margo was hiding in my apartment.

I chose a dark sheath that looked lovely with my black wrist support. I had worn the dress once before—to a successful pitch for a superglue account. I stared at myself in the full-length mirror on my bedroom door. I could see I was gaining weight. That was the way I was—on the way down or on the way up. I reassessed the triumphant dress. It was tight. It was short, and I hated my legs. I remembered that I had found the dress online after a spell on Pound People.

From high school on, I had started and restarted the well-known diet program dozens of times. Always my last-ditch effort, my only hope. My mother would suggest it, and then I would feel as though I had to do something. Each time, I went to a new meeting in a new place, and each time, I lost fifteen pounds. Usually, my experience went like this: lose six, then three, then three, then two, then one, then zero, then cupcakes, please. To be candid, the reason I lost a gratifying six pounds the first week was simple: Before I signed up for a diet program, I ate like I would never see food again. A plow had nothing on me. In any case, I had lost fifteen pounds—as usual—and was heading skyward.

I glanced at the clock on my dresser as it clicked eleven a.m. The baby shower was called for ten thirty. I had thought of telling Allie I wasn't up to it but lost my courage, mostly because I was trying to be valiant, hear-me-roar after the Great Humiliation. One day I got as far as knocking on her door to tell her I couldn't attend, that going was the psychological equivalent of Three Mile Island, but she wasn't home. I took that as a sign. I should go. It was a test of strength. Wrong. I should have known that going to a baby shower required a soul made of steel. Why did I always have to do what was right? Shut up, take off the superglue dress, and find something to wear, Lauren.

I pulled out a somber tunic, my black go-to trousers with the fake zipper and half-elastic waist. I settled on my bed to buckle my ankle boots. I added jewelry. I glanced in the mirror again, decided I looked nice and should have selected the pants in the first place. I smiled at myself. *You're not so bad.* I sprayed perfume Stephanie had given me after I cared for the girls the last week of December when Steinbach Kraus was shuttered and my sister went on vacation with Rob. I was delighted to babysit. It gave me alone time with my nieces.

I grabbed the shower gift, bought before the Great Humiliation and wrapped in Peanuts paper. Margo had one more observation: "You're a good man, Charlie Brown."

Allie worked for American Airlines out of her apartment. It was odd she was employed by an airline because she hardly ever went anywhere. Allie was married to Marc, whom she had dated since her first day of college. When she traveled home for a weekend, he missed her so much, he used to go into her dorm room and sit on her bed. One day, Allie's roommate stopped in for a textbook she had forgotten. She saw Marc, with his head on Allie's pillow and his zipper open. So I guess he was very lonely. I still can't believe Allie told me that story. I also can't get it out of my mind.

When I was away, Allie was kind enough to feed my cat, change the litter, and take in my mail. She let in the cable guy and supervised the repair people. She was there to open my door when my friends arrived from out of town. Of course, I would do all the same for her, but like I said, she never went anywhere.

Allie offered all the convenience of a great doorman without the overhead of a full-service building. No tips. And tips run New York. The last place I lived had been a high-rise with twenty-four-hour security. The doorman on weekdays was Twenty-dollar Larry, a burly man with a big mustache who instead of standing next to the door planted himself on a chair inside the lobby. If a resident said, "Larry, I'm locked out. Could you open my door with a master key?" Larry remained motionless, seated, until he saw twenty dollars.

In any case, I was fortunate and grateful to have Allie as a neighbor, and even though I'd rather be shot at sunrise than attend one more baby shower, there I was at her door, gift in hand.

Allie's mom, Mrs. Forman, greeted me at the door. She wore a knee-length, silk shirtdress the color of Cabernet. Her layered bob was a shade of red that does not exist in nature. Mrs. Forman stood back, inspecting me up and down.

"You look wonderful," Mrs. Forman said as she hugged me to her bones. I was positive that the last time she ate a meal, dinosaurs were starving for vegetation.

"Thanks," I said, releasing myself from bondage.

I knew code, and "You look wonderful" was scrambled letters for "Finally, you lost a few pounds."

"How have you been?" she asked, as though someone had died.

"I'm good," I said, not wanting to get into a conversation about being jilted.

"There are plenty of men out there," she assured me.

Time to go.

"I have to lose weight before we leave for Boca. Allie tells me I am way too thin. But you know the saying . . ."

"You're never too rich or too thin."

"I wonder who coined that phrase," she said, bemused.

"Someone wealthy and emaciated. So where should I put my present?"

"I'll take it."

I handed her the gift—a half dozen picture books that I had loved as a child. As I passed the present to her, my throat tightened. These were the books I would have liked for my children. This shower was going to be nothing but reminders, no way to turn the bells off.

Allie had lived in the apartment with a roommate until Marc moved in. Her place was similar to mine but had an alcove off the living room. Allie planned to convert the alcove into the baby's room. This was luxurious in our zip code, where newborns were often stored in cleared-out walk-in closets.

Allie was on a salmon-colored chair with presents stacked in front of her on the table. Women were seated on her coral couch. Allie liked pink more than a three-year-old girl.

I took a head count. There were fifteen women. They all resembled Allie—petite with perfectly blown hair; most wore short dresses and pointed shoes with heels that could be used to kill a man. A few were pregnant as well.

I waved to Allie and stood behind one of her cookie-cutter friends who looked like she might deliver on her way home from the shower. If I were pregnant, I would be jubilant sitting in my apartment in a new rocking chair thinking about the baby. No shower, no celebration, no gift-wrapping necessary. Why did women always make parties for the friends who were already happy, already had what they wanted? Why didn't they round up a crowd, buy expensive gifts, a sheet cake, flowers, and balloons to throw a surprise bash for someone depressed? Depressed people deserved to register at Macy's.

Allie was unveiling a baby stroller when her mother pointed to me. "Allie, Allie, look who's here now. Doesn't she look fabulous?" Everyone turned to stare. Allie smiled. She blew me a kiss. One woman waved.

As Allie unwrapped each gift, she exclaimed, "It's just what I wanted!"

Yes, Allie, that's because it was on your registry. Don't mistake sarcasm for anything else. I was glad for Allie and looked forward to having a sweet baby next door, but I was concerned that hearing the baby cry or watching Allie's parents arrive on a Sunday laden with diapers and toys would make me envious and, most of all, sad.

My gift was the last to be opened. Allie shouted "Books!" and everyone acted like they had never seen a book before.

"What a great idea for a gift," Allie said.

The whole shower situation, like anything uncomfortable, made me want to eat, and I did. I concentrated on the buffet and what was going into my mouth, until Allie's high school friend, Rachel, made her way to Allie's chair and took over.

"Is everyone ready to play a game?" she cheered.

Silent groan. Showers where they play games should really be outlawed. And the hat thing—when they make a hat from the gift wrap—that should be a decision left to each individual state.

"I am going to name an item for a baby. Your job is to guess what it cost. Is everyone ready? One hundred diapers!"

"What kind?" someone asked.

Wet ones.

"Pampers."

"What size?" someone shouted.

"Really, Leah? You need to know the size?" Rachel said.

Leah, Rachel—was every woman in Genesis at this party?

"Don't roll your eyes. Just tell me what size," Leah said.

"I wasn't rolling my eyes."

"Allie, was she rolling her eyes?"

"You were rolling your eyes," someone said.

"I wasn't rolling."

"Just tell us what size diaper," Allie said.

"Newborn," Rachel said.

Allie's best friend, Sara, raised her hand. "This is confusing. After all, the price depends on where you buy it. Costco is cheaper than Walgreens."

"But you probably do best if you order it on Amazon," Eve said.

"I'm not sure of that," Sara put in.

The conversation was killing me. I wished I could leave, but departing would interrupt what was happening. All the attention would land on me. I imagined Allie asking if I was okay, her friends whispering I had been jilted at forty-one and a baby shower was the last place I should be. Why hadn't I listened to Margo? Why couldn't I be like Margo? For distraction, I took out my cell phone and checked the news.

"I can't believe it," Rachel cried out. "Lauren is cheating," she continued, pointing at me. "She was looking up the answer on her phone."

The accusation, as silly as it was, cut like a cleaver to a piece of my favorite pie. Apple pie. Not Dutch apple. Plain apple.

I was an outsider in a room full of women talking about babies. Why had I come? Was not disappointing Allie more important than my sanity? When would I stop trying to please other people? Allie. Eric. Eric's parents. And the big one, my mother.

I had been moving forward, but I felt as though this event had thrown me back. What could I do? I decided to pace myself. I was in recovery from a wipeout. I needed time. No more pretending I was fine. I waited a few moments, plastered on a smile, and went for the door.

Mrs. Forman approached. "Too soon?" she said.

I burst into tears.

And I bolted.

I was beyond consolation.

❦

At home, Margo, in a Japanese robe, was planted on the couch with her laptop.

"How was it?" she asked.

"Worse than I thought—and all the windows were closed. No jumping."

I went into the kitchen to soften my blows with ice cream.

My cupboards were open. Pots were haphazardly piled in the sink. Spices from around the world lined the counter.

"What happened?" I shrieked. How dare she? She had no respect. She had turned my place into a disaster area in the time it took me to decide I was never going to a shower again. I could kick myself for not telling her up front she couldn't stay with me. I was in no condition for this mess.

"I cooked dinner."

"For a battalion?"

"No. For us." She removed the cover on my largest frying pan, which was on the stove. "Paella," she said.

"Oh, so you haven't cleaned up yet?"

"The person who cooks doesn't clean up. The other person cleans up. Besides, I was planning to bake a cake."

I took in the catastrophe that was my aisle of a kitchen. I envisioned flour all over the dark tile floor.

I was short of spitting venom. "No baking. Ever. No baking if there isn't a slice of bread left in the world."

She took a step back. "All right, then."

The phone rang. It was Kate.

I must have sounded as angry and awful as I felt, because she asked immediately if I was okay.

"I just returned from hell on earth." To find a second perdition in my kitchen.

"What happened?"

"I went to a baby shower," I said as I shifted around Margo's mess to clean my cat's bowl, refill it with water. Tuesday was a sweetheart, calm and never curious. Curiosity would not kill my cat.

"Are you nuts? Haven't you been through enough lately?"

"I had no choice. I had to go. It was for Allie next door. But new decision—I'm not doing anything anymore that I am not ready for."

"Stay away from weddings."

"Would you believe she received three breast pumps—a pump for each breast and a spare?"

I opened a flip-top can of Finicky Feast, which was the only brand Tuesday would tolerate—and it had to be Gravy Lovers in seafood or chicken. I had tried other food, but Tuesday shook her head and slinked off as though I had insulted her. If only I could be more like my pet—a picky eater.

"What's her husband's name again?"

"Marc," I said.

"I still can't get over that story about how Marc used to masturbate on her bed in college."

I told Kate everything. She was up-to-the-minute on the severe knocking pain I once had in my vagina.

"I'm happy for Allie. She tried to get pregnant for years."

"So how was the basket of cut vegetables?"

"Guess what else they had?"

"Hummus."

"I wish I could keep my weight off," I said in a defeated, bratty voice.

She whined back at me. "Pout. Pout."

"Like you don't have something you wish for."

"I wish you were thin, but not thinner than me," she said.

I finished forking out cat food as I spoke, then checked the highest shelf in my cupboard. I moved balsamic vinegar to a side and discovered a Tootsie Roll lollipop, the sole survivor from when my nieces visited. Best of all, it was chocolate. Olivia preferred orange. Liza always chose purple.

I unwrapped the lollipop.

"Lauren, you worked so hard to lose that weight."

"I could start Pound People, but all I want to do at those meetings is study the rack of low-calorie snacks for sale. And I detest killing time in line to be weighed. It's torture. I would rather await my execution. I get on the dreaded scale. The leader says, 'I'm sorry,' and I think I have gained five pounds in a week. Then she says, 'Oh my. You're up an eighth of a pound.' I could belch an eighth of a pound. I am not signing up for Pound People—even if I can eat all the fruit and vegetables I want."

"You can eat all the fruit you want? What kind of diet is that?"

I adored Kate. But she didn't understand overweight people.

"You're saying I could have three fruits a day if I wanted?"

I couldn't help myself. "If they're small. Like three green grapes or three blueberries."

"You know the secret of being thin?"

"Diet and exercise," I mouthed to myself, pretending to lift a weight.

"Diet and exercise," she said.

"Easy for you to say."

"Do you think I actually enjoy staying in shape?"

"You're not staying in shape. You were born in shape. I weighed twelve pounds at birth."

"Lauren, what are you eating?" she asked as I crunched into the chocolate center of the Tootsie pop.

"Nothing. Not a thing."

⁓

I found Margo on my bed, watching the news.

"How's your wrist?" she asked.

"It's all right. I have Oxy."

"How many?"

"Forty-two. That's the limit."

"Can I have one?"

Margo was such a moocher.

"When you damage your wrist," I said.

I knew if I started yakking about family, she would become as annoyed with me as I was with her, so I plunged in. "By the way, Mom and Stephanie texted. I mentioned I had damaged my wrist. They called me immediately. Very nice people. You ought to get to know them—or maybe simply divulge you're in town."

"Why do you care so much?"

"Because I feel as though I am lying for you. And can you please move over?"

I plunked down next to her. I noticed her bare feet poking out from my thick comforter.

"What's with your toe?"

"Oh, those damn boots."

"It's off color."

"That will go away."

I bent to look. The toe was dark, and she was wearing blue nail polish, so it was literally black and blue.

"I don't think so," I said. "Could you shove over a smidge?"

She groaned as though I had asked her to haul bricks on her naked back to a construction site.

"Move." She had always been a bed hog. Often, as kids, we'd slept on Grandma's convertible couch in her living room. I was a sucker—I always wound up in the middle of the bed, which was so thin, you could feel the metal bar in the center. One night, I stood my ground and insisted on an end. Incredibly, Stephanie agreed to sleep in the middle—making it clear this was a onetime offer. I rose to go to the bathroom. When I returned, Margo was across the bed—diagonally. Her feet were at Stephanie's thighs, and her head was where I had been sleeping. I woke her to tell her to move over. Margo cocked one eye, looked at me, and fell back to sleep. My grandmother heard me. She came out of her kitchen and asked why I was up. I pointed to Margo.

Grandma put her arm around me, walked me into her bedroom. I woke in the morning to find myself cuddled next to Grandma on her queen-size canopy bed with the fat mattress and the patchwork quilt. Her face was fair and beautiful. She wore a cornflower-blue cotton nightgown. To me, she smelled like the best grandma in the world.

I shoved Margo. She made a face but shifted to the right.

"I was thinking about Grandma," I said.

"Which one?"

"Dad's mom."

"She was great. All that unconditional love. She had five children, a dozen grandkids, but you could never tell which one she liked best."

"What are you talking about? She liked me best," I said.

"No, it was me," Margo said.

91

My grandmother had her own language. The language of love. She added "aleh" to each of our names. I was Lauraleh. One day when I was home from college, I rang her bell. Three times to be sure she would hear it.

Behind the door, Grandma said, "Who is it?"

I told her to guess.

"Mitchaleh?"

"No."

"Debaleh?"

"No."

"Sherraleh?"

"No."

"Nu, who are you?"

"It's the burgaleh."

She chuckled as she unlocked the chain.

By this time, Grandma had short, sparse white hair. She wore a zip-front housecoat I recognized from years ago. She ushered me into the kitchen. Her table fit four and was smooshed against the wall. I settled into a vinyl seat with a chrome bottom facing the wall with the Jewish calendar.

"What do you want to eat?" she said, of course.

"I'm trying to diet."

"Feh. Diet when you're *not* with me. I made a pot of pierogi."

"Potato?"

"Potato."

"Do you have sour cream?"

"Do I have sour cream—that's a question?" She took Breakstone's from the fridge. "You'll bring my apple cake to your father. He starves in your mother's house."

That morning, I had argued with my mother. She wanted me to sign up for a weight-loss program. "I will pay for it. All you have to do is go," Mom said.

"I'll pay for it. You go," I replied.

War broke out. As per my modus operandi, I rushed out of the house. Yes, I rushed out of the house, out of Allie's shower, out of the synagogue. I was a grown woman now. When would I learn to stay and fight?

Grandma placed the pierogi on the table. There was enough to feed a family.

"How are you getting along with your mother?" she asked.

"Mom insists I go to a diet program."

I dipped the object of my desire in sour cream. Heaven. The dough. The potato. The delectable cream.

"She doesn't understand your hunger."

True, but what could I do about it?

I stopped reminiscing. I addressed my sister. "Margo, listen up. You've got to tell Mom and Dad and Stephanie you are in New York. I don't want them to find out by default. That would be hurtful."

"Bug off, Lauren."

"And you need to see a doctor about that toe."

"It will be fine."

That was my last shot—about the toe. I was now dropping it. What was the point of telling anyone anything?

Chapter 9

Margo was tilting on a chair, her feet up on the dining table, when I returned home from a client early the next day. Around the room, I saw the evidence of everything she had consumed. Any detective on a series could follow cookie crumbs to track her. I had had enough.

"Margo, we have to talk."

"I was thinking of you too."

"How long are you planning to stay?"

"Until you're feeling better."

"I'm feeling better," I said.

"Okay, then until *I* am feeling better."

I followed her to the living room, where she opened the sliding door to my terrace where I had grilled salmon when dieting for the wedding.

As we looked out, I said, "Do you think you could shut the light when you leave a room?"

"Now you sound like Dad." She imitated my father. "Do you have any idea what I pay for electricity?"

"Do you?" I screamed.

"You're yelling," she said.

"You're an ungrateful slob, Margo."

"Okay, so I'm not a clean freak, but I'm good company. Would you prefer someone clean who bored you to death?"

No. I wouldn't. Because I don't want anyone here at all.

The dismissal buzzer rang at the school across the street. We watched as students flooded the yard.

"You know, Lauren, if you want a baby, you should find a sperm donor. Or have sex with the first guy you meet. Or ask a male friend. Or adopt a child."

Thanks, Margo, because I could never think of any of those things on my own. The truth was, I was a traditionalist. I wanted a baby in the confines of a conventional family. Was it too late in the history of womanhood to admit that?

"But you want a family in the outmoded, old-fashioned way, which makes me wonder how you can possibly consider yourself a feminist. You want to break the ceiling where you work but nowhere else."

"And what about you?"

"Me?" Was she not on the terrace?

"Margo, did you ever think about having children?"

"No. I despised my childhood."

I thought she would expound on this, repeating every sentence she had ever said about growing up in the Leo household. How many times had she told me that Mom was a relic who went through life as though conducting a symphony while Margo was meant to be the lead in a rock band? Individuality in our home was out of place.

I was surprised when Margo directed the discussion another way.

"I'm sorry I didn't come to your wedding," she said.

I sniffed not to cry.

"It was wrong, but I thought Mom would go on about how much weight I had gained. I belonged at the wedding, but I didn't want to be shamed."

Bingo. I knew what she meant. I understood. I had lived it. But still . . .

"No one wants to be shamed," I said.

"True. Tell that to Mom."

"Believe me. I've tried."

That's what I said, but I knew it wasn't true.

"No, you haven't. You don't have it in yourself to tell her off. You need to come out guns blazing."

"So I put her in her place. She'll stay there an hour."

"Let's get out of here," Margo said. "Do you want to go shopping?"

"Not really."

"Oh, come on. Do it for me."

I thought getting out might improve my mood.

In an elegant boutique, part of a national chain I had never visited, a sales Barbie greeted us. Admiring the chic clothes, I became tense when I realized the store might not carry Margo's size.

The woman asked if she could help us. Short of ignoring the customer, the least effective approach. A good salesperson would know to show the customer merchandise, to suggest.

"We're looking," Margo said.

"My apologies. We do not have your size in store," the Barbie said as she scanned Margo up and down.

I took in her knee-length knit dress, so formfitting, she must have painted it on.

"I'm wearing your brand right now," Margo said, pinching her V-neck on top.

"Yes, we carry plus-wear online."

I tugged Margo's hand, turned to go. But Margo persisted.

"Let me guess," Margo said, stepping close enough to see the saleswoman's brain. "You believe large women—or 'mature' women, as you mistakenly call us—never leave home."

The saleswoman rubbed her nose job with one finger. "Not at all. There's just no room in the store."

"For large sizes or large people?" Margo sneered.

"Margo," I said, taking her gently by the arm. She wouldn't have moved if I attempted to drag her out of the store.

"What about handbags?" Margo said. "Do you carry large handbags?"

Once on the street, I expected my sister to blow up, but instead she smiled and said, "Let's have a sandwich somewhere."

I understood she wanted to eat her pain. Sour as it would taste in the long run.

She shook her head then, sounding defeated. "No, no. Let's go straight home."

"Let me in, Margo. What are you thinking?"

"I've gorged my way to type two diabetes."

It was no surprise she had diabetes, but why was she blaming herself for it?

"You didn't gorge your way to diabetes," I said.

"Then how did I get here?" Margo said, holding her hands out to display her body.

"Plenty of people eat the way you do, never exercise, and are fine."

"Name one."

That was easy. "Okay, me."

"So far," Margo said.

"Well, there's no history of diabetes in our family."

"Great. I'm the first! And you're wrong. I have no one to admonish but myself. I can't even point a finger at Mom. I was a thin kid. I was an adult when I picked up a fork and forgot to put it down. Killed my career with calories."

I had no idea what to say. But it didn't matter, because she ran on.

"Tell me the name of one substantially overweight actress in Hollywood."

In a tone that said I was clearly joking, I said, "Do you want me to google it?"

"Go ahead."

"That's ridiculous."

"No. Google it."

I stopped walking, typed "overweight actress" on my phone.

She waited, looking up at the sky.

Under "People also ask," the first question was, "Who is the fattest actress?" My heart sank. I couldn't believe there was a human cruel enough to ask such a question. I had dieted my way down; maybe there was a way I could help Margo. Trouble was, I had no idea how to make a suggestion without sounding like my mother.

I began with, "I lost weight for the Great Humiliation."

"And have you kept it off?" She said it like she was sure the answer was going to be "no, of course not."

"I'm afraid to look." I was depressed enough. I wasn't getting on a scale. My scale was my judge and jury. And I rarely got acquitted.

"The sequence is sick, vicious, untenable. I can't nab a part weighing what I weigh, and the more I don't work, the more time on my hands, the more I eat."

I got it.

We continued walking toward the Max.

"I know a movie producer who went to a residential weight-loss facility, but those places are few and far between. Very expensive. I'd have to stay a long time. I can't lose this weight in a day. I've really done myself in this time."

"Maybe we could find a facility covered by insurance."

"We?" She said "we" as though it were the strangest word in the dictionary.

I wanted to help her. Besides, it was easier to support her than it was to help myself. If she lost weight, maybe she could get a role on television, a recurring role. She would be happy.

That took care of one of us.

As we crossed Madison Avenue, where ad men in prehistoric times had smoked cigarettes and dumped on women, I said, "My friend's aunt went to a residential program in New Jersey."

"I hate New Jersey."

"Pretend you're in Hawaii."

"Where in New Jersey?"

"In an oil refinery. What difference does it make?" What was her problem? I liked Jersey. Bruce Springsteen liked New Jersey. Bon Jovi was from New Jersey. It was a musical state.

Tentatively, she said, "I guess all that camaraderie with people in the same boat could be motivational."

I patted her on the back. "There you go."

She stood still in her tracks.

I waited. I understood I had been walking barefoot on shattered glass.

"On the other hand, I might clean out a Wawa or a Cumberland Farms with my newfound friends."

Did anyone know better than me how easily that could happen?

◌෨

On Sunday morning, Margo moved from the couch to my bed.

"By the way, do you know where my remote is?" I asked her.

"To this TV?"

"To the one in the living room."

She checked around the bed, lifting the covers.

"Here," she said, handing it to me.

"Why is it in here?"

"I was holding it."

My phone rang. Steinbach. I could count the times—three—he had ever called on a weekend. Was there an emergency at the agency? I wondered what was up. I knew he was in Toronto with the creative director as well as the sterling new account guy, Matt Hutchins, pitching a yogurt company. Hutchins had played lacrosse with the CEO.

"How's your shoulder?" Steinbach said briskly.

My wrist, I thought. *It's my wrist, Steinbach.* I was about to tell him that, but he continued talking.

"There's bad news at New England Can. Personal, not professional."

"What happened?"

"Arthur passed away."

"Oh no," I said. "Oh no."

I had teamed with Arthur starting as an assistant on the Can account. The account executive, Jumping Jack—everyone called him that because he couldn't stand still—was scooped up by a larger advertising agency to service a feline litter account, and I was promoted to his position, meaning the account was mine to lead. If the business did well, I did well. A great deal of my success at Steinbach Kraus was due to the growth of New England Can.

"He had pancreatic cancer."

"I know," I said softly. My sadness stuck in my throat.

"My father had it. Gone in a month at seventy-three. What a killer."

"I'm sorry." "Sorry" didn't sound sympathetic enough. But what was? "Is there a funeral?"

"Yes. He'll be cremated. The memorial service is April 15 in Far Acres at the Moore family burial grounds," Steinbach said. "I have to go to Idaho to pump up the potato people, but I'll return early to see Arthur off."

It occurred to me I couldn't drive to Massachusetts.

"I can't drive—due to my injury." Only a week and a half had passed since the accident, and my wrist was wrapped in the band.

"We'll go together."

"Thank you. I appreciate it."

"No worries."

Eric always said "no worries." He picked it up on a trip to Sydney, Australia, to attend the International Conference of Condiment Connoisseurs.

When the call ended, I turned bleary-eyed to my sister. "My favorite client has passed away. My wedding. The accident. Now Arthur."

"Bad things come in threes."

"Spare me the cliché," I said.

Margo cocked her head. "'Spare me the cliché' is a cliché. Three things have occurred already. You're in the clear."

False. There were four things if I included my open-blouse assault of Steinbach. He hadn't mentioned the incident, likely chalked it up to my fragile state, but I would be embarrassed about my stupidity until I died.

There was a hill of inside-out apparel capped with leopard-print pajamas. I stared at it, wondering why it was on the floor.

"My laundry," Margo said. "When I go on a trip, I pack my laundry."

"You pack dirty clothing?"

"Yes."

"Arthur and I were tight," I said sadly.

"How tight?" Margo said with a smirk.

"Oh, stop it. I learned a lot from him, and I will miss him."

"Would you feel better if I did all the laundry? I mean yours too?"

I looked over to where her clothing was near my desk chair, her suitcase was wide open, and shoes were scattered about. She was an environmental hazard.

"The washer is in the basement. You need quarters."

"I prefer a laundry service—pickup, wash, dry, fold, drop off."

Apparently, if Margo offered to clean my apartment, I'd see a housekeeper.

Chapter 10

I met Joanna for drinks at a nearby bar. We convened at a high table in the rear of the room, chatting about her husband's new job as the maître d' at a well-known restaurant, lack of diversity in our advertising agency, Arthur's funeral—everything but being jilted by Eric. Talk about the elephant in the room. My no-wedding was a herd—and keeping it off the table took a lot of energy.

Joanna ordered a gin martini dry with blue-cheese olives. I asked for a glass of wine, sauvignon blanc from Sonoma, another, then another, until it was apparent that I should have ordered a bottle. There were cashews mixed with raisins on the table. I finished the bowl. Joanna didn't have any. She said she was going home for a late supper. What? What did one thing have to do with the other?

When I returned to the Max, I stepped off the elevator into the pungent scent of weed. I sniffed at Allie's door, 5A, but the marijuana was not from her place. I wondered what the rules were. Was it safe to smoke when you were with child? When Stephanie was pregnant, she gave up coffee and liquor. My mom said, "I drank coffee. I had wine. Look how nice you turned out." When Stephanie chose to breastfeed, Mom said, "I didn't breastfeed, and you're not fat." Well, she didn't breastfeed me, and she couldn't get off the subject of my weight.

Mrs. Tomolonius, 5C, lived on the other side of my place. She was eighty-five going on 110. Someone would have had to wake her up to give her a joint. Then they would have had to puff it for her. Mr. and Mrs. Hecht lived in Longboat Key, Florida, six months a year. It was clear Margo was having a party for herself.

I entered my apartment to see Margo splayed on the couch. On the coffee table, there were two large pizza cartons from Amadeus. I had no idea why a pizza place was named after an Austrian composer. There was also a half-eaten Greek salad in a huge aluminum tin, spots of dressing she had obviously ordered on the side, and one finished and one started bag of popcorn. My favorite bowl, the one I used for cereal, was now an ashtray. The mahogany bar cabinet with brass knobs and accents that had belonged to my grandmother was agape. On the serving shelf was Belvedere Vodka, Botanist Gin, and a bottle of Dewar's turned on its side.

"Oh, you're home," Margo said drearily. She was stoned, wearing a pink top—her boobs protruding, a turquoise necklace the girth of a giant's knuckle, rings, bracelets, a turban worthy of a fortune-teller, heavy makeup, fake eyelashes long enough to be tied.

"What's going on?" Had all of New York been invited to my apartment? And why didn't she ask me first? I would have said yes if given the opportunity. Now I was annoyed.

"My theater friends heard I was in New York."

"They heard?"

"All right, I paid for a billboard in Times Square."

"Illuminated?"

"Of course."

"Margo, the floor." Had she been tossing popcorn in the air? I couldn't imagine what her place in Santa Monica looked like. However, I was positive the Board of Health had visited.

"Stop getting upset. The popcorn is not alive," she said dramatically. "It's caramel. You couldn't eat something that wouldn't stick?"

I felt like our mother, a feeling I didn't enjoy. I couldn't believe I had to contend with Margo after battling the need to bawl all day. Earlier, in the bar with Joanna, I had noticed a thirtieth birthday celebration. My eyes watered at the sight of friends surrounding the birthday girl in song, cheering as she blew out her candles. Happy people should be sequestered from unhappy people.

From the couch, Margo almost toppled reaching down for the sticky popcorn. She deposited a handful of kernels in my former cereal bowl. She clapped her hands. "Voilà," she said, "the place is immaculate."

Not exactly. There were kernels too far to reach from the couch. Frustrated, I reprimanded her, which made me feel old and even more morose.

"Margo, I don't care if you have friends over, but you must clean up."

"You'll never see popcorn on this floor again. Maybe potato chips. But no popcorn."

I looked around the room, the dirty glasses, the crushed Amadeus napkins, and I worked up the courage to tell her it was time for her to crash with a friend or get a hotel room or sleep on the street wrapped in the blanket I would be glad to give her. No need to return it.

"Okay, so I'm not as spick-and-span as you. But I have other good qualities."

"Name one."

"I," she said, emphasizing the pronoun, "have an audition."

"Wow. Congratulations. That's great," I said sincerely.

I didn't want to ruin her shining moment. After all, she had an audition. I checked out the pizza. "Mushroom pizza? I hate fungi. Even the word is awful."

"Lauren, you weren't here when I ordered."

"What difference does that make?" I demanded. "What's the other pizza?"

"White with extra ricotta."

"What about regular pizza? The kind people from New York miss when they are anywhere else. If you're going to mess up my house, treat your friends to my liquor, the least you could do is order the pizza I like," I said angrily. I could give her a pass on the mess, but the pizza?

"I didn't know there would be any left over."

"Well, there is, and it's mushroom. And I don't understand white pizza. It makes no sense."

"So eat the salad."

"Why did you order salad?"

"The actresses barely eat at all. If a chorus girl puts ranch dressing on her salad, she considers it a buffet."

"You owe me a pizza," I said.

She tore off a slice, picked off the mushrooms, handed it to me.

"The only thing I dislike more than mushrooms is capers."

"Why capers?"

"I can't waste my time eating a food that small."

"Do you want to hear about my audition?" She patted the couch for me to sit next to her; then she consumed the mushrooms from my pizza, eating one at a time.

"Sure, of course." Despite everything, I was excited for her. Throughout our lives, I had rooted for her success.

"So listen to this. The director Robinson Mulvaney was here. Do you know who he is? Because everyone does."

I didn't, but I was too bushed to listen to his résumé, so I nodded.

"He wants me to read a part in a play."

Margo was on the upswing. It was great for her and for me. If my sister got a role in a play, maybe she would rent her own place.

"If the reading goes well, and if he can find deep pockets, real big money, the play could be produced off Broadway, but only if Mulvaney can get the right actress for the part I am reading—in his office in Soho on Thursday."

"Sounds promising," I said, confused. From what she said, I deduced she would perform at the reading, probably in someone's office, but if the play was staged, her role would go to a more famous actress. I didn't burst her bubble.

"I'm sorry about the mess," she said contritely.

"And the mushrooms?" I asked.

"And the mushrooms. Especially the mushrooms."

"Stephanie would have never ordered mushrooms," I teased.

"Funny, I don't see her here in your moment of need."

I gave her a look that said, "Stop." I wasn't in the mood to pile on Stephanie, who had been wonderful to me at the synagogue, or to entertain Margo by dissing her. "Eric hasn't called."

"Amazing, but I told you to remove his name from your phone."

"I did—for a day."

"I would slash every picture of him."

"I'm not you."

"I'm sorry," she quipped, and I had to laugh.

Margo toted tumblers into the kitchen, returned with paper towels, all-purpose cleaner, and furniture polish. I was surprised she wasn't afraid to break a finger pressing the pump.

"But why hasn't he texted or e-mailed or something?" I said, hoping Margo would respond with a reason that would make me feel better. Although I didn't think there was one.

"Maybe he's dead. That would be wonderful," she said, grinning.

"He's not dead. Only the good die young." I wandered to the terrace, stared at the schoolyard.

Margo hung an arm around me. "You need to get on with your life. Like me."

I was surprised she was networking. Maybe there was a lesson in that? Maybe I should get off my duff? Do something besides my job?

"Margo?"

"Yup?"

"You have caramel popcorn between your breasts."

Chapter 11

On a sunny morning, unappreciated by me, I waited on the sidewalk in front of the office for a lift to Westport, where I had to see the Bag Lady, international wholesaler of shopping bags for specialty stores. Due to the condition of my wrist, Steinbach had suggested I call on one of his chauffeurs whenever I traveled to an out-of-town client. He gave me the number of his favorite "guy," told me to sit in the back seat, and go for the ride until I ditched the brace.

I was greeting a coworker when a shining and spotless three-row Cadillac Escalade—raven black with chrome trim—pulled to the curb. Hallelujah. The car was sumptuous. I wouldn't knock myself out at the wheel—and big benefit, I could work as I traveled.

Steinbach's "guy" climbed out of the Escalade. "It's you again!"

"I remember you." *But I am not as excited to see you as you are to see me.*

"You remember me." He clutched his hands to his heart.

I still didn't need a charmer. "From the hospital. Thank you again."

"Rudy Cohen."

As I had forgotten his name, I reminded him of mine. "Lauren Leo."

The inside of the Escalade was futuristic, luxurious, spacious, leather with stitching. I sat in the heated second-row captain's chair behind the front passenger seat, noticing the speakers in the ceiling. I took in the bottled water, the healthy snacks.

I looked forward to opening my laptop in comfort. Wasn't that the point of a driver? But as Rudy started the car, I found myself sitting on Magna-Tiles, toys for building in assorted colors.

"How old was your last passenger?" I said to Rudy.

"An account guy from your office. Late sixties."

"He was playing with Magna-Tiles."

"No. Those are mine."

"And how old are you?" I asked as I discovered another tile.

"Thirty-six going on six," he said. "My half birthday is next Tuesday."

I put the Magna-Tiles together, then to a side.

"I drove my nephew to school."

"That's nice of you." I buried my head in my laptop, my forehead short of touching the keys. I had to look busy or this guy would yak the entire way to Westport. When I got to the Bag Lady, I'd want to put a bag over his head. I had never been big on random chatter. My current state of mind made responding downright grueling.

I checked my phone for any sign of Eric. This had become a tic. Stephanie and my friends were in touch, but only Kate would broach his name, which she altered to "that asshole," as in: "I can't believe that asshole hasn't called. Who does this?"

Eric Farkas. That Fark Ass.

"Last night, my nephew built the Eiffel Tower with Magna-Tiles," Rudy said proudly. "It looks like the Eiffel Tower anyway. That's what I told him. Would you believe he knew the Eiffel was in Paris? And he knew Paris was in France?"

I didn't respond.

"He did think France was near New York."

I was trying to work. What's more, I couldn't suffer Rudy's happiness so early in the day. Couldn't Steinbach have found a despondent driver?

"I'm surprised you knew those were Magna-Tiles."

I wasn't one to be rude. "I have two nieces."

"What are their names?"

"Olivia and Liza."

"How old are Olivia and Liza?"

"Forty and forty-two," I said, hoping to conclude the conversation. But he laughed. I had spurred him on.

"No. Really?"

"Eight and four."

I pictured the girls at my place, checking to see what I had in the fridge and the freezer. When I knew my nieces were coming, I stocked goodies Stephanie would never purchase. Happiness is a box of Cap'n Crunch.

"Do you smile when you're with them?"

I wondered why he asked.

"You don't smile much."

I hadn't thought my detachment was obvious. I felt contrite about that. After all, it wasn't about him. He couldn't be more pleasant. Was it possible to be too pleasant?

"You have to fight it."

"Fight what?" I had no idea what he was talking about.

"Bad days," he said. "I know from experience that talking helps."

Despite myself, I took interest in the conversation. "How long have you been driving for Steinbach?"

"Since before I could drive."

I almost laughed. Not quite. "How long ago was that?"

"A few months. He was friends with my father."

"Was your father in advertising?"

"No. They robbed banks together." He laughed at his own joke.

111

I smiled, my first full smile since the Great Humiliation. "What did your father do?"

"You've heard of Bonnie and Clyde?"

"Of course."

"He was Bonnie."

Rudy was entertaining. But I wouldn't allow myself to be cheered up.

"I have work to do," I said.

Creeping on a local road, we stopped behind one school bus, then another, and whenever I looked up and out, I saw yellow. Every few streets, there were children with mothers waiting on corners. Most wore sneakers, sweatshirts, khakis, or jeans. Monogrammed knapsacks sat on the grass near the road. Rudy hit the brake. I watched as children skipped up to a bus and a few mothers waved goodbye. I wondered what the moms did when their children were at school. I guessed mother by mother who was going to work and where, who was headed to the gym or the tennis court or the library to volunteer, who needed to straighten up the house.

If I had children, which mother would I be? I had thought about packing it in and staying home after I had my first baby. In one Mommy and Me scenario, I would leave Steinbach. I would start my own advertising agency. I could do what I loved yet make my own hours, be on call for my kids, invite their friends to the house with the awesome mom—and the best treats. I wouldn't have to oblige Steinbach or anyone else. Dreamy-eyed and naive—because to remain in business, I would have to answer to my clients.

The children in the rear of a school bus were waving at Rudy. I watched as he waved back—first with one hand and then with two. *Put your hands on the wheel.*

When would I ever be in a good mood again?

"I love kids," he said as he gestured some more. "Look how thrilled they are by a wave. Adults want this and want that. Nothing is good enough. All these kids ask for is a wave. You should wave."

Maybe you should leave me alone and drive.

"Come on," he said.

I waved. Twice. Then I sat back. I memorized the snacks in the car, but I didn't take one. Instead, I thought about the food I had been shoveling in. I had to maintain a size 12, my current size. If I started gaining weight, I would plummet into the cycle of the damned—swallowing feelings with carbohydrates, burping up self-hate. I had taken many surveys. Check one. Do you overeat when happy? Unhappy? Anxious? Calm? All of the above.

My phone interrupted the rant in my head.

"How's your frame of mind?" Kate said.

"Okay."

"Tell me you're not thinking about that asshole."

"No. Never. Not at all, but I decided there was a positive side to being left at the altar."

As I said it, I saw Rudy's head lean back as though he were listening, and I regretted that he could hear me, but I wanted to talk to Kate.

"What's that?" Kate said.

"I lost weight for the wedding."

Kate laughed. "With you, everything is about weight."

"Story of my life."

"Are you honestly okay? Because I'm thinking maybe you should speak to someone. A shrink, a psychologist."

"I'm talking to you."

"I mean a professional. My friend Jackie is seeing someone she swears by."

"Jackie, who keeps a dozen feral cats in a studio apartment?"

"Well, yes."

"Thanks, but no thanks."

"Consider it," Kate said.

"Do you think I'm going to let an insignificant event like being left at the altar upset me? Worse things have happened. I just can't think of any at the moment."

"What about meds? Something calming?"

"I am not medicating. Somehow I'm going to yank myself up."

"Weed? If you want, I will google the address of a dispensary."

"Kate . . ."

"Okay, how can I help?"

"Just don't tell me I'll meet someone else. I'm finished. Seven percent—seven percent is the chance of a woman over forty getting married in this country. Easier to get into Harvard—without graduating high school."

"Well, you can't go by statistics. When my mom succumbed to her disease, there was a ninety-five-percent survival rate. Okay, then. No medications. No shrink."

"Thank you."

How many friends like Kate does a woman get in life?

"What are best buddies for?" Kate said.

"For this, I guess. By the way, I have more news. Margo showed up."

"Really?"

"She's staying with me."

"How's that?"

"She abducted my apartment."

"Not good. Fish and visitors."

"I think you meant fish and sisters."

"How long is she staying?"

"I don't know. I probably made a mistake letting her move in."

"Can't she go to Stephanie's?"

Guffaw.

"You're taking on too much. Look after yourself."

I lost my bravado. "How pathetic would it be to say I wish Eric would call me?"

"You could call him. But I wouldn't."

"What would you do?"

"By now, I would have killed him."

"I could do that. But I'm too claustrophobic to spend my life in prison."

"I would bring you a file," Kate said.

"Make sure it's in a cake."

I watched Rudy lean forward again. I felt like saying something outrageous to Kate, like that I drove by Eric's house, shot bullets through a window while he looked out.

Off the phone, I was relieved Rudy didn't say a word about what he had heard. I read e-mails, several from the synagogue asking when I was planning to retrieve my possessions from the bridal suite. I erased each message with a flourish.

"You don't need to be any thinner," Rudy said.

Can you repeat that? And say it louder—on the radio. Maybe I should marry this driver. Or not listen to a word of his baloney.

"Thank you, but commentary on a person's appearance is inappropriate."

"Even if the comment is a compliment?"

"I think so."

"Okay, then I won't say nice things."

That would be a shame. And leave me wondering what the nice things were. "Did you have something nice you wanted to say?"

He shook his head. "No more nice things."

I went back to his original comment. That I didn't have to lose weight. No one had ever said that to me before. I had reached size 12, but if I didn't start gaining, I could lose more. Kate was a 6. That's right. Always feel lousy about yourself, Lauren. To take my mind off making myself more miserable, I talked to him.

"How much do you weigh?" I asked him.

"195," he said.

"Would you date a girl who weighed more than you?"

"How much more than me?"

"Ten pounds," I said.

"Of course."

"Thirty pounds?"

"Absolutely."

"Two thousand pounds," I said as though it was my last offer.

"Why are you suspicious of me?"

"Because you were eavesdropping on my conversation?"

"It's a small car." I could see from the side of his face that he was grinning. He was having a good time. He considered me amusing. He was a good way to pass time.

"Anyway, it's not you. I find men an unreliable source."

"All men? Now that's far-reaching."

"No. Just the ones who ask me to marry them."

"Sounds like you took a pounding."

"Watch out," I said as a school bus halted in front of us. I remembered taking the bus. It was awful. My stop was one of the last on the route. I rode with Stephanie. When we climbed on, Stephanie's popular friends were in the far back, calling her name. Every day, my sister was hailed to the last row. I might as well have sat on the bus driver's lap. Although they all rode the bus, they referred to it as the Loser Cruiser—and I was queen of the losers. I told Mom I was lonely on the bus. "Lonely?" she answered back. "It's a school bus. It's filled with kids."

"How'd you knock off the weight?" Rudy said, interrupting my memories of mustard-yellow hell.

"I went on a diet, no carbs, to fit into my wedding gown. Then, as you accidentally overheard, I was jilted."

"So you were about to marry a jerk?"

Well, that was a good way to look at it. Now I had to hope a litany of "wise" sayings wasn't coming.

"His loss." Like everyone else, Rudy had a way with clichés.

"I hope so, and I wish someone would tell him that instead of plying me with advice. My mother is petrified I will regain the weight before I meet someone new."

"Does she say this to you?" There was surprise in his voice—as though he had never met a person who would say such a hurtful thing. But then he hadn't met Ellen Leo.

"Repeatedly since I was born."

"You must tell her to stop."

"The woman couldn't be stopped by a train—if she was standing in the middle of the tracks. Weight is her big issue. Pardon the pun."

"Is she heavy?"

I laughed. "For a wafer."

"When is the last time you told her to quit harassing you, to lay off?"

"I guess I didn't. I just ignore her. Or I change the subject. Or I leave."

"But you're not ignoring her."

Maybe "ignore" was the wrong word. In any case, what gave him the right to judge my behavior? I knew him about as long as it took to stop at a red light.

"You're taking every bit of it in, and it's hurtful. She's abusing you. Tell her to stop."

From his tone, you would think my mother was brutalizing me with a red-hot iron.

I defended her. "Abusing me? That's overstating things."

"It's verbal abuse."

"I don't think you understand." I didn't know how to explain that my parents were good people, but weight was the sword my mother would die on.

"I understand plenty."

Who died and left him Freud?

On the other hand, I found myself interested. "Look, I'm not great at confronting my mother. I'm her fourth-favorite daughter, and she only has three daughters." What I really hated about that remark was that I had been using it as material since I was in junior high, and it was still true. Even though Margo aggravated my mother, she had always excused Margo. "You have to give her credit," my mother would say. I had no idea when I would get any credit.

"You need to confront her."

How many times a day? My mother mentioned my weight whenever there was food around, whether it was a billboard for McDonald's, a Little Debbie delivery truck, an apple-cider-donut stand, a holiday meal.

"You only have to say it one time the right way."

"What's the right way?" Who knew? Maybe he had all the answers.

"So she will never forget you said it."

"Do you read advice columns?"

"No."

I stationed my laptop next to me. "Well, in every situation, they tell the person asking the question to confront the person they are having a problem with, to tell the person straight-out to knock it off. But if you do that, the person will despise you, probably never speak to you again. I try to avoid that."

"You are a milquetoast because you don't want to be disliked."

"Wow. Is there a couch in this car?"

"Better to speak up, to stand your ground, rather than be assaulted. Your mother has no right to make you feel less than."

"She's my mother." I was now annoyed. "Besides, when is the last time you spoke to your mother?"

"Two years ago."

Two years? I was happy he wasn't my son.

"I don't see her often now that she has passed away."

I regretted my lame attempt at a "gotcha" moment.

"She lived in Boca Raton. When I dropped out of law school, she told her book club I was going blind."

"You went to law school?"

"Yes. My eyesight was twenty-twenty, but I didn't want to be a lawyer."

"No one wants to be a lawyer."

He bit. "What do law students want to be?"

"Writers. Tell me more." I had to admit to myself that Rudy was entertaining, and I would rather talk about him than myself.

"When I visited, Mom played canasta for hours in her clubhouse at Heaven's Gate Village."

"Heaven's Gate Village? Isn't that the place where the man drove his Lincoln Town Car over a woman sleeping on a chaise, dragging her into the pool?"

"You win some. You lose some."

"Wasn't that man one hundred years old?"

"Yes, but he didn't look a day over ninety."

It was easy to talk to Rudy, and he was quick-witted. I wondered why he was driving for a living. I didn't want to ask. After all, I hardly knew him.

"What did you do after law school and before this?"

"I was a magician's assistant."

"I would have liked to have seen that."

"Keep your eyes out for a rabbit."

"On the road?"

"In the car."

I enjoyed his company despite myself.

Chapter 12

The visit to the Bag Lady went well. Sales were up, and she credited my agency. On the ride back, Rudy and I chatted about advertising. I was surprised. He knew quite a bit from simply listening to the partners and clients in the Escalade. He said he mostly learned from overhearing Steinbach on the phone. I teased, "Don't tell me you listen in!" The whole day had perked me up, yet I was as foul as the weather the next morning. Out my living room window, the city was gray and overcast.

"I need an umbrella," I thought aloud to Margo.

She yawned, jacked up her head to see the sky from her makeshift bed on my purple couch. "It's not going to rain."

"If I don't take an umbrella, it will pour."

I went to the hall closet, where there was a lifetime supply of inexpensive, compact black umbrellas I had bought when I thought it wasn't going to rain. I stashed one in my briefcase. I walked to my office. I waited outside for Rudy, who was to drive me to the client, Dara Casey. Rudy had taken my mind off Eric, and I was looking forward to more psychotherapy. People took advice from their bartenders and stylists, so why not confide in my driver?

As Steinbach and Hutchins exited the building, I watched Steinbach pat Hutchins on his back. Already an adopted son. Hutchins's navy suit fit so well, it had to be a custom order. I was annoyed, certain that while I had hid Ring Dings wrappers in my night-table drawer, Hutchins was a teen model for Abercrombie & Fitch.

Steinbach approached me. "Cutting it close. Isn't Dara Casey at nine a.m.?" He explained to Hutchins: "Dara is the daughter of Howard Raff, the retail magnate."

"Of course," Hutchins replied. "He's a media mogul too."

"Dara is dallying in upscale boutiques for women. Lauren will land the account—and who knows from there."

To Steinbach, Dara was a little girl. He wanted her father.

"I look forward to meeting her dad," Hutchins said.

What a creep.

Rudy pulled up.

"Good morning," he said, robustly, to the three of us.

You're late, I thought. But I didn't verbalize it, because Steinbach was in the mix. I had no reason to embarrass Rudy.

As soon as Rudy was in "Drive," I said, "I prefer punctual people."

"I texted," he said.

No. I don't ever need another text from a man. Well, at least Rudy didn't text Stephanie.

I called my client, apologizing, assuring her I was on my way.

"That's fine," she said, "but this doesn't reflect well on your agency. Please be on time from now on."

I detested a reprimand, a remnant from my overcriticized, underadored childhood. My mother assessed, called out, corrected every microcrime I committed. My dad studied my report cards, believing he was being of help pointing out a B-plus that could have been an A-minus if I worked a bit harder. Therefore, as an adult, I lay low, keeping quiet for fear of a "scolding." By the time I was twelve, I knew everything Margo did would be considered outrageous or belligerent. I would be viewed as incompetent. Golden Girl Stephanie skipped through life triumphant.

I didn't want to say anything to Rudy I would regret, so I read the *New York Times*. A great thing about the *New York Times* is how long and wide it is, covering your face when you read it.

"What's with the mood?" Rudy said.

"Honestly?"

"No, make something up," he said.

"Why were you late?"

"Miss Escobar-Diaz asked to have a chat."

"Miss Escobar-Diaz?"

"My nephew's teacher."

Didn't his nephew have a mother or a father?

"He kicked a kid."

"Did the kid kick him first?" I said, in an attempt to lighten up.

"Yes," Rudy said.

"Self-defense!" I declared.

"Thank you for not saying I was delayed in front of Steinbach."

I was impressed by his appreciation. "You were late?" I said, kidding.

"You're kind," Rudy said.

"Sometimes too kind."

"Well, you're not a yes-man."

I opened a small bottle of Evian. "No. I'm a yes-woman." And I needed to stop.

"Oh, come on. I don't believe that."

I asked him, "Were you ever overweight or did you stand out in some way?"

"I stuttered. Heck of a time with the letter 'L,' as in Lauren."

I was surprised to hear he had stuttered as a child because his speech was fine. Also, he was outgoing and easy to talk to. Despite my defense system, I had revealed more to Rudy Cohen in the Escalade than I had to anyone I had known for such a short time. The Escalade was intimate.

"Well, I was overweight. Not that overweight. But heavier than my sisters. I was vigilant—about diverting attention to me, to my size. I feared the first tomato thrown would be salted with the F-word."

"F-word?"

"Fat. Cruelest word in the dictionary." It didn't take more than that sentence to dredge up the time two girls behind me in gym class had whispered the adjective and suggested I looked like the giant ball we were about to toss.

I was astonished I was talking to Rudy as though a patient on his couch. He was the driver. I was the employer. Well, Steinbach was the employer. Who knew what Rudy and Steinbach discussed? I wanted to clam up, but apparently the Evian in the Escalade contained a powerful truth serum.

"So?"

"I was agreeable."

"And now?"

"Habit."

"You have a habit of being a nice person?" He grinned. "That's awful. You should end that immediately."

"I have a habit of people-pleasing," I said, laughing at his mock outrage, cajoled out of my lousy mood.

∽

To Die For was the name of the business now owned by Dara Casey. Dara's customer base consisted of young suburban moms whose credit cards had no limits. For this reason, I was stupefied when Rudy pulled in front of the shop where we were to meet her. The signage was lifeless, the windows dreary. Were we in the wrong place?

Inside the clothing boutique, Dara Casey wore a taupe dress, a beige cardigan. She had long, dark curls. Her eyes were big, her cheekbones high. She was unfolding a raspberry sweater. Three saleswomen, in neutral colors, hung on her words.

"What a marvelous sweater," I said. "Lauren Leo from Steinbach Kraus."

She shook my hand. "Dara Casey. Do you love it?"

I lit up in approval. "Love it."

"You must try it on."

The last thing I wanted to do.

"You must," she repeated, pointing to the fitting room.

I pasted on a smile, followed her instruction.

"Is it the right size?" Dara said from the other side of the curtain.

Thanks to my wedding diet, she had figured me a medium. The fitting room did not have a mirror. I would be forced to exit, uncertain of my appearance. I groused at the thought of modeling for the saleswomen. I looked down. Was the sweater pulling? Was I stretching it out? I would rather lie on a bed of nails than come out. But this was business.

As I stood breathless, waiting for the horror to be over, Dara adjusted the fuzzy bell sleeves, the colossal cowl neck. She stepped back to assess. The three saleswomen nodded approval. Did I mention I didn't like to call attention to myself?

"Check the mirror," Dara said. "You are about to fall in love."

I was too tense to fall in love.

"I have to have this!" I said, because that was the smart thing to say.

"Yes, it is you," Dara said. "Do you worship the color? You must wear raspberry often."

I stopped myself from saying navy was my most vibrant fashion choice. I once had something in raspberry—a yogurt. I kept the sweater on—twinned with my black skirt. We sat at a round oak table beside the mirror. Dara asked me what I had done before I was in advertising. I told her I was a camp counselor, and she laughed.

"I've been in advertising since I could buy a glass of wine."

"Good thing," she said. "I hear it's a tough business to be in if you can't have a drink."

We chatted on. She mentioned she had gone to camp. Lo and behold, it was mine. I was older, so I never knew her or didn't remember her. Within half an hour, we were as good as singing "Kumbaya."

I told Dara I would visit all her stores but asked to see some photographs. Was this the dowdiest? The others had to be better. She flipped through pictures on her laptop. The exteriors were all dated, many different dates.

She leaned forward. "Tell me what you think so far."

Start with the positive. "To Die For could set the pace for boutiques all over the country. The choice of merchandise is stunning."

She kissed her fingertips. "You should see what we ordered for fall."

"I know you called me here today to discuss advertising, but I must be honest. There's a lot to consider before we start the creative process. Your boutiques require unification. A new logo, a facade and windows as up-to-the-minute as the fashion in your stores."

Dara took it in.

Had I hurt her feelings? I had to tell the truth. The haphazard storefronts were a turnoff.

"And in the meantime?"

"There's the existing consumer base, pleased to see the store updated. And to reach new patrons, clearance sales due to the renovation. You can carry some great lines of clothing—special offers—for that purpose."

Slowly, she smiled. I could tell by her expression that she would consider change but was hoping to get by—for now—without a massive investment. I waited for it all to roll over her; then I said, "What do you think?"

She nodded. "I like you."

"I tell it like it is." I was relieved I wasn't going to be dressed down.

She placed her elbows on the table, locked her hands together. Her fingers moved. "This is big."

"Yes, it is."

I guessed Dara Casey would have to deliberate, ruminate, discuss it with her investment partners, her bank, her accountant, her palm reader, whoever. I wondered whether other agencies she interviewed had broached the exteriors. If she decided against us because of my suggestions, Steinbach would slaughter me.

"I have to leave to attend a play at my son's school," she said. "He's Miss Hannigan in *Annie*."

"*He's* Miss Hannigan?"

"They needed someone taller than the orphans."

I liked her. I wanted to go with her to see her son in *Annie*.

"Next time, lunch," Dara said.

"You're on, my friend. And let me pay for this sweater."

"$499, but for you, it's $479. Not bad for the quality," Dara said.

"A deal," I said, choking at the price—but I slid my AmEx through the credit card machine.

She slipped the receipt and the black suit jacket I had come in with into a bag.

Once the shop had a new exterior, I would tell her to avoid bargain-store price points. To round up to $500 and down to $475.

Since I had packed my umbrella, the sun was now shining. I was hot and itchy in the raspberry sweater. Rudy was in the Escalade, a few yards down the empty, tree-lined street. I slid in.

"New sweater?" Rudy said.

"From the client," I said, wishing he wouldn't wag on. I had spent myself at the boutique in more ways than one.

"I guess you get a lot of swag."

"You should see my haul from the Emmys. I'm a celebrity."

"That's why I look out for you."

On a dime, I turned gnarly. "You don't have to look out for me. You're a wonderful driver, but this is not *Driving Miss Daisy*. We don't have a lifetime of endearing friendship in front of us. I'm not southern. I don't have a son, and he won't realize how much you have done for me in the end."

"Whoa. Where did that come from?"

"I've been through a lot lately," I said, backing up my biting verbiage because I realized that I had way overdone it because I was uncomfortable with Dara and the Three Wise Saleswomen fussing over me in the sweater; I had squandered $479 on an unnecessary purchase, as I could have closed the deal without it; Rudy was a man, the same species as Eric; the sun won't come out tomorrow.

I continued. "Don't take this personally."

"Never," he said.

"Because it's not personal."

"I get it. It's general," Rudy said.

"Exactly. I hope I never meet another man again."

"Ouch!" he said as he shook his hands above the steering wheel.

My head hurt, and I reached into my bag to find Tylenol. I swallowed two with Evian. In addition to Evian, there was Perrier as well as dried fruit—apricots, apples, banana chips. I took a package of apricots. I loved dried apricots. I wanted another pack, but there was only one more, and I didn't want Steinbach to complain of no apricots to Rudy next time he was in the car. *What the heck,* I thought as I plucked the pack and ripped it open. Steinbach could eat banana chips.

My phone rang again. It was Arlene Flakowitz, coordinator from Temple Sons of Abraham. I answered because she had reached out to me multiple times, and I wanted to be rid of her. Arlene had a heavy Queens accent. Queens the borough, not the ruler. She spoke as though her nose was stuffed and her throat had a chicken in it.

"What's a matter? You don't answer e-mails?"

Just what I needed, reprimanding. I loathed reprimands, even picayune, innocent ones. I cringed when the dental hygienist told me I didn't floss often enough. In fact, I switched my dentist multiple times to avoid being scolded. It was easier than training myself to floss.

"How can I help you?" I realized I had pressed "Speaker" but didn't care that Rudy was listening. "Is something wrong?"

"I have gout," she said. "Too much uric acid. But that's not the problem."

"What is the problem?" *And why are you calling me about it?* I didn't want the presents, reminders of the wedding, I didn't belong to the temple. I hadn't booked the wedding. I was an innocent party to my own destruction.

"I'm sorry your wedding didn't work out. But you know what they say?"

Let's see. One door closes, another one opens. There are plenty of fish in the sea. Every pot has a cover. You miss one bus, you catch the next. Talk may be cheap, but three-hundred-year-old sayings are free.

"I'm fine, thank you."

"Well, you may be fine, but I'm not fine. Your wedding gifts are in the suite for the bride. Not as many as I would have thought for such a large crowd, but still."

"The groom of doom can have them all."

Most guests were from his side, many his parents' friends—Myrna's event-planning clients as well as anyone who had ever given Stanley a business lead. My family, my friends had a practice of sending cards in advance with checks I had already deposited.

"Where's your head? You don't leave wedding gifts for a man who left you at the altar. Did your mother teach you anything? What school did you go to?"

"I thought he would return the gifts."

"You have a lot to learn, *mamaleh.*"

Oh no. Now she was talking my grandmother's native language.

Arlene went on. "If I gave you a gift, I wouldn't want it back simply because you were humiliated."

Rudy turned from the road to peek at me as he heard this statement. He was shaking his head. Arlene was unbearable.

"Look, Arlene, call Eric."

"I did. He hasn't returned my calls."

"Then call his parents."

"I called Myrna. She said she was too embarrassed to come to the synagogue."

"For the gifts?"

"Ever again."

"I don't care who you call. Just don't call me. I don't want the wedding gifts."

"Listen to me, Lauren. We haven't had an event here since your wedding, but there's one on Sunday. We need the room. Her name is Aviva. She's nineteen."

Who ties the knot at nineteen anymore? By the time she was my age, she would be married two decades—or not.

"Arlene, I have to go. Please don't call me again."

I understood the woman was doing her job, but I refused to recoup the gifts. Too painful. Too many gifts from Eric's family and his parents' friends, strangers to me. If Arlene had to empty the room, she could donate everything. There. Something good could come from something bad. That had to be Talmudic.

"Wow," Rudy said. "It was so awful, you don't want the goodies?"

"Yes, it was horrific. Besides, how many espresso makers does one girl need?"

"What did he do?"

"He texted my sister Stephanie immediately before the ceremony."

"Did he have someone else?"

"That question is personal."

"Well, did he?" Rudy lifted his head so I could see his face in the mirror. Did he think I would lie if I didn't see his eyes?

I didn't need to hesitate. I did not believe Eric had someone else. And if he had, by now the camp grapevine would have spread the news. And although that gossip would not have gotten to me in a game of telephone, I knew Kate would have told me, because there was no doubt I would have flown to Chicago to tell her if things had been the other way around. "Eric wasn't ready to grow up. He was immature."

"That's what Steinbach said."

"Excuse me?"

"Yesterday Steinbach was discussing you in the car."

"He talks about me?"

"Everybody talks about everyone. There are no secrets," Rudy said, as though this was something I should have already known.

"Whom do *you* talk about?"

"You." He raised his eyebrows purposefully in the mirror so I could see his expression.

I wondered what he said about me.

"Let's go get the gifts," Rudy announced, as though it was undoubtedly, unmistakably the thing to do.

I lowered my window to let in air. "I'm not getting the gifts."

"Why?"

"Too traumatic."

"Not if you have company. We can do it together. We'll bypass this Arlene. We'll grab the gifts from the room, load the car in a hurry, scoot into Manhattan. Then one day, when you're in a decent mood, you'll tell me what you received. We'll laugh about it."

"Okay, we pick up the gifts. Then what?"

"It's simple. Keep what you want. The rest—donate."

"Is that what you would do?" I said, curious to hear about his endgame.

"There must be a homeless shelter in need of a designer ten-speed blender imported from Italy and sold exclusively at Bloomingdale's."

"Must be."

"So you agree."

He hadn't changed my mind. I reached for another Evian. It was refreshing. I guess water tastes good when you have been left high and dry.

"Did you receive such a blender when you got married?" I said, fishing.

He arched his back, straightened up in his seat. "Me? I'm single. I lived with my girlfriend for four years, but we wanted different things. For example, I'm never leaving Brooklyn. It's the promised land. She was done with New York City. What's more, she believed she should move to Los Angeles to make it as a performer."

"So she left?"

"Yes."

"And?"

"She made it."

"Good for her."

"Have you heard of Lady Gaga?"

"You almost married Lady Gaga?"

"No. I'm asking if you ever heard of her."

I laughed. He laughed.

"We're going in, partner. We're going to get the gifts."

"Okay," I said, throwing up my hands.

Chapter 13

At the entrance to Temple Sons of Abraham, a guard was stationed inside a prefabricated booth. He wore a hunter's hat with ear flaps. He asked our names. I said John Lennon here to see Paul McCartney. This cost me. Because I joked, Rudy and I were told to display two forms of identification.

In the lot, Rudy chose the spot that said RESERVED FOR CLERGY.

"Maybe you shouldn't park here. This is for clergy."

"Yes, but if you're John Lennon, I am clergy."

"Oh, come on. You're not really taking the rabbi's spot."

"Just testing to see if you're awake."

There was another guard at the door to the synagogue. It was impossible to miss his gun in a holster.

Rudy said, "It's heartbreaking that a synagogue has to be protected this way."

I agreed.

The guard studied us, top to bottom. He zeroed in on Rudy.

"Can I see your license?" he said.

Rudy showed his identification. Rudy responded to a question in Hebrew. I was surprised he knew Hebrew.

The guard decided we weren't dangerous, and he let us in.

"What did you say to him?" I asked.

"You can't judge a book by its cover."

"How is it you know Hebrew?"

"Three months in the heat on a kibbutz picking tomatoes."

"Sounds like you didn't enjoy it."

"I no longer eat tomatoes," he said.

I was delighted to discuss his dislike of tomatoes or anything else to postpone entering the bridal suite. It was akin to returning to the scene of a massacre—all the gifts were bodies yet to be removed.

I peppered Rudy with questions in order to delay. "How long were you in Israel?"

"I told you. Three months. After I graduated college."

"Which college?"

"Harvard, then Yale, then Princeton," he joked. "Lauren, you're stalling."

I stopped dead at the door.

"Come on, champ. You can do this," he said.

"I can, but do I want to?"

He waited. "Fine. Let's turn around."

The choice of leaving gave me courage. "No way. We're going in."

Apparently, the wedding business had been slow. Dead of winter wasn't a top choice for a wedding date. All that worry about the weather. But most important, a wedding in a synagogue wasn't as popular as it had once been. Couples preferred art museums, galleries, parks, barns— but Myrna and Stanley had browbeaten Eric, and I should have noticed he was a juvenile then and there. It wasn't Eric's fault alone. I was too eager to please. I went along to go along. I wanted to marry Eric much more than I cared about the location of the wedding.

Everything in the bridal suite was as I had left it. I half expected the exact spot I had been standing when Stephanie told me about the text to be circled in chalk, the way police outlined a body found in the movies. Someone had stacked the presents in a corner. The vibrator was sideways on the vanity, where I had left it.

"Was that a gift?" Rudy directed my attention to the vibrator, raising an eyebrow. He was having fun.

"From the groom," I cracked.

"Good thing he ran off."

His sense of humor eased my nerves. "Actually, it was a gag from my bridesmaids—something blue."

"You had bridesmaids? In matching dresses?"

What a waste of fabric.

"How do you know the vibrator was a joke? Maybe your friends were serious, and it was a warning."

"Very funny." I shook a finger at him. "The balloon I was in when we became engaged should have been the warning."

"How so?"

"The balloon was stop-sign red. Full of hot air like the groom."

"I wouldn't donate the vibrator to a homeless shelter," he said with a smile.

"Why? It would be more useful than an espresso machine."

I settled on the couch Stephanie had been on when I spoke on the phone to Eric, when Eric dumped me from his cell in Starbucks waiting to use the bathroom. A new low for dumping.

"You okay?" Rudy said.

"Life goes on." I didn't mean it, but what was the point of dragging him down?

"Your face isn't saying life goes on."

My face was saying I was a fool not to perceive before the wedding that Eric had reconsidered. Or had I not noticed because I didn't want to? Because I had wanted sorely to move into the next stage of my life.

I needed to unload. Rudy would hear me out. The man liked to talk, but he also enjoyed listening.

"You know what my mother told me? She said I was fortunate Eric didn't leave me with a baby. But I wish he had left me with a baby. I wish we had married and I had gotten pregnant and had a baby. Then he could leave me."

A tear trickled. Another. The past was painful. The truth was awful.

"That wouldn't be great for your child." He handed me a tissue from the vanity. He nestled next to me, as sympathetic as a friend I had known for many years.

"Plenty of children are brought up by single mothers."

"My nephew has a single mother, but she's ill and now he lives with me."

I was surprised. He had mentioned a nephew, but I was unaware he was raising him. Rudy was easygoing and mellow—as though he didn't have an obligation in the world. I figured Rudy drove for a living because he didn't want to exert himself. He lived with, cared for his nephew. The Magna-Tiles had new meaning.

"What's your nephew's name?" I asked.

"Aidan," he said.

"I like that name. Where is he?"

"School, of course. Then afterward, he goes to the community center. I get him at six thirty."

"Every day?" There was more to Rudy than I had thought.

"My friends pitch in. Stacy and Sheri live in my building. Stacy is a graphic designer. She works from home."

"Can I ask what's wrong with your sister?"

"She's in a coma."

"That's terrible." I was complaining about gifts to a man who had a sister in a coma, a nephew to raise, while working a full-time gig. What a hardship. I thought about the fight Aidan had at school, the reason Rudy had been late. I wondered if Aidan's mother would recuperate. I scolded myself. *Be grateful for what you have, brat.* I observed the back of Rudy's neck. He was perspiring and sort of nodding. I tapped his shoulder in sympathy.

I asked, "What happened?"

He told the story in one tone—as though an outline for his book report. "It was late October. Libby and I dropped Aidan at his grandparents' home in Suffern for the day. Aidan's father, Jeb, is missing in action, somewhere in Colorado. Jeb abandoned Aidan, but his folks stay close and involved. Anyway, my sister and I cycled on a bike trail. We did that a lot. We were miles in. Having a great time. Libby hit a boulder on the otherwise vacant road. She fell forward. Hit the ground, bruised her head."

I gasped. "Oh, Rudy."

I recalled biking the trail in Cape Cod. For a while, Eric was way ahead of me. I could have tumbled, and he wouldn't have noticed until he hit the brake to wait up. But Rudy was riding next to his sister. He saw her topple off the bicycle, onto the ground. "Was she wearing a helmet?"

He looked annoyed, so irritated I half expected him to repeat my helmet question in a high, squeaky voice. I regretted I asked.

"Of course," he said as though I was a fool.

"I'm sorry about your sister. Sorry her son has to live with you."

"Hey, watch that. It's a treat to live with me."

I gave him an elbow. "I didn't mean it that way—and I'm sure it's a treat to have you for a buddy. Who knows what happens, what the real story is in someone else's life? It reminds me of that poem."

Then Rudy recited, "Whenever Richard Cory went down town, We people on the pavement looked at him: He was a gentleman from sole to crown. Clean favored, and imperially slim. And he was always quietly arrayed, And he was always human when he talked; But still he fluttered pulses when he said, 'Good-morning,' and he glittered when he walked. And he was rich—yes, richer than a king—And admirably schooled in every grace: In fine, we thought that he was everything to make us wish that we were in his place. So on we worked, and waited for the light, And went without the meat, and cursed the bread; And Richard Cory, one calm summer night, Went home and put a bullet through his head."

"Wow. You know the entire poem."

"It's famous. What do you think, I drive for a living so I couldn't possibly know a poem?"

"I didn't mean it that way."

"My apologies," he said.

I wished Eric had offered apologies to me. The man ran as though from a raging fire. The fact that he had never reached out to explain or ask forgiveness was cruelest.

"Let's get this stuff out of here," I said abruptly, before more thoughts of Eric filled my head.

Rudy piled packages, all different sizes. I grabbed a box, the basket, the vibrator.

Arlene was at the entrance. She wore putty pants, a brown shirt, both some kind of wrinkly crepe. She completed her fashion statement with round-toed, beige orthopedic shoes, Velcro closures.

I was not looking forward to a conversation.

"You're here!" Arlene held my face between her hands. She hadn't been affectionate on the telephone. I guessed she was relieved I was doing my duty.

I backed up slightly, as did Rudy.

She looked Rudy over. Top to bottom and back again, her eyes landing on the fly of his pants.

"You might have told me you were coming—as a courtesy."

"I intended to leave a note," I said.

"I see you brought a boyfriend."

Rudy introduced himself, extended his hand.

Arlene concentrated on me. "Here I was—feeling sorry for you. I guess you'll be okay."

"He's not my boyfriend," I said, because he wasn't.

"Whatever you say."

What I said was nothing. Write this one down: if you're left at the altar and return to the venue for your gifts, bring a man everyone will think is your boyfriend.

Arlene studied Rudy yet again. "Don't take her for a ride."

༄

We didn't speak much on the drive to the city. I sat with my head tilted back, in no mood to chat. Returning to the scene of the crime was as painful as I thought it would be—even with Rudy helping me. When we could see the Max, Rudy offered to park and help me carry everything up to my apartment. Despite his kindness, it had been a long day—I wasn't up for a visit. I would've told Santa Claus to come down the chimney another time. What I required was Tylenol and my head on a pillow. After my nap, I wanted to pour vodka like lemonade.

Also, I had no clue as to the condition of my place. Thank you, Margo the Mess.

"Rudy, you've been great, and I don't want to bother you any further."

"No bother." He seemed disappointed.

"You've done a lot already. If we empty the trunk on the street, I can handle it from there."

As I climbed out of the car, I saw Margo. Hard to miss. She wore a getup—a lime-and-orange swing coat with Dolman sleeves in zebra stripes, earrings the circumference of pancakes, a leopard-dot turban, and movie-star sunglasses. Her lipstick was fire-engine red.

"Costume party?" I commented to Margo as Rudy surveyed her outfit. "Margo, this is Rudy Cohen. Rudy, my elder sister, Margo."

Margo frowned. "Must you say 'elder'?"

"Rudy, this is my great-grandmother Margo."

It was obvious Margo thought Rudy was attractive. She sashayed closer to him. Any closer and I would be an aunt in nine months. I had never mentioned Rudy to Margo, and that was easy to tell by her annoying questions.

"Lyft or Uber?" she said in the sexiest voice of her ex–TV soap character, Mirabella. "If you drive for Uber, I will change my app pronto."

Oh no. Fasten a gag on my sister.

"Neither. I work for Mr. Steinbach," Rudy said.

Margo tapped the hood of the Escalade. "Nice car. Is it yours?"

"Yes."

"Hmm," Margo said.

"Rudy has been taking me to out-of-town clients." I had no idea why I was explaining, but I kept going. "Because of my wrist."

Rudy excused himself to unload the trunk.

"Are these your wedding gifts?" Margo said.

I nodded.

"Where were they?"

"At the synagogue."

"All this time? Didn't you want them?"

"Not really, Margo."

"You're kidding. That's ridiculous. I'll take them. It's amazing what people will buy on eBay."

A horn. She glanced across the street.

"That Amazon van is pulling out. Rudy can park and help carry your dowry upstairs."

"Not necessary," I said.

"Rudy," she yelled, pointing to the departing van.

Rudy slammed the trunk, jumped in the car.

"I don't want him to come up."

"Why not? Don't you like your handsome driver?"

"Margo, lay off. I am not ready to see anyone. And even if I was interested, I don't mix business with pleasure."

"Okay, then he's your business. And my pleasure."

Margo was an outrageous flirt, so shameless, Stephanie called her the Man-eater. I was surprised she was heaping it on for Rudy. She preferred heftier guys. All three ex-husbands were older men, wisecrackers. I met her first husband, Arnold the Ex-terminator (because his name was Arnold, and he owned an extermination business), at their wedding in a chapel in Las Vegas with a clerical comedian officiating. Arnold hadn't left her as much as a cockroach. She called home to say she was about to marry again so a Latvian friend—remove the *r* in friend—could remain in America. My folks went wild—as she knew they would. Once he gained citizenship, they parted amicably. She wasn't talking to Phil or Ellen or Stephanie, so I flew to Los Angeles and represented the family at Margo's third wedding. She married an established actor/director/producer. A true triple threat: He drank. He did drugs. He was addicted to sex.

Rudy was not Margo's type. But he was coming up, and it was too late to alter the situation without appearing ill-mannered, ungrateful for his generous assistance.

In the elevator, we came upon Allie, who had been in the dank basement, considering the contents of her storage bin.

"Lauren, I have news. Great news. I went for an ultrasound yesterday. It's a boy! Marc and I are having a boy."

"Congratulations," I said, which was what I would have said if she expected a boy or a girl.

I introduced Allie to Margo and Rudy.

"So you're Lauren's sister from California. Are you staying awhile?"

As I shook my head to indicate Margo's apartment visa was running out, Margo said a hearty "yes."

"So you can feed the cat when Lauren is away."

"I don't cook," Margo said.

Rudy laughed.

"Wedding gifts?" Allie asked with sudden melancholy.

"Yes," I said.

"Intense."

No kidding.

"I send presents early, but I heard in a podcast that guests have up to a year to give a wedding gift."

"Well, in my case, I think if they didn't send it by now, they won't."

Allie was about to laugh, but then she reconsidered.

In the apartment, we stationed the gifts around the couch. I thought that would be it for Rudy's visit, but Margo asked Rudy if he would like wine, and before I knew it, she was pouring. Rudy held his wineglass, scanned my living room. I presumed my bedroom was a jumble. I was relieved the door was shut.

Rudy petted Tuesday. Margo scratched Tuesday. I retreated to a corner of the couch. Rudy settled next to me. Too close. I waited a few moments, then stood. Margo took to the armchair, consulting her cell. Then, out of the blue, she got to her feet, something she generally avoided once seated. As children, we had one overstuffed tartan armchair facing the largest big-back TV. The other seats were ladder-back, uncomfortable and narrow. Once Margo plopped herself on the tartan, I'd have to wait hours, until she needed the toilet, to claim the armchair. Upon her return, she stood in front of me like a palace guard, commanding I give up my seat. If that didn't work, she shouted to my mother, "Lauren is in my chair." Mom had her fill of Margo. From somewhere in the kitchen, she bellowed, "Give Margo the chair." Margo piled on top of me until I gave up. It was the history of our sisterhood.

"I forgot I have an appointment," Margo said briskly.

I understood. Margo had invited Rudy up to the apartment for me. A favor I could have done without.

I couldn't help myself. "Really?"

"Oh yes, a wax. Look at these," she said, pointing to her brows. "I could braid them."

I was embarrassed by Margo's obvious ploy. I hoped Rudy didn't think I had put her up to leaving us alone.

After the door had closed behind her, Rudy said, "Margo is a character."

"I have another sister, Stephanie, Margo's polar opposite. She's a teacher."

"In addition to Libby, Aidan's mom, I have an older brother named Jason. He took a birthright trip to Israel while in college. He stayed, became ultrareligious. Jason and Shira have six children he refers to as his starter kids."

"So, including Aidan, you have seven nieces and nephews. I'd like a few more little people to spoil myself, but Stephanie is done—and you met Margo."

"Let's open presents!" Rudy said.

I surveyed the bounty. I pointed to an oversize carton. Rudy shook his head. I held up an envelope, waving it like a flag on a windy day. Rudy shook his head again. I selected a small, narrow gift, less than a foot in length. "How about this?"

"Definitely a seventy-two-inch TV," Rudy joked.

I read the card as Rudy walked to the back of the couch and stood behind me. He was leaning. I could feel his breath by my neck. He was too close. I wasn't ready to be that close again to anyone. I read the card. "Always and forever, may you be as happy and full of love as you are this day. Here's to a lifetime together.

"Sure thing," I said to Rudy.

"Do you want me to laugh or be sad?" he said.

"Let's laugh. Do the honors?"

He circled the couch. He was in front of me, my eyes level with his belt, brown with a thin brass buckle, strapped two holes in. I felt myself staring. I glanced upward. He unwrapped the gift neatly, preserving the paper. He showed me a red Cartier box. He lifted the lid, kidding around, peeking in.

There were ten sterling silver salt-and-pepper shakers, each the size of a thimble, what every newlywed needed. I imagined the shakers at a dinner at the White House.

"How have I lived without these?" I rotated one between my thumb and index finger.

"Well, this gift shakes things up," Rudy said, launching a pun storm. Because I was laughing, I forgot I was opening gifts from a wedding I didn't have.

"My turn," he said, perusing the haul.

"Be my guest."

He went for an envelope. The card said, "Today is the day."

"Wow," he said. "A gift certificate for a weekend in Nantucket. Now, this was given by a good friend."

I took the card. "Best wishes from Cousin Hallie Blaire."

"Ahh. Delightful woman," Rudy joked.

"I don't know her. She's somewhere on the groom's side. But I love Nantucket. I stopped going because it became too expensive."

He handed me the certificate.

"Yes! This inn is the best place to stay. My friend Kate from camp stayed there."

"Was Kate at your wedding?"

"Everyone but Margo and the groom were at the wedding."

"Margo missed your wedding?"

"That's why she is here now—or so she says."

"What do you think?"

"She wanted to help me, but also she was lonely and gig-less in California."

"Do you think she's here to stay?"

"If she is, it won't be in my apartment."

"You are a tough one," Rudy said as he pointed at me.

"I wish."

But it was more than wishing. I longed to speak out. I was tired of hoping Margo would leave instead of telling her time was up. Not addressing the insipid, hurtful asides made by my mom. And the big one—agreeing to a wedding at Eric's synagogue when I preferred something else. Since I was a teen, my bridal fantasy was a reception in a white party tent by the lake—at camp. I had told Eric my dream, but he never mentioned it to his parents, who for sure wouldn't have liked it. I imagined Myrna's response: "An outdoor wedding? Ridiculous. Where will people go to the bathroom?" Which is why and how I thought up the wedding cans.

"A drink would be nice. Let's check that out," I said about a gift that was the shape of a bottle. The wine was Montepulciano d'Abruzzo, my favorite red. "I tasted this in Italy," I said to Rudy. "I was nineteen, on spring break, the Basilica di Santa Croce in Florence."

"You uncorked wine in the Basilica?"

"Another American whispered hello to me at the tomb of Michelangelo. When I moved on to Galileo, he was there too. We agreed to lunch in the plaza. Voilà, Montepulciano d'Abruzzo."

I didn't mention my one-afternoon stand.

I uncorked the bottle.

Rudy went to the kitchen and brought back two clean goblets.

"Let's look up the wine," Rudy said.

"The wine—or the price?" I chuckled.

"The price, of course."

"Isn't that tacky?"

"So we're tacky." Rudy checked Google. "And this bottle is very inexpensive."

Rudy poured as we stood facing each other.

"What should we toast?" I asked.

"To envelopes," he said. He flapped one. We clinked glasses.

"I like gifts that fit in envelopes."

"Envelopes are good," Rudy said, nodding.

We toasted.

"To envelopes," he repeated.

"To envelopes!"

I reached for a pink one. "Lauren and Eric Forever" in cursive.

"Ever and ever," Rudy said.

"A regular fairy tale. Boy meets girl. Boy leaves girl at the altar. She wins a weekend in Nantucket. You know, there once was a man from Nantucket . . ."

I collapsed on the couch. He sat next to me. Our shoulders were touching. I didn't move.

"The envelope, please," I said as though I was at the Oscars.

He passed it to me. "Go ahead, Reese Witherspoon, you open it."

"All right, Tom Hanks. And the Oscar goes to . . . dinner for two at the Brazilian."

"Have you ever been to that restaurant?"

"No," I said. "What's it like?"

"No idea," he said.

"Let's go," I heard myself say as the wine buzzing through me told me I deserved some fun.

He looked at me. "When?"

"Now! Let's walk." The restaurant was blocks away. My head was spinning. I needed the air.

"Great, but I have to make a call first."

He hit one number. I heard a woman's cheerful voice on the other end. Who was Rudy speaking to? Why did I care? Why did I want to know? I hadn't considered he might have a girlfriend or maybe someone who lived with him.

And what if he did? He had taken me to get the gifts because he was driving. We had a professional relationship. At most, we were friends. Rationalizations weren't helping. I was about to grab my coat when I decided I might not be going anywhere.

He said, "Everything okay, Stace? Great. Well, I shouldn't be home too late."

I didn't interrupt. I waited until he slipped the phone back into his pocket.

"Stace?"

"She's the best," he said.

"You said you were single. Lady Gaga left you."

"You care whether I'm single?" he said, busting a smile.

I was annoyed. "Well, are you single or not?"

"Do I look single?"

"You were coming on to me, so I assumed you were."

"I was coming on to you?"

"Ever since the hospital."

"You had an auto accident. I was being kind."

I was mortified I had accused him.

He winked. The charm. "I thought I mentioned that Stacy and Sheri are my neighbors, enormous help with Aidan. Stacy is babysitting Aidan. At this juncture, my friends are the equivalent of aunts to him."

I was an idiot, but mostly I was embarrassed that it appeared I cared about his status.

"Oh," I said demurely.

He raised an eyebrow.

"Shall we go?" he said. "We okay?"

"Yes."

"Good."

Chapter 14

The Brazilian was all windows out front, string lights dancing on the flashing, colorful sign. I assumed dinner would feature steak, because steak was a significant product of Brazil. Don't ask me how I knew this. I had never been to South America. Mostly because I had no wanderlust. When I graduated from college in Boston, all I wanted was Manhattan, no Astoria or Brooklyn or Hoboken for me; to find a solid job in advertising; to build my career. Once Stephanie met Rob, I wished to find a guy as loving and trustworthy. I worked diligently, billed impressive hours, but success at the agency seemed incidental, something to aim for while awaiting the real prize. A family.

Inside the colossal restaurant, Panama fans whirled from the white ceiling. The furniture was rattan, rockers in the front where we were greeted. The place was loud, deafening. I could barely hear the maître d' ask how many in our party. Over the din, Rudy said we were two and raised two fingers. The maître d' led us to a table at the rear of the restaurant. Any farther back and we would be in Bolivia, not Brazil. Most tables were for groups—such as the multigenerational family next to us—toddlers in booster seats, babies in high chairs, their crumbs on the floor.

Once seated, I said to Rudy, "This place is a party."

He said, "What?"

I repeated myself, speaking louder, enunciating, cupping my lips.

He pointed to his ears. "Can't hear you," he mouthed.

I was ready to give up on conversation. There was no alternative.

Rudy held up an index finger as though to say, "One minute, please." He reached for his phone. He pointed to it, and I thought he needed to make a call. I waited, glancing at business buddies drinking beer to the right. I thought I heard my cell. I picked up. No reason not to. After all, Rudy was on his phone.

"Hello," I said.

"It's Rudy."

I stared across the table at him.

"Turn your volume up," he said over the phone.

I adjusted the sound, amused.

"Now, what did you say?" he said, laughing.

A waiter approached. "Welcome to the Brazilian. Have you dined with us before?"

Still holding our phones, we shook our heads.

"Then an introduction is necessary. The endless salad bar is the focal point of the room. Help yourself. You'll find a bounty—everything from olives and bread and sushi to fresh, cold shrimp." He placed two round cards, about the size of the bottom of a glass, on the white table-cloth. One side was green, the other red.

"Leave the cards on red while enjoying the salad bar. When you are ready for our waiters to serve meat, fish, and poultry on skewers, turn the card to the green side. When you are done eating or wish to rest for a while, turn the cards to red again. Very easy. Stop and go. We also serve polenta, fried bananas, rice and beans as side dishes."

"Brazilians eat like this every night," Rudy said into his phone when the waiter departed. "In fact, there are places in Brazil where this is considered a snack."

Rudy asked whether I would like wine.

"It's not polite to talk on your telephone at the table," I joked.

"It is if you are speaking to the person you are at the table with."

A steward came by, and Rudy ordered wine.

We strolled to the salad bar. Rudy chose cold beets and string beans, marinated mussels, deviled eggs as well as bread. I filled my plate with olives, cheese, and sashimi. I had no idea sashimi was a Brazilian food.

After our first run, Rudy stood to return to the salad bar. I remained seated. I didn't need to demonstrate to Rudy how much I could pack away.

"You're not going for seconds?" he said, disappointed.

I shook my head, waved him on.

"But I'll be lonely," he said.

"I wouldn't want that."

As I refilled my plate next to Rudy, who was sampling every kind of cheese, I lost my inhibition. I told Rudy I was playing follow the leader—and refilled my plate with every item he chose.

"This is my idea of fun," he said.

It was fun. And at that moment, I felt I could tell him anything. "I'm addicted to food."

"Who isn't?"

Nice to be accepted, but Rudy had no concept of the level of my madness. "No. I am really addicted."

"It wouldn't be entertaining to be here with someone who wasn't a foodie."

We flipped our *ready, set, go to hell with yourself* cards. Green side up. Rudy and I were characters in a vegan's nightmare. Waiter after waiter stopped by with our choice of anything that had been an animal—once upon a time on a farm in Brazil. We sampled pork chop, top sirloin, tenderloin, filet mignon, chicken, turkey, barbecue ribs, lamb sausage, lamb chops, leg of lamb. Honestly, so many parts of a lamb were offered, I wouldn't be surprised if the restaurant had also served wool.

The waiters sliced the meats off long skewers. Rudy and I caught a few pieces with metal tongs and situated the offering on our crowded plates. As soon as we bit into a Brazilian specialty, a waiter arrived tendering another type. It seemed as though months of our gluttony had passed before I turned my card back to the red side, signaling I had eaten enough. Rudy continued. I watched him enjoy himself.

Rudy called my phone.

"Yes?" I said, laughing.

"I forgot to tell you—".

"What?"

"I'm a vegetarian."

"Not anymore."

The out-of-towners next to us dressed in pastels and patterns rarely seen on a New Yorker crooned "Happy Birthday" to Grandma, a slight woman wearing a gold tiara that said 90. Afterward, a song I had never heard before, "May All Your Dreams Come True," topped by an ear-ringing rendition of "For She's a Jolly Good Fellow." How nice to have a family who gives you your due.

For dessert, Rudy ordered sky-high Brazilian chocolate cake but then realized there was no way we could eat it. I said he should bring the cake to Aidan.

When we returned home, he asked whether he could come up.

Margo was networking, seeing a play written by a friend. She was planting seeds for theater work. Before she left, she said, "If I can make it here, I can make it anywhere."

Was inviting Rudy up a signal I was interested? That I was ready to step out? I wasn't. No. I wasn't. I needed time to heal from the last disaster. I needed to stay away from men until I pulled myself back together.

Besides, there was the matter of Rudy's position as Steinbach's employee. What would Steinbach think if he knew I was with Rudy? What did we really have in common besides being in a car together all day?

As I ruminated, Rudy touched my arm. He said, "I'm only asking because I might need to use your bathroom."

I was such an idiot.

"Of course," I said, blushing inside myself.

"We need to hurry," he said, increasing his pace.

In the elevator, I fished my keys from my bag, fumbling under the pressure to unlock the door. Rudy raced to the bathroom. He was there for an eternity. I started to wonder if he was one of those people who went on the internet while on the toilet and never surfaced until someone started knocking. Once, I had erroneously opened an occupied stall at a concert to find a girl playing Words with Friends. She slammed the door back in my face in embarrassment. Too bad. I'm really good at Words with Friends.

Time was ticking. I knocked at the bathroom door. "Are you all right?"

"Fine. Be with you in a second."

I heard a flush. Another flush. Another. There was the sound of the sink. Then Rudy was before me. His black hair was wet and shiny, as though he had doused himself with water. His complexion was a tinge of green.

"Meat sweats," he said weakly.

"Never heard of it."

"Cow's revenge," he said.

I handed him a guest towel. He wiped his forehead, held it to his neck.

I helped him to my couch, placing a throw pillow behind his back.

"Are you okay?" he said, concerned I was about to break out with meat sweats as well.

"So far. Do you want to lie down?"

"I can't. I have to pick up Aidan." He hurried to the bathroom, leaving the door ajar. I watched as he soaked his face, splashed his hair so the curls were back and flat. Even with a rare animal disease, he was handsome. I watched as he dried off.

"It was fun," he said on his way out. "You are fun."

"I have other gifts we can use," I said, immediately lamenting and regretting the come-on tone of the words.

"You have many gifts." He winked, and his big brown eyes regained their pre-Brazil shine.

When he left, I stood still, my back to the wall, thinking how I wanted to stop thinking about him.

Chapter 15

In the morning, I was relieved to have my place to myself. Margo had texted to tell me she was staying overnight with Patricia, an actress she knew from Summer Stock. Patricia had a loft in Soho. I imagined Margo saying I was a hurting fool and she had invited Rudy to my apartment. My sister thought I was ripe to become involved again. She was incorrect.

I had not weighed myself since before the no-wedding wedding. I stared at the floor scale, my nemesis, about to step on, but then I had a better idea. I turned on the shower, sloughing with a loofah, shaving my underarms, my legs. The dead skin, the body hair, had to account for a few ounces. I dried off. I tiptoed onto the scale. I was motionless, a statue. I glanced down, wincing at the number. I was up. The scale was up. I had gained weight—and worst of all, I was in an all-new decade of numbers. For a nanosecond I was candid—considering what I had consumed since the wedding, the weight gain was not that bad. I stepped on the scale again. I weighed the same as moments before. I held a foot in the air. Same. The scale was obstinate. It would not move.

I applied makeup carefully. I wore my hair down. I chose a dress I had bought a month before the wedding. It was tight. I returned to the rack for a long-sleeve V-neck with two front pockets, definitely on the clingy side but not too snug for work. It was springtime. No need for pantyhose. I hopped into black pumps. Then, noise at my front door. Margo jerking a key out of the lock. In the apartment, she dropped her bag. She peered at me with a dead-serious face. "Nice," she said about the way I looked. "And it's good you look nice. Because guess who is downstairs outside?"

"George Clooney," I said.

"Think more available."

A cold creep, a shudder. "Eric." Without a doubt, Eric. Eric had surfaced. Once I had wanted him to show his face, but his random appearance shook me. Why now? What was up his sleeve?

"I was in his path. He didn't know me, but I recognized him from your pictures—short and childish."

"He's not short."

"Well, he's not tall. You're five eight. He's about five ten." Margo dropped on the couch. "He is shot to hell. Wretched, miserable. He wants you. He needs you. He can't live without you." She was an actress—swooning, pressing her palms to her heart.

"Are you done yet?"

Most likely, Eric had shown up to assuage his guilt. He owed me an apology—and that was it, no more, no less. He didn't want me back—and I didn't want him. I wouldn't return to Eric if he had the only sperm on the planet.

"You would think you were the one who left him. The man is haggard."

"Why do you think he's here?"

"Maybe he's moving into the building."

"That's not funny."

I rushed to the armoire in my bedroom. Margo followed, her toes at my heels. I jerked the top drawer. It almost fell out. I moved it about until it fit back into its slot. Nervously, I reached behind socks for a small velvet box. My diamond engagement ring was inside. I didn't open the box. I didn't want to look.

"You're returning the ring?" Margo's tone reeked of outrage.

"Yes," I said. Get off my back. I am doing the right thing.

"To him?"

"No, to the diamond district. Why? Do you want it?" I said, guessing she had all her engagement rings. Perhaps she wore three at the same time.

She dangled her head as though I was a lost cause.

"Margo!" Defiant, I pocketed the ring in my dress.

"Give him hell," Margo said, waving me on.

Outside, the sky was clear, the clouds puffy—a beautiful day about to be ruined.

In front of me, a few feet away, leaning on his car, I saw him. I saw Eric. Looking at him, his smart-aleck stance, his legs stretched before him, made me feel sick.

Margo was right. Eric was a hot mess, swimming in his jeans, a black T-shirt with paint splattered on it. He didn't paint. Did he buy it like that? Was there no justice? I pile on weight while struggling—he shrinks without trying. His hair needed a cut. He needed a shave. His eyes were bleary. Bombay Sapphire for breakfast? Who cared what he was drinking or when? Why was he here?

My mind raced back to the day in the balloon. Yes, yes, yes. No, no, no should have been the answer. I doubted I would ever say yes to anyone about anything again.

I stopped in my tracks, a few feet away from him. "You're stalking now?"

"Do you have a minute, Lauren?"

Do you have an apology? No, because that would take longer than a minute.

"You're loitering here."

"Please, one minute."

"I don't have that kind of time."

Eric smiled. Watching him spread his lips enraged me.

"You don't get to smile. You don't have the right to breathe."

He stood straight. "Whew. I anticipated incoming fire, but I didn't expect this."

What did he expect? A welcome committee? A parade?

"In retrospect, I should have spoken up sooner." Eric wasn't apologizing for humiliating me. He was sorry he waited to make amends after he humiliated me. I wanted to throttle him. What a loser. I was done with men.

He proceeded slowly, in measured sentences—as though answering a customer complaint. "I planned this—to catch you in the morning on your way to the office. I didn't want to call, set an exact time or a place to meet, because I felt I might not have the courage to appear."

That would be in character.

"I should have come over weeks ago."

Well, you're here now. Spit it out. Make me feel better about myself.

"Anyway, you left some stuff at my apartment."

I suppressed wild laughter, the chortle of a woman beyond reason. What? This was about stuff? Stuff? How about, "Sorry, lady"? "Excuse me, I might have done you wrong"? I didn't need my underwear, my bras, a few books. If looks could kill, he would be embalmed. Or cremated. Or dropped at sea. The choice was his. I looked on the street for something sharp I could pick up.

"I called a service to deliver, but I thought that was a little cold."

Anger rose from my toes, steamed out my head. Worst of all, I did not need this setback, this new emotional hurricane, while trying to lift myself off the ground.

"Lauren, I knew in the balloon."

Shock. "In the balloon. The balloon! You knew you didn't want to get married the second you asked me?"

He nodded, then doubled down with the word "yes."

Tell me, Eric. Have you seen your psychologist lately? If so, you should ask for a refund.

"Are you insane? You invited your parents. Your mother met us with her guest list. You told me she was an event planner, and I should let her plan. So I did."

"You didn't let her plan. You let her walk all over you."

"Why didn't you stop her?"

"Because I had no interest in the wedding. I didn't want to get married."

How many times was he going to stab me?

"I was not ready to have kids."

Stunned, I stepped back. I felt faint, as though I would fall. "Eric, I'm forty-one. I don't have the luxury of waiting. We discussed it. We agreed. A compromise. One child."

"You settled on one child because you thought I was the last boat out."

"Out of what?" I resented the way he portrayed me as desperate. I loved him, and I felt like a woman who knew what she wanted in life.

"Out of being single, out of never having kids at all."

"That's not true."

"Think harder."

"Is this the conversation you came here to have in the street?"

"I had no idea how you would feel about seeing me."

"Oh, it's downright delightful to see you. Awesome to see you. What else would you like to rehash? Maybe we could go all the way back to when we kissed at thirteen."

A homeless woman passed by. She pushed a cart, loaded with a bag full of empty soda cans and her possessions. Teenagers wearing plaid uniforms and knee socks headed to school.

"I think we should keep it down," Eric said.

Keep it down? It was New York. We could cannibalize each other—no one cared.

"Why did you ask me to marry you?"

"Honestly?"

"Are you capable of honesty?"

"I didn't want you to move on, to find someone else, another man, and I didn't know how long you would stay with me because I knew you wanted to have kids. For crying out loud, you were talking about quitting Steinbach, launching your own agency so you could be your own boss, be available for childcare, work at your own pace. The wedding train departed the station, and I didn't have the balls to stand in front of it."

This was all my fault? "Screw you, Eric. You were driving the wedding train."

"Bullshit. You weren't really in love with me. You had invested two years. You were thirty-nine when we met at the reunion. There wasn't much time remaining to find someone and have kids. Besides, you approved of my résumé. You can't deny the life you wanted."

"I was in love with you. I was in love with you," I repeated.

"You thought you were in love with me, but you were in love with the idea of me."

I lifted my hand. I did something I had never thought of, never ever done. To anyone. I whacked him. I slammed Eric across the face. As I slapped his cheek—twice—my hand grazed his nose and an eye. I staggered—taken aback. Stunned, shaken by my own behavior.

But also proud.

"You know what, Eric? I have no hint, not an inkling, of what you are looking for here, but you won't find it. Not now. Not ever. How dare you tell me what my feelings were when you didn't have a clue what was going on in your pathetic excuse for a heart, your immature, hollow pit of a head."

He patted his cheek, stroked it. "You're smacking these days? Perfect, Lauren. I'm leaving."

"Again? Really? I thought you would stay and double down some more."

"I didn't come here with that intention."

"Take your accusations and leave. We have nothing left to discuss, Eric."

"Well, there is one thing," he said haughtily. "You know the honeymoon I bought, the two-week cruise to Spain and Italy? I am shipping out. Myself."

Bon voyage. "The *Courageous*? I hope the boat sinks."

∽

Margo was in the lobby of my building, by the desk with the pre-Easter eggs and the enormous stuffed bunny, the lame Passover decorations, waiting with compassion, empathy, and wet eyes when I came inside. She had watched us, guarded over me, from the window in the apartment.

She hurried my way. She clutched me.

"Don't let go," I said to my sister as I cracked into pieces.

Hours later, I realized Eric had driven away with the goods he came to deliver.

And I had never given him the ring.

Chapter 16

A frozen fruit pop in my hand, I stewed over Eric's accusations, amazed I had slapped him, pleased I had acted out on the street the day before. Yes, I had wanted a family—but I wanted that family with him. Yes, I liked his résumé, but my own was not shabby. Yes, I let his mother walk all over me, but only because he agreed with her. Temple Sons of Abraham or bust.

Margo was already in her pajamas, though it was only seven in the evening, jabbering to someone in my bedroom—on my bed—plotting her comeback as an actress. Apparently, Margo was willing to stand—but it had to be on a stage. She was trying for a part in a play in which she would star as a part-time accountant who becomes a full-time sleuth. As I was about to raid the freezer for another pop, Kate called.

She was sorry she had dropped the ball, not been in touch enough since her return to Chicago. "No worries," I said. In the next breath, I revealed Eric had shown his face, spinning the details. When I mentioned I had brought out the heavy artillery—my slapping hand—she said, "Good for you. That SOB. He deserved it."

I drank in her approval. But enough about me. "How are you?"

"I'm fine," Kate said. "Awesome!"

She was way too cheery to convince me. "You are not fine."

She took a breath. "Glenn and I are separating," she said bluntly.

She startled me, as she had never spoken about her marriage in any way that would lead to the conclusion there were problems worth parting for.

"Separating?" I said, a trill in my voice.

"Glenn is involved with my neighbor."

Thud, my heart. "No. Oh no, Kate. I am sorry."

"You know what I thought when I discovered my husband was having sex with my next-door neighbor?"

"That you should move." This was not a joke. I was serious.

"That maybe you were the lucky one."

"You can't think like that. You have two kids."

"I know," Kate said. "They don't deserve this."

"How did you find out?" I supposed someone had told her—not Glenn, but someone else.

"I found them together."

"Where?"

"In my bed."

"Oh, Kate." I imagined her California king–size bed, the two good-for-nothing scoundrels, personally trained, lactate-free bodies meshed under the patchwork quilt Kate's mom had sewn as a wedding gift. If it were me, I would never sleep in that bed again. Hello, Mattress Firm.

I conjured Kate, my Kate, at the entrance to the bedroom. Kate, dumbstruck—as good as bludgeoned in the head. Speechless. Ascertaining she was seeing correctly. Then—Kate with the kerosene, setting her six-bedroom Colonial on two landscaped acres ablaze. There were movies about that.

I lived hundreds of miles away, but I was ready to lead her battle. "How can I help? What can I do? Do you want me to come to Chicago?"

"Not necessary. The nanny is here, and my mother is helping out."

"That's good, but I'm worried about you."

"I will be A-OK. You know why? Because I'm tough."

I was astounded by her attitude, so up, like she wasn't going to let a little thing like this stand in her way. *Emulate her,* I thought. She was my role model. I had always wanted to be like Kate when I grew up.

"I can't control that idiot I married. I'm a bright, capable woman. Gorgeous, if I have to say so myself."

"You don't have to say so yourself. I'll say it. Kate Kaufman is a knockout."

"I have to do what's best for my children. They won't be happy if I'm not happy."

I was amazed at her get-up-and-go.

"I'm on Tinder. And other sites."

Tinder? I cringed. Not what I had in mind.

"Do you want to know why? Because one door closes, another opens."

Please. No adages. "Where's Glenn?" I asked.

"My neighbor's husband moved to a townhome, and Glenn has already unpacked next door. Real nice for my kids. Daddy living with her three children. Funny how he takes the trash out each morning. I had to plead with him to dump the garbage. Yesterday, I saw him outside in sweatpants and a hoodie attempting to fix her garage door. Glenn! He couldn't repair an appliance if the only thing he had to do was hold a beer for the contractor."

This was awful. Far worse than what had happened to me. My problem was a tremor. Her problem was an earthquake. I had known and liked Glenn since their second date. Never would I have expected his awful behavior.

"Even though Margo is here, you're welcome to come," I said, unsure why I was offering this, as she probably couldn't leave her kids. There was little room in my apartment—plus she would want to discuss her situation, and Margo would be a distraction. On the other hand, Margo had been divorced multiple times, so maybe she would commiserate.

Kate ignored my offer. "Glenn never pulled up from the office until after dark, and now I see him in her driveway at five every night. He swings his briefcase as he walks from the car. Swings it. Even his briefcase is happy."

I thought it was terrible about his briefcase. Mostly that she had to see it.

When I finished college in Boston, I had no intention of returning to Connecticut. In the advertising capital of the world, I shared a tenement with Kate Kaufman and two other girls. Our place was in the west 40s, where the sign blinked for the Lincoln Tunnel. Kate and I halved the bedroom. The others split the living room. For this luxury, Kate and I kicked in $100 extra a month. Soon, we could afford the entire apartment and asked our tenants to move out. Kate and Glenn met through our camp friend Jillian. She had invited both to her birthday party in a crowded Irish bar on the Upper West Side. It was a miracle they found each other—the old watering hole was pitch-black. Kate gave up her position at Estée Lauder, moved to Chicago when Glenn joined a medical practice. He was an anesthesiologist. I thought he was supposed to eliminate pain.

As for me, I'd met Glenn's friends. Where would I be if I had married one of those guys—pacing outside my neighbor's Tudor with a shotgun? I wondered, what was marriage? A promise. A promise people broke. There were no guarantees. Couples in their sixties and seventies were separating, planning divorce—in droves. My parents remained an anomaly, together forever. Was this love or persistence? I never envisioned a marriage to Eric failing in the long run, what it would be like when we were old, whether our goals, our dreams would change. I had never considered a pileup like the one Kate was in. On my wedding day in the size-12 gown, I was optimistic—but also blind. Kate had the twins. She would be linked to Glenn through their children for a lifetime. After our encounter on the street, Eric was gone for good.

"Here's my thoughts: if I meet a few new men each weekend, quantitatively I have to find Glenn's replacement. I'm out there, and you should be too."

"Are you kidding? I'm in recovery mode. I dress for work in the morning. I take off my bra and change into my pajamas as soon as I return home. If I didn't have a driver, I wouldn't speak to anyone about anything but business all day."

"You have a driver?"

"Rudy. You would like him."

"Is he handsome?"

"Yes, but looks aren't everything," I said.

"Not when you're staring at the back of someone's head all day. Maybe I should meet your driver. Wait. What about you and the driver?"

"We're friends. He's fun." I was recovering from heartache, not in a condition for anything else—with anyone.

"Fun?"

"He makes me laugh."

Kate was sarcastic. "Awful, just awful. Don't ever get in a car with him again."

"I made a big mistake with Eric. I didn't see what was right there in front of my eyes. I'm not plunging in. In fact, I don't even want to tiptoe."

"What are you doing?"

"I'm concentrating on my work."

"You know what they say. All work, no play makes for no sex. I have to go. I think my tech guy from the J-Fig site walked into the bar. He told me he would be in a gray sweater vest with brown leather buttons."

"You would date a guy in a gray sweater vest?"

Kate chuckled and said goodbye.

I thought about my situation. What happened to Kate could have happened to me. Getting married ensured nothing. Eric might have left the day after he said "I do." There was no way to control another person. All I had for sure was me.

☙

Stephanie, who like my mother reached out to me daily, was in the city and suggested we meet. I would've invited Margo to get off the couch and join us, but she still hadn't told Stephanie she was in town. I waited for Stephanie in a well-lit Sixth Avenue café.

I checked my e-mails. My mother had forwarded several articles. Of course, there was one about nutrition. Another about aging and posture. The kicker was a lengthy exposé: "Why It's Difficult for Single Women Over Forty to Meet Men." Answer: availability of younger women. I punched in Mom's number, knowing she wouldn't pick up because she could never find her phone. I left a brief message. "Mom. Don't forward articles. If you have to send something, send money."

Stephanie arrived, in pants, a formfitting jacket with a wide belt. To my surprise, Olivia was with her. I brightened, enveloping my niece. She was wearing a T-shirt that said, ONLY HUMAN. I told her I loved it.

"Hi, best niece in the world."

"If I'm your best niece, what is Liza?"

"My best niece when you're not listening," I joked.

I felt strange hiding Aunt Margo, who believed Stephanie would tell my mom she was in town. I could swear Stephanie, even Olivia, to

165

secrecy, but then what if? Why couldn't we all grow up? Why was this on me?

"What are you doing in the city?"

"Seeing a potential new dermatologist," Stephanie said.

"How did it go?"

"Not well. I was told I would be evaluated by a physician's assistant. I said I expected an MD. The nurse asked if I had specifically asked for a doctor."

"You have to specifically ask for a doctor?"

"I said, 'Of course not. I assumed when I made an appointment at a specialist's office, I would see a doctor.'"

"And we are talking about your face here, not your rear end."

Olivia grinned—her mouth wide open. I grinned back.

When Olivia went to the restroom, I told Stephanie about Kate.

"No marriage is flawless. If a woman tells you she has never had a problem with her husband, the woman is a liar."

"Have you?"

"What?"

"Had a problem?"

"Not a one. Never ever," she said, grinning, then laughing.

When Olivia returned, Stephanie went to the counter for two lattes and a milk.

"Aunt Lauren, I miss you. You need to visit," Olivia said.

"I will soon."

"Bring the chocolate from Godiva, but don't tell Mom."

"Anything else?"

"Liza likes Skittles."

Stephanie set the drinks on the table. "I'm getting ready for Passover. The Seder will be at my house."

"Of course. It's always at your house."

"I love making the holidays. You know that."

I asked what I could bring to the dinner. I never went anywhere empty-handed. She suggested wine, which implied she didn't think I could cook anything she would eat. This annoyed me, so I offered to bring a dessert. I asked what she would prefer.

"We don't need any desserts. Helena is making the desserts."

My sister's housekeeper was a Polish woman in her late sixties who always wore a skirt that stopped at the knee and a short-sleeve blouse, embroidered with a round collar. She had braided blond hair wrapped around her head.

"Besides, the dessert has to be kosher."

My sister was more religious than I was. She had always been so. Plus—she married Rob, who came from an observant family.

"I will make the dessert kosher."

She shook her head—overvigorously. "You don't know how."

Now I really wanted to bring dessert.

"Count me in for macaroons." We devoured macaroons on Passover. My favorite was almond, but my nieces loved chocolate.

"Your kitchen isn't kosher. What's more, your baking pan isn't kosher."

"I'll use aluminum foil. I'll buy a new roll. I'll have a rabbi say a prayer over it."

"Helena is making everything once she cleans my house and koshers my kitchen and changes the plates to the special ones I use for Passover only."

I was beginning to wonder who was actually celebrating Passover, my sister or her housekeeper.

"Just bring wine. From Israel."

"Got it," I said. "What's Mom bringing?"

"Her brisket." We always referred to the brisket Mom made as "her" brisket. Mom was a horrible cook. Beef with root vegetables was way out of her league, but each Passover we told my mom the brisket was better than last year.

I remembered the first time I brought Eric to a family event. It was July 4 at Stephanie's weathered beach house in Wellfleet on Cape Cod. I remember thinking that if Eric and I got married, we would buy a house, and I would throw family parties—minus Stephanie's rules.

This would be my first holiday without Eric. I hoped my mother could keep her mouth shut about it. I would feel lousy enough.

I sipped my mocha latte. Would Margo go to the Seder or stay hidden from my family? Maybe by the Seder, Margo would lighten up, but I doubted it. Margo's main problem was not Stephanie. It was Stephanie's relationship with my mother, which she liked to refer to as "parasitical." "Two pisses in a pod," she called them. I ignored what Margo deemed unbearable. Some of it she brought on herself.

The last big blowout had been years before. Margo was at my parents' house—the place we grew up—we all were, on Yom Kippur, the highest holiday, the day of atonement, a fast day. Fast as in nothing to eat. Purposefully, Margo ordered food to the house. My father blew his stack, called her out of line, told her to take her stuffed shells and leave. Mom was embarrassed for our more religious next-door neighbors, who had certainly seen the delivery. She recited every minor infraction Margo had made since entering the world. Margo blew like a cannon. She swore she would never visit again.

I guessed I was going to Passover alone.

"Have you heard from Margo?" Stephanie asked, thinking about our sister as well. Weren't holidays supposed to bring families together? So they could argue—and fall apart again?

I didn't want to lie. I switched the subject.

"I have a funeral tomorrow," I said sadly.

"Someone we know?"

"My favorite client, Arthur."

"From the toilets?"

I didn't appreciate Stephanie's tone. I corrected her. "They are not toilets. They are porta potties. What's more, New England Can is the

Apple, the Microsoft, maybe the Tesla of porta potties. And we are introducing a line for weddings. There's a flower vase in each one."

I teared up. Arthur in the urn. Eric on the street. Kate on Tinder. It was all too much.

Stephanie rolled her eyes at Olivia. "May Arthur's memory be for a blessing."

Chapter 17

Arthur's funeral was April 15, the day taxes were most often due. I had gone on extension because my accountant friend, Steve Strauss, had called and suggested it. Steve had attended the Great Humiliation in March. He said, "Maybe you will feel more up to it in October."

I waited for my ride in a black belted dress coat, a cashmere scarf, knee-high black boots. My dress was also black—with a turtleneck. A sea-blue Bentley pulled smoothly to the curb. It was a luxurious all-terrain SUV.

A young driver with a body pumped hourly hopped out, sprinting around the SUV to the curb. I deduced from the dangling drape of his navy blazer that he was not a suit kind of guy. His light-blue tie was woven. I hadn't seen a woven tie since my biology teacher wore a red one on test days. Mr. Frey said his tie was red because he was out for blood. He was joking, but back then, I took it seriously. I wish now I'd had a sense of humor when I was a kid. Adolescence would have been easier.

"Where's Rudy?" I asked, bewildered and disappointed by his absence. "And where's Steinbach?"

"I'm The Rock. I drive for Steinbach too."

The Rock?

"Steinbach flew out of Idaho, made it to Chicago; then his flight was delayed. One of those not-chill situations where the airline announces a delay, then extends takeoff fifteen minutes at a time until the entire month is over."

"I hate when that happens."

"Yes, ma'am."

Ma'am? I looked in the seat next to me. There was no Ma'am.

It was a colossal no-no for Steinbach to miss the funeral for any reason. He should have flown back a day early, ensuring his presence. After all, we had plenty of notice. Certainly, Steinbach was aggravated to be stuck in Chicago. He considered every social encounter, even a funeral, as a business opportunity. Corey Steinbach was disingenuous, but perhaps this resulted in his great success.

"Ready to go?" The Rock said.

As I settled in, my phone rang.

It was Steinbach. He was still in the airport, attempting to get another plane to New York. A Top-of-the-World Diamond Flyer, he couldn't believe how poorly the airline was treating him. Worst of all, they were out of hard-boiled eggs in the Diamond Flyer concierge lounge. I had traveled by air with Steinbach. He carried an egg slicer in his briefcase.

"How's your shoulder?" he asked.

"It's my knee," I wanted to say to see if he would detect a change in body part.

"You'll extend my regards, my sympathy."

"Of course."

"Listen carefully. Keep your nose to the ground. Report back to me today if there's anything going on."

Going on?

"George has to replace Arthur. The new guy, the new vice president, will want to bring in his own advertising agency, an agency he has worked with before."

Guy? His? He?

Maybe one day Steinbach would launch himself into the next decade, which for him would be the 1990s. My egg-eating, sixty-nine-year-old boss was an old-fashioned "fellow" with a newfangled office.

I looked at the back of the head of The Rock. I wished he was Rudy so we could talk. I missed Rudy. I wondered if there was a way without calling attention to myself that I could request only Rudy, because if I couldn't get Rudy, I was willing to walk.

The Rock pulled through the gates of the cemetery, behind an old stone church built before the American Revolution as a meetinghouse. I could see the plaque that deemed it a historic site.

"We're here," he announced.

"Do you make many trips to cemeteries?"

"Only when someone dies." The Rock was deadpan, unaware that he'd made a joke.

The cemetery was flat, backing up to woods. There was no path, and it was too early in spring for the grass to be green. I passed memorial stones dated as far back as 1750, when most men seemed to be named Ebenezer. The women were Abigail. There was a flock of mourners, most in their late sixties, like Arthur. Drawn, narrow faces, blue eyes, thin hair. Arthur's assistant, Paul Stuart, waved me over. I nodded, stood beside him, somber and still.

I recognized Arthur's wife, Camille, the mayor of Far Acres. She was in her late fifties, slight, fair with sunny hair in a pearl-and-shell clip. I imagined her shopping at Talbots and asking if they had anything more conservative. Beside her were Arthur's sons, tall and taller, Harvard and Dartmouth. Both men had passed on the family business but appeared at the company Christmas parties, thrown the first week in December, always at George's impressive farmhouse. Next to the sons were Arthur's daughters-in-law and his grandchildren. Arthur was gone, but he had had what I had considered a full life, a career and a family.

I imagined my burial at the cemetery next to the expressway in Queens, where bodies were packed like sardines and there was only one way to find your relative's gravestone: stop at the office, cooled by a noisy fan in summer, to request a map. I would die single, no descendants to argue over my engagement ring from Eric. While shoveling dirt to cover my simple pine casket, my mother would tear up and say, "I warned her to watch what she ate." There would be a shiva, held at Stephanie's house, mirrors covered with sheets so no one would think about anything but me. My family would be seated on black boxes meant for mourners. My mother would say, "So sad she died alone."

As I considered my own demise, Arthur's ashes were buried in an urn made by his great-great-great-grandfather, one of the first silversmiths in America—in business with Paul Revere. The sons spoke, and that was it. I shook hands with the people I knew. I waited around to speak to George Moore and let him know how apoplectic my boss was to be unable to attend.

George greeted me. He smelled of his favorite single-malt scotch and powerful cologne, wore a custom blue suit and kelly-green silk tie. He took in my black wrist support. He asked what had happened.

"I split lumber without an ax," I said, pretending to chop with the side of my hand.

He smiled. I didn't mention my crash. It was a big deal to me because it was on the heels of the Great Humiliation, but people do not want to know the particulars of your minor injury or serious illness. No point delving into specifics. Few who asked remembered whether you had gallbladder surgery or a tumor removed from your brain. Exhibit A: my boss confusing my wrist with my shoulder.

"Arthur would be a happy guy to see you here," George said.

I felt a thump in my heavy heart. "Thank you," I said warmly. "He was always good to me. I learned a lot from him. And I will never forget it."

"Where's Steinbach?" he asked briskly.

"He planned to be here, but his plane was grounded. He's sorry. He said to say he is with you in spirit." And he's searching for a hard-boiled egg in the airline lounge.

"Let's talk." He steered me to the right under a tremendous oak yet to unfurl for spring. I was confused, wondering why he chose to speak alone with me during Arthur's funeral. "Did you know Arthur played the piano by heart?"

"Yes, of course." Arthur entertained at the Christmas parties. I could feel George's pain.

"A sucker for the Beatles." George hummed "Eleanor Rigby." "My favorite. Hum with me—in memory of Arthur."

What? Oh well. I hummed. Poor Eleanor. Poor Arthur. Poor me. I had almost married a man-child who stalked me before work to return my underwear and let me know he was going on our honeymoon, the least of his transgressions.

"I don't do business at funerals," George said out of nowhere.

"Understandable," I said.

"It's in bad taste," he said, nodding from his chin. "But since you're here and I'm here, I want you to contemplate something. Consider this. Consider succeeding Arthur at New England Can."

What? He was offering me a job. Arthur's job. At Arthur's funeral. Although the sudden proposal—mostly the timing—was dumbfounding, this scenario was common in advertising: an employee of an agency crossing over to work for a client, in-house.

My stunned silence must have been golden, because George spoke again. "I would make it worth your while. This could be your hole in one."

I wondered what my while was worth. I would have to move to Far Acres. I had never lived in the country. It would be as good as living upside down. Where would I order a pizza? Nothing was open after eight at night.

On the other hand, having imagined my funeral moments before, moving might be the panacea to an empty life. *Stop thinking and listen, Lauren.*

"With our current growth, I'm ready to offer substantial remuneration. I'm talking Big Apple money. Also, the down payment on a house in town. Company car. You pick. They say the Tesla is amazing, and now there's a charging station at every rest stop on the Pike."

I was surprised by the offer, but I didn't think it would benefit me in any way to discuss it while Arthur's ashes were still warm. And something else bothered me. George Moore and Corey Steinbach had been great friends since high school. Why was George poaching—behind Steinbach's back? Did I want to accept a position with someone who would do that?

"I'm flattered," I said as the sun came out. Was the sudden glare a sign of something? Had I realized a funeral might result in a job offer of this magnitude, I would have followed obituaries in the *New York Times.*

"Don't be flattered, Lauren. Be smart. Here's the thing. We have a lot of balls in the air. In fact, we may be buying another company. Also, mull it over and be patient. I'll need time to pull a proper proposal together."

I was flabbergasted. It was a funeral.

"Back to the party," George said.

⌒♡

In front of the church, The Rock was in the Bentley, his head back, his eyes closed, listening to a podcast about weightlifting.

"Ready?" he said as he sat forward, turned off the podcast.

"All systems go," I said as the ill-timed, yet awesome, offer from George led me to think about my career.

I had always worked in an advertising agency. I had never considered going over to the client side. During college, I was employed by Sage Martindale. A single mother raising three kids, she owned an award-winning agency. I was mesmerized by her. Sage was the first woman I knew who ran a business out of an office, the first woman I watched balance work and family life. What's more, I liked working in a place where I had a chance to learn a little about a lot. After graduating, I moved on—to New York. Eighteen years later, I wanted to be the first woman partner at my agency, but I didn't know if Steinbach would diversify the board. What were my choices if he didn't? Go to another agency. Open my own agency.

Or switch—to the client side.

What if I did take the job? I could relocate to Far Acres, eviscerating painful reminders of Eric. I would relish the drama of announcing I was going somewhere unexpected. It would show I had recovered from heartbreak whether I had or I hadn't. Take that, Eric. What's more, no one in Western Massachusetts knew I was the broken woman who had been jilted at forty-one.

There was nothing to deter a move. My dreams of a nuclear family had exploded. Could this be my rebound? A change might be good.

⌒☙

I imagined myself living in Far Acres—in a farmhouse, a renovated farmhouse with white trim, six eight-pane windows in front. I would give my new home a name. After all, I was in advertising. I loved coming up with names. I would bring Tuesday, who had spent her life in an apartment. Maybe surprise her with a kitten friend. I would adopt the dog I planned to get with Eric. Not that exact dog. Eric was committed to a purebred Scottish terrier. He was down on mutts. I wanted to find a shelter and save a dog. Now that I thought about it, maybe Eric didn't want a dog any more than he wanted a kid. In my new state, I would grow my own vegetables—or I would hire someone to do it. I would paint the picket fence—or I would hire a handyperson to do it. I'd ride out of the three-stop-sign town, visit my nieces, in my yellow Chevy pickup. My vanity plate, ADWOMN.

In time, I would heal from the Great Humiliation. I would meet the community's only single heterosexual man. He would be the polar opposite of men like Eric and Glenn. His land would border my farm. We would meet for breakfast at Colleen's Café since 1932, open six a.m. to two p.m. I would order egg whites and be perfect on my diet. We would enjoy hikes so steep, we would need to slow ourselves up on the way down. In summer, we would attend theater in Williamstown to see plays, the music festival at Tanglewood to hear the Boston Symphony Orchestra, picnicking on a plaid blanket from the Vermont Country Store. We would rock on chairs on the wide porch of the Red Lion Inn in Stockbridge, drink margaritas, watch senior citizens (New Yorkers with Florida plates) arrive for the weekend. I would become close with other expats from the Upper West Side and hold a potluck dinner on Sunday nights. No need to RSVP. Show up any Sunday from seven p.m. on.

I envisioned sharing my news with my family and friends, all of whom would agree I had lost my mind. Moving out of New York to promote toilets. But a product was a product. When you had to go, you had to go.

I gazed out the window. Whether I took the job or not, it was great to be asked, to have an ego-building alternative. Something good had happened.

The Rock checked the rearview mirror.

I wished he was Rudy. I was itching to call him for company, so I did.

"Ahh. It's the woman who took me to Brazil. Are you calling to schedule a ride?"

"No. I'm just calling." As I said it, I realized I had never called him to talk before.

"Sorry I couldn't drive you to the funeral. I heard you got The Rock, so it should be easy to sleep in the car."

I laughed.

I told him Steinbach had missed the funeral.

"Steinbach must be disappointed. Once, I drove him to a wake. Steinbach asked me to come in with him. Bald man in his sixties, open casket."

"And?"

"The funeral home is about to become a client."

"Gorham's Green Pasture," I said. "It's a national chain."

If I told him about the job offer, The Rock might overhear or worse, Rudy might squeal. Could he be trusted? After all, Eric was a man. Glenn was a man. Rudy was definitely a man, a man who worked for Steinbach.

I decided not to say a word. "I should text Steinbach and give him the lowdown on the send-off."

"I want a Viking funeral," Rudy said.

"I'll remember that."

❧

The Rock dropped me at home. Margo was in the apartment in a burgundy felt beret. She said she was on her way to dinner and a Broadway play.

"What will you see?"

"A new play about internet privacy called *Right to Be Forgotten*. I'm friends with the playwright. What a talent."

I was sizzling with my news, and glad to have Margo to confide in.

"I received a job offer from New England Can."

"At the funeral?"

"From the grieving CEO."

"Wait, are you saying you might move to Massachusetts?" She grabbed my forearms. "But I like it here."

"I'll keep that in mind." I took the beret off her head and put it on mine. "How's it look on me?"

"I can't move to Boston. I need to stay here for the theater," she said.

"The job isn't in Boston. It's north of the Berkshires."

"What city is that near?"

"Very funny, Margo. You go. It can wait."

"I have good news too. A callback tomorrow," she said, animating the words with her hands. As much as she liked to sit, she was not sitting around. Neither was Kate.

There was a lesson in this. I should consider the job. It was my turn to move on as well.

Margo left, returning in a moment to swipe the beret off my head.

I had to think, which meant I had to eat. Literally chew things over. I changed into a T-shirt and ankle jeans, settled in my armchair, studied restaurants on Seamless, the food-delivery app, as though I was going to be tested in school the next morning. I didn't know if I preferred pastrami with mustard on club with a diet cream soda from Chaim Meyer's Kosher Delectable Deli or Chinese food from House of Wonton. I couldn't decide, so I ordered from the deli and then chose diced chicken with cashews from Wonton. When the doorbell rang, I saw a young man in a skullcap and an Asian man with a bike helmet, both delivery people arriving at the same time.

"Kids," I yelled, "dinnertime."

I was sure I couldn't order pastrami from a kosher deli in Far Acres. But that might be the price of success.

Chapter 18

It was good to feel wanted. I was so valuable, I was being stolen. I took a walk to Central Park, where people were everywhere, strolling in shorts, running in tank tops, licking ice cream, reading on the grass. I leaned back against an isolated mound, studied the sky.

I thought how great it was that Rudy kept the Escalade well stocked. There were bottles of Evian, cans of sparkling Pellegrino. One time, I noticed a sudden abundance of dried apricots.

"Thank you for the apricots," I had said to Rudy as we returned from a client. "But how did you know I like apricots?"

"Inventory control," he had said.

"You notice everything."

"About you," he said.

"You notice everything about me?"

"I do."

I wanted to say, "Like what?" but we pulled up at the office as Joanna waved to me from the sidewalk. She wore a short dress with a coordinated blazer, a scarlet headband in her silky hair.

Rudy and I climbed out of the Escalade. He definitely gave Joanna the once-over, but who wouldn't? Joanna had always been a magnet. When she was single and we went out after work together, we never paid for a drink. I was her sidekick, and there were benefits to being friends with a woman who had her charm.

"Joanna, this is Rudy Cohen. And Rudy, this is Joanna Wells."

They shook hands warmly. Joanna said she worked in media and she was planning an auto accident so Steinbach would hire a handsome driver to take her around, but she didn't think her husband would like it. Although Rudy smiled, even chuckled, I could see he was not falling under her spell. Did that mean he actually meant the flirtatious things he said to me?

"No need to go that far, Joanna. But I could use a new passenger. I'm only driving your friend here until May 1."

What? I had no idea of that until he said it.

He turned to me. "Steinbach assumes you'll be better, ready to drive on your own, by then."

"Not true. I can't drive as long as I wear this support. I'll mention that to Steinbach. He must not be aware."

Joanna knew me well enough to know I was milking my injury until the udder collapsed. I had a strategy. I planned to ride with Rudy as long as possible. He cheered me up.

"Please don't rush it," Joanna said, attempting not to grin. "If you remove a support early, you wind up with more damage later. That's why my cousin suffers from early-onset arthritis."

Okay. She could stop now.

"I enjoyed meeting you, Rudy."

⁓

That night, before bed, I found the counter in the bathroom swamped with cosmetics. Also, there was Margo's hair dryer, her electric toothbrush, Crest without a cap, a retainer, lens solution, and a Walgreens' worth of aerosol sprays. It was no longer my bathroom. It was backstage at a beauty pageant. I dug up a basket I had received when Eric had sent flowers. I gathered Margo's paraphernalia, loading the basket, placing it to a side. I scooped the clumping cat litter as Tuesday supervised. I washed up, moisturized my skin, actually laughed when I tripped on one of Margo's heeled furry slippers in the hall as I risked my life by walking to the bed.

I could feel that something had lifted in me. Maybe Margo's efforts to find work made me realize I had to get on with my life. Kate was an inspiration as well. She had hired a divorce attorney she called Mr. Fix-It, claimed it was the best $800 an hour she had ever spent, and hoped it wouldn't take more than an hour to leave Glenn without a pair of pants. Kate was seeing a psychologist and relying on help from her family in Chicago.

My phone rang. My mother. "How are you? Tell me you're not eating."

"Okay, I am not eating."

"I keep forgetting to ask. What happened with the wedding presents?"

I thought back to the day Rudy had insisted on picking up the presents, something I would never have done on my own, how opening the gifts had been fun, how I would never use the tiny salt-and-pepper shakers or eat Brazilian food again. "I picked them up."

"All by yourself?"

"With my driver."

"What driver? Since when do you have a driver?" she asked.

"Four weeks? Steinbach hired him because of my wrist."

"I loved that movie *Driving Miss Daisy*, but you know you should be walking more."

I thought how Rudy had advised me to confront my mother, tell her to cut her body-shaming crap. But why start an argument now? It was easier to say goodbye. Besides, if I did say anything, I would hear her accusation, "You're starting an argument before a holiday?" The holiday being Passover. Lucky for my mom, there were so many Jewish holidays, especially in the fall, she could use that line almost all the time. By the way, she did not consider the Fourth of July a holiday we couldn't bicker before.

"Mom, whatever. Tell Dad I said hi."

"Don't eat. You'll blow up."

I rolled my eyes. For exercise.

When Margo came home, I was sitting up in bed, reading a novel. Tuesday was a lump under the covers. Margo, in a tent dress, joined me with a platter—Cabot cheddar and French brie, olives and crackers. She opened a twist-top chardonnay from Down Under. I was amazed she was serving, and sure she had no intention of cleaning up.

"Any news on that job in Massachusetts?" she asked.

"I'm trying not to think about it until I have a written proposal. George Moore said it would take a while."

"Maybe that's good. Maybe he's trying to up the ante."

"Maybe he's interviewing other people."

"Nope. He wouldn't have broached it at the cemetery if he was doing that," Margo said. "Would you take it?"

"What do you think?" I said, contemplating how nice it was to have a late-night chat with my older sister.

She laughed. "I would have to see the written proposal. And tell me, how is Rudy, our favorite driver?"

I took a breath. "Honestly, I'm afraid that I like him."

"Why so negative? Because he drives for a living?"

"No. Not at all. It's not about what he does. It's about who he is."

"Who is he?"

"A man."

"Shameful."

"I think of my track record. How after two years I didn't figure out Eric was a child, that he was completely full of it. I worry about making another mistake with another man. I don't trust my judgment. Can you imagine being left at the altar two times?"

She laughed. She poked me. "You're not marrying Rudy, silly."

"I know. I know."

"And even if you were, he wouldn't leave you stranded at the aisle. He would drive you home. Stop being so damn serious. You're a funny girl. Lighten up."

I adjusted my pillow. I waded in. "Margo, Mom called earlier."

"Did she make you want to eat? Is that why you're feasting on cheese with me?"

"You need to tell Mom and Dad and Stephanie you are here. You need to get in touch. I don't want to lie about your whereabouts."

"You're not lying. You're leaving me out of the discussion. Besides, I was in touch with Mom. She was speaking through the saleswoman in that horrid store that didn't carry my size."

Holidays meant nothing to her, but why couldn't she understand how important they were to the rest of us? "You're in Manhattan, near Connecticut. Hiding in my apartment. And you're telling me you're going to lounge around here while I go to Stephanie's house—alone, still single—the imperfect daughter. Margo, I need your support. By the way, Stephanie mentioned you when we had coffee."

"Don't tell me you told her I was here."

I shook my head. "I didn't."

"Good, because that would be a really mean thing to do after I flew across the country to save you."

And because your own life was falling apart.

"We could surprise her," I said, ready for Margo to go nuts on me.

"These crackers are awful." She made a face, gritting her teeth.

I sipped wine. I needed wine to say the next sentence. "We are a family. We should be together for the holiday. Please come to the Seder."

"Over my dead fat body."

"What if I tell Mom not to say anything about your weight?"

"She'll be thinking it."

"Let her think," I said.

"I hate when she thinks. Watching her think makes me want to eat."

I understood, but I continued. "It's nice for family to be together."

"Maybe family, but not our family." She rolled her eyes to the heavens.

"Come on."

"You know what I'd like. I'd like Mom to be extremely overweight for a day. One day." She put up one finger in case I didn't hear the word "one." "Besides, for me right now, Mom is a sideshow. I'm going on calls, trying to land a part. Trouble is my weight. My weight is a huge problem."

"Huge?" I joked.

"Huge," she said.

"I understand," I said. I was empathetic—and copathetic. I did not ask about her plan for weight loss. Inquiring would result in dragon-size fume and fury. Suggest a solution and I would be pushed out the window, splat on the avenue. And who was I to tell her what to do when I had spent a lifetime disliking my body, obsessing over my weight? I had starved for the wedding and was now in bed with a buffet of cheese.

She didn't need my advice. She needed me.

"We could tackle our weight together," I offered, because I could lose a few, and she was my sister who I wanted to be healthy and employed.

She begrudged me a smile and shook her head.

I had gone far enough. Who knew better than me that an overweight person did not want suggestions about ways to lose weight? That most of us had already tried it all.

I swapped the subject matter—back to the Seder.

"Whether you go to Stephanie's or not, I will give you until Passover to tell Mom you are here."

She nibbled more cheddar. She swished some wine. "All right. I'll mull over the family hoo-ha. Does Stephanie still serve that sweet almond cake with the icing?"

Chapter 19

The day of the Seder, I called Kate to wish her a good holiday.

"I'm going to my mom's house. My brother dresses up as Moses."

"What does that entail?" I asked.

"Sandals," she said.

"Do you have the kids?"

"Of course. Glenn's new woman is Catholic. Glenn will be celebrating Easter."

"I guess that worked out."

After speaking to Kate, I realized I was doing better too. I had gotten an X-ray, and my wrist was fine. Of course, I continued wearing the support to work so I still "needed" my driver. On my sunnier days, I was able to admit how much I liked Rudy. He was smart. I enjoyed talking to him. He made me laugh. At other times, I convinced myself that getting involved so soon after Eric was a recipe for disaster. I swayed back and forth, a palm tree in the wind in the middle of Manhattan.

Margo had not only agreed to come to the Seder—she'd offered to split the price of the Israeli wine I had sent Stephanie.

I had lunch at a corner diner, Good and Greasy. I ordered a sandwich. I had to have a sandwich because during Passover, I did not eat bread for eight days. I was in a booth when the waitress delivered my tuna on thick sourdough. I ordered a chocolate egg cream. An egg cream is a New York drink made by stirring chocolate into whole milk, filling the rest of the glass with seltzer, stirring again. Once I ordered an egg cream in Connecticut, and the waitress asked how I wanted the egg in the cream. I was pretty far up in Connecticut. Maybe Litchfield. I thought how I had asked Margo to diet with me and she had turned me down. Neither of us was done eating.

I went to Angel for a haircut. My first since the Great Humiliation. Angel said my brown eyes looked bigger than ever. Did he tell that to all the girls? He said I had the most beautiful skin he had ever seen. I hoped he wasn't charging for every compliment. When he was done, I smiled at cascading chestnut curls, shining from an expensive half-hour conditioning. I had bought a new dress. It was knee-length with a round neck and a glossy wide zipper in the back. I was excited to wear it.

Margo greeted me at the door to my apartment. She was wearing all of Estée Lauder's makeup, striped leggings with pink trim, a long gold tent top, enough jewelry to sink a ship. She slipped on her long, super-puffy black coat.

"Margo, it's way too warm outside for that coat."

"My shield," she said. She was coming to the Seder.

I was elated, as though the most popular girl in the seventh grade had agreed to host my birthday party. My family would be together for Passover for the first time in many years. Everyone would be solicitous of Margo, and no one would be all over me.

Stephanie, in a navy cardigan set, pearls, and a cigarette skirt, answered the door, shocked to see Margo. Stephanie's blunt cut was blunter than ever.

"Look what I found in your driveway," I said as though I had run into Margo, as though she had been dropped off by taxi to my surprise.

"Oh, Margo!" Stephanie smiled from one side of the house to the other. She hadn't seen Margo in years.

I remembered Margo had come east when Liza was born. She was at the ceremony in the synagogue when Stephanie named Liza with an *L* in memory of my dad's mother. I was relieved Stephanie didn't know Margo had been hiding in my apartment for weeks.

My dad came into the room. Upon seeing Margo, he sniffled as a tear ran down his cheek. Then he joked, "Has anyone heard from Margo? It would be wonderful if she was here."

He grinned. She grinned. He hugged her. It was all as I had imagined it. Things were going well. How great it would be if we had a lovely, trauma-free Seder and everyone got along.

Stephanie's great room was navy and white. The wood floor was washed gray. There was a fireplace. An elevator to the second floor. Her sectionals were light blue, large, low, and deep. There were comfortable side chairs as well. Abstract paintings brightened the walls.

"Lauren, is that you?" my mother bellowed from the kitchen. Margo gave me the eye as though to say, "The fun is now over."

I took Margo's hand, leading her toward the smell of beef brisket, onions, carrots, potatoes, and Mom's Chanel No. 5, a perfume that had always overwhelmed me. I was hoping my mother would be so delighted to see Margo, she would edit her comments. But I was tense, uneasy. This was a game of Jenga. Move a crucial block and all the blocks could fall. If Mom said a single provocative word, Margo would return to the city.

Mom stood back to take Margo in, then squeezed her cheeks the way an aunt in her eighties might take a chunk out of the cheek of a toddler at a family function. "Oh, my Margo. My Margo. You've made my holiday. Such a surprise. What a surprise."

You'd never know Mom had tangled with Margo almost every time she had spoken to her since before the invention of the microwave. But whose fault was that? The blame had to be shared. It belonged to both of them. My mother was cemented in her ways, clung to her practices long after their shelf time had expired. She had no concept of evolving. I was amiable, detested conflict, especially in the family. Margo got a kick out of sticking it to my mom. As a teenager, she attracted friends Mom didn't approve of. Mom had no use for Margo's best friend, Cecil. As in, what kind of name was Cecil? As in, Cecil needs a good hairbrush. My sister kept Cecil in my mother's face.

When Mom clammed up and did something nice for Margo, it backfired. For example, Margo fell into a depression following her first divorce. Mom reached out. Margo mentioned a lack of mental-health insurance.

Mom said she would be happy to pay for a shrink, which Margo translated to me as, "Can you believe Mom had the nerve to tell me to see a shrink?"

"She was trying to help," I said.

"Is that what you call it?" she said.

"What do you call it?"

"Interfering. Maybe we should chip in and buy Mom an hour."

"Hi, Mom," Margo said flatly in Stephanie's kitchen. She'd give warmer hellos to sharks in choppy water. "Imagine meeting you here."

Mom's smile was wide. *Please, please, Mom, don't mention Margo's weight. Don't do it.* I was practically chanting "don't do it" in my head— as though I could warn my mother by telepathy and miracle of miracles, she would heed me. I was astonished when my mother went whole hog to the other side.

"You look beautiful," Mom said as she surveyed Margo in her Michelin Man coat.

Margo threw me a look. She thought my mother was full of it. I tried to remember the last time my mother had told me I was beautiful. I came up with nothing.

"Doesn't Margo look wonderful," my mother said to Stephanie.

I wished she would come up with a new line.

"How many times are you going to say that?" Margo asked.

Stephanie stepped back to remove herself from the line of fire.

"What did I say?" my mom asked, mostly to me.

"That I look wonderful," Margo said like the Queen of Nasty.

My mother threw up her hands. "What are you carrying on for?"

The air was sizzling.

"As you know, because you were there, I wasn't born an hour ago. I gain a ton of weight and you tell me I look wonderful. What's that about?"

My heart sank. They were off.

"You gained weight?" My mother was aghast. "I thought it was the coat."

"Are you here only for the day?" Stephanie asked Margo.

"Let's convince her to stay longer," I said as my dad joined us.

"Actually, I've been in New York for weeks," Margo said.

There went Margo. I had told her not to mention that she was practically a New Yorker now, but she couldn't leave well enough alone.

"Weeks?" my mother said. "You've been here for weeks?"

Silence.

"She's been here for weeks, Phil," my mother said to my father.

"Well, I'm sure you've been busy," I said, dashing from the outfield to save that ball.

"Not really," Margo said, shrugging.

191

"You've been in New York, and you didn't call us? Not one of us? Where are you staying?" Mom asked.

I assumed she knew better than to say she had been in my apartment.

"At the Hotel Lauren," she said, smiling at me.

Damn, I thought from under the bus.

"You were hiding in Lauren's apartment?" My mother turned to me. "Why would you keep such a secret, Lauren?"

My dad intervened before the guillotine dropped on my head. "Let's get this Seder started."

"We're waiting for Rob," Stephanie said. "He's coming from work."

My father walked out of the room.

"So, what have you been doing in New York?" my mother asked Margo.

"I had a few auditions."

"For commercials?" my mother said.

Margo couldn't stop herself. "No, Mom, for a revival of *A Chorus Line*," she said with sarcasm. "One singular sensation."

"But you don't dance," my mother said. "You quit Introduction to Ballet because you preferred tap. I sent you for tap lessons, but you were annoyed by the sound of the shoes. Then, when you attempted modern dance at Little Folks Feet, the instructor said you should try singing lessons."

"I can learn to dance," Margo said, digging her fists into the deep pockets of the puffy coat. That was good—with her hands tucked away, she couldn't punch anyone. "You don't think I can learn to dance?"

Was she actually that desperate to ignite my mother?

Once I would have stood by, but I was changing.

"Margo," I said. "Cut the crap."

"What crap?"

"The crap you brought from Los Angeles."

My dad returned to the kitchen. "We can hear you all over the house. There are children here. It's a holiday. Enough."

I felt four years old.

"Margo, Lauren. Wait for Rob in the dining room. Where is he anyway? Doesn't he know it's a holiday? Who's late for a Seder?"

I turned to Margo. "Excellent performance."

⌐∘

Stephanie's long rectangular table was set in white. White tablecloth, white cloth napkins. A white cover on the plate of three special matzot used in the ceremony. A white Seder plate with each of the symbols of the holiday. What wasn't white was silver, polished to perfection. The wineglasses were crystal and matched the water goblets. The kiddush cup was handblown glass—as was the cup for Elijah, the ancient prophet said to visit all Jewish homes on Passover. At the center of the table were candlesticks and the floral arrangement. Every chair had a white slipcover, a pleated skirt, a bow in the back.

Next to each place setting was a paperback the size of a coloring book—a slim Hebrew-English Haggadah. Before dinner was served, we would recite the Haggadah, which was basically the tale of the slaves fleeing Egypt. In fact, there were endless versions of the Haggadah— reform, conservative, Orthodox. Feminist. LGBTQ+. With illustrations. Without illustrations. There was an edition free in grocery stores when you bought Maxwell House coffee. For the past few years, because of the girls, Stephanie favored the equivalent of *Passover for Dummies*. Cover to cover, this Haggadah ticked off at a total of thirty minutes with songs.

When Rob arrived, in a navy suit, a white shirt, and a cranberry tie, I introduced him in jest to Margo. He didn't laugh. In fact, he seemed tense, a bit sweaty. Not himself. I wondered what was on his mind. Maybe he wasn't thrilled to see Margo because he thought she would create her usual turmoil. Little did he know that commotion had already taken place.

The two girls, in new dresses and sneakers, came down from playing upstairs. Great squeezes all around. I thought how fortunate Stephanie was to have children, how great it was I had nieces, how I would love a nephew. This made me think of Rudy. He hadn't mentioned what he was doing for Passover. Was he at the home of Aidan's grandparents?

We settled in the dining room. Rob commanded the table. When we were seated, he lifted a wine goblet and said, "Happy Passover," smiling across the table at his girls.

He picked up his Haggadah, the story of Passover, with disturbing disdain.

"What is this?" he said to no one exactly, as though there was something he had never seen before on the table. "I'm not using this Haggadah," he said.

This was unusual behavior for Rob. For anyone, really.

"Steph," he called out in a bizarrely commanding tone.

Stephanie was carrying short white candles to light in the exquisite candelabra my grandmother had given her as a wedding gift. She glanced at Rob. The first question in the Haggadah was, why is this night different from all other nights—and for sure, Rob was acting different.

"I told you last year I don't like this adaptation of the Haggadah."

"Well, I donated the old edition years ago, and these are the new ones."

"I don't want this abbreviated Haggadah. It's like the CliffsNotes. Do you want to read *War and Peace* or do you want to read the CliffsNotes?"

I had read the CliffsNotes in college—for a world literature course.

"Okay, next year, I will buy new books, or you can choose what you would like," Stephanie said, annoyed and bewildered. Margo pursed her lips, shook her head. She didn't care if we used a Haggadah or a Marvel comic.

"This won't do," Rob said loudly.

The girls were wide-eyed. My mother looked like she had swallowed a goat. Margo pinched my leg. I pinched back. We were slaves. We are free. Let's eat.

Rob turned to my father, seated next to him.

"Phil, will you look at this?" Rob said, irate. "The Jews struggled in the desert for forty years, and Stephanie wants to tell the whole story in five minutes. This Haggadah is so brief, I bet they cut the ten plagues down to four."

My father looked at me. I looked at him. We both looked at Stephanie. What was wrong with Rob?

"Rob, are you okay?" Stephanie asked. "It's only a Haggadah."

"Only a Haggadah? And is the Torah only a Torah?"

Oy—as my people say. Rabbi Rob, I thought. Where was this coming from? He had grown up more religious than any of us, but he could only be described as a secular Jew. His Shabbat ritual was travel soccer games on Saturday mornings. And what had they done with perfect Rob? The guy with the brownies and coffee at my apartment?

Stephanie gave it another try. "Next year, I will purchase brand-new editions with commentary from a thousand rabbis, the longest, most involved version of forty years in the desert. Maybe it will be eighty years in the desert. The girls will be older. They'll enjoy an all-night prayer fest more."

Olivia grunted. Liza rolled her eyes. "Daddy, we like the short one."

Rob stood. "Barnes & Noble is open. I am going to get a comprehensive Haggadah."

"Rob, that's ridiculous," Stephanie said from her seat. "Everyone is here. We are about to start."

Had Rob gone bonkers? Who cared about the Haggadah? Get the show on the road. I thought we were done with the turmoil in the kitchen.

Rob stood. "I will be right back. Is there anything else we need?"

Like what? An encyclopedia of religion?

Dad stood. "Sit, Rob." He pointed to Rob's empty dining chair. My father was a jovial, quiet man, but he had a fuse, and it was overheated.

Rob seemed to sway.

"It's the holiday. Start the Seder," Dad said.

Defiant, Rob remained standing. A showdown between Rob and my dad. Never in my wildest dreams.

The doorbell rang. Thank heavens. An interruption. *Bless whoever is at the door.*

"Must be Elijah the ancient prophet," Margo said, breaking the tension.

"Funny," I said. "Elijah never rang the bell before."

Olivia laughed. "Maybe he rang because he's early."

My father and Rob ended the duel, settled back into chairs, and I went to answer the bell. No imaginary prophet—no long gray beard, no white robe, no sandals. Instead, there were two men, serious men, square jaws, suits and ties, clean-shaven with crew cuts, about fifty years old.

"I'm Agent Martino. My partner is Agent Bowler."

I wasn't sure I heard right.

"We're looking for Robert Jeffrey Levine," Martino said.

"Are you friends of his?" I asked, probing because I knew Rob didn't have a single friend who looked like either of these guys. Rob's friends were suburbanites. So who were these guys, and why were they here?

"FBI," Martino continued, and flipped out a badge.

I froze in place.

I had never seen an FBI agent or a badge in real life before. But I had on TV, so I knew what to ask. "Do you have a warrant?" I heard myself say right out of an HBO show.

"Who is it?" Rob called out.

I opened my mouth to speak, but before I could respond, Rob shouted, "Tell them to come in."

The two men followed the direction of Rob's voice.

I had no idea what to do—so I trailed behind.

Martino and whatever the other one was named strutted up to where Rob was seated at the head of the Passover table. One man on each side of my brother-in-law. "Please stand."

Stephanie lost all color. I wasn't sure she was breathing, and I wouldn't have been surprised if she passed out. Margo's eyes shifted from one FBI agent to the other. My mother rose to say something. My father tugged her—back into the chair. Olivia and Liza were crying. I wanted to comfort my nieces, but I did not speak or move.

Hands quivering, Rob picked up a Haggadah, Stephanie's *Passover for Dummies*, rubbing the cover with his thumbs. I felt as though he wanted to open the book and read from it. He wanted to pray. I made eye contact with Margo. I could not look at Stephanie or the kids.

Martino spoke: "Robert Jeffrey Levine, you are under arrest. You have the right to remain silent . . ."

I felt paralyzed by the words. Stephanie slumped over, her head on the table. The two girls ran to her. She put an arm around each one. The rest of us telegraphed our disbelief.

Once in handcuffs, Rob became strangely calm, as though he expected what had happened and was relieved it was done. He took command. "Stephanie, stay here. Don't leave the house. Call Armstrong. Tell him what happened. Girls, your dad will be home very soon. This is an error, a mistake, a screwup."

Olivia's mouth was agape. Liza had tears on her little face.

What had Rob done? He was a straight arrow. Was he another person I had misjudged the way I misjudged Eric? We weren't a crime family. But now, I guessed we were.

"This can't be happening," Stephanie said to the ceiling, her hands in midair.

"Don't you worry. Everything will be okay." My dad stood behind Stephanie, his hands on her shaking shoulders.

"It's an error. An error," my mother kept saying.

Olivia held Liza's hand. Did this have to happen in front of the kids?

Filled with fear for them, I turned to the girls. "Don't worry. Everything will be okay."

Olivia was not fooled by my words. "But those were handcuffs."

Margo stepped in—as though she had rejoined the family. She took Liza's hand, telling the girls she would explain upstairs. Olivia froze. She wouldn't move. Margo tapped her on the head. "Last one upstairs is the last one upstairs," Margo said as she bolted. But the girls remained seated until my dad told them to go.

"Lawyer, lawyer," Stephanie said, her voice cracking. "I have to call Armstrong. That's what people do."

"Your phone, Stephanie," I said. "Where's your phone?"

As Stephanie searched for Armstrong's number, my mother said, "I've never seen anyone arrested before."

Stephanie fired back, "Zip your lip. The FBI wants to talk to him. End of story. That's it."

"On Passover, they came." My mother tapped all her fingers at once on the table to make her point. "On a holiday. And they knew it was a holiday."

Leave it to my mother to blame my brother-in-law's arrest for we-know-not-what on the anti-Semitism of the FBI.

"Mom, they didn't know it was a holiday," I said.

"Maybe not before they came, but they could see it was a holiday when they got here—candles, matzah, wine."

Did she expect them to leave and come back in eight days when Passover was over?

"Do you think they arrest people celebrating Christmas?" Mom continued. "It would never happen."

Stephanie called Armstrong. She left a message.

What did the FBI think Rob had done? Did Stephanie know what was going on? Or was she an ostrich, her head buried in the sand? The same way I had been with Eric. My heart pounded for her. Why would the FBI arrest Rob? Perfect Rob. It was beyond my imagination that he had done something criminal.

I climbed the stairs and heard voices emanating from Stephanie's bedroom. I entered to find my nieces on her king-size bed with the carved headboard, hiding under the quilt. I tiptoed across the room past the fireplace.

I yelled, "I found you!"

Liza said, "No one is here."

I pulled the quilt off the kids.

"And where is Aunt Margo?" I said, casing the room like a spy.

"Right here," Margo said as she jumped out from behind the divan. The flatscreen was on.

"What are you watching?" I said, glad the show was keeping their minds off what had happened.

"Some old HBO show called *Sex and the City*. Aunt Margo said it was very good."

I glanced at Margo. But I got it, distraction.

"I loved that show," I said.

"Aunt Margo told us you would tell us to turn it off," Liza said.

"Did she? No, it's a good show. I think I saw this episode."

"What's it about?" Liza asked.

"Friendship," I said.

"It's about sex—in the city," Olivia said.

"Which city?" Liza asked.

"New York," Olivia replied.

"You live in the city. Do you have sex?" Liza asked me.

I would have answered that question if only I could have their father back at the Seder table.

"Why did those men arrest Dad?" Olivia said sadly.

"Wrong house," Margo said.

I wished. If Rob himself hadn't done something to bring on the FBI, could be he was involved with someone who did. And why would that be?

"If it was a mistake, he'll be back soon, right?" Liza said.

"Yes," I said. "As soon as his lawyer explains what happened."

Liar, liar, pants on fire. We had no idea when he would be back.

"My friend's dad is a lawyer," Olivia said. "I bet he could solve this."

"But what if it wasn't a mistake?" Liza said.

"It's a mistake. This is your dad we are talking about," I said, patting her head, hoping to make things better. I was overcome with the maternal desire to coddle and protect these children I loved.

Margo said she would stay with our nieces. I went downstairs to rescue Stephanie from my mother. Helena was crying as I passed her. "This is terrible," I said, hoping she would reveal what she knew—after all, she was at the house almost every day. But Helena was smarter than me—all she did was shake her head in sorrow.

In the dining room, Mom was interrogating Stephanie a bit short of water torture.

"Do you know why Rob is in trouble?" Mom asked.

"I don't know." Stephanie's tone made me think she had said it a few times before.

"You don't know?" my father said. "Something must have happened."

Stephanie homed in on me, silently begging me to put an end to the questions.

"Let's give Stephanie a chance to think," I said to my parents. "We won't know anything until she reaches a lawyer."

"I wish Armstrong would call me back," Stephanie said. "Waiting is the worst."

"If he doesn't call soon, you'll call my brother," my mother said. Her brother, my uncle Felix, was a lawyer, a total bottom-feeder, and the original lawyer/shark joke. My sister was not enlisting him.

"I need a good lawyer," Stephanie said abruptly.

"He's not a good lawyer because he's my brother?"

"He's not a good lawyer because he has lost his license three times," I said. "And he has no discretion. He told me flat-out what cousin Lisa received in her settlement."

"Oy. That divorce. What did she get?" my mother asked.

Stephanie collapsed into a dining room chair only partially facing the table. "I'm positive this is a misunderstanding. If Armstrong doesn't call, I'll reach Barton Michael, the attorney who handles Rob's firm. I taught both his kids, I'm friendly with his wife, he comes to all our barbecues. Barton will manage the whole thing and bring Rob back tonight."

I had no idea what attending barbecues had to do with experience as a lawyer. My head throbbed. I was petrified for Stephanie, for the girls.

"What are my daughters doing?" she said, as though it was an average day in the neighborhood.

"TV with Margo," I said.

"Maybe you should go," she said, glancing at my parents. "I'll phone Barton when you leave."

"Let's go, Ellen," my father said. "Stephanie will call us if anything happens."

"The FBI had guns," my mother said.

"Mom, there were no guns," I said.

Stephanie shot up. "Leave now, Mom! Go home! There is nothing you can do!" Stephanie never raised her voice. The shouting shocked my mother into finding her bag in a hurry.

What had Rob done? Certainly not drugs. What do people get arrested for? What did an upstanding citizen like Rob get arrested for? I didn't believe he was taken into custody by mistake. Rob was in trouble. I thought about my sister calling the white-collar lawyer from his firm. Rob's arrest had to do with business. Otherwise, wouldn't she need a criminal lawyer? Well, at least he hadn't robbed a bank. Taxes, maybe he hadn't paid their taxes—or his firm's taxes? Could he be arrested for that? Did the FBI arrest you in your house in front of your family for a white-collar crime?

My mother and father approached the front door.

"What are we to do?" my mother said to me.

"Let's wait. Let's see what this is about. Maybe it's a misunderstanding," I said to calm my parents.

Rob had done something, something to someone. But what?

❧

I waited until my parents settled in the Lexus and I couldn't see it anymore—to be sure they were on their way home. I found Stephanie upstairs with Margo. We whispered outside the bedroom where the girls were still watching Carrie and friends.

"Did you call the lawyer?" I whispered as though the FBI could hear me. Was the house bugged? I looked up and around the hallway.

"Yes," she said. "Barton Michael can't handle it. There's a conflict of interest. He said Rob had already been in touch. He referred Rob to another attorney."

There was a conflict of interest? So it had to do with the wealth-management firm.

"The new lawyer handles white-collar crime exclusively."

"Stephanie, tell us what's going on. Maybe we can help." Margo was trying.

Stephanie snickered. "Now you're here to help, Margo? That's rich. You probably didn't even want to come to the Seder. I'll bet Lauren had to break your back. Do you have to kick up the dust with Mom every time you see her?"

I stood still, hoping to be left out of the ridiculous confrontation. But then she jumped on me.

"And, Lauren, you think I have it easy. Well, this isn't easy. Marriage is work. Every day. Work. And I have two daughters. And I teach. And there are the kids at school. And I get paid next to zero, nada, for hours and hours of dedication. Summers I heal my heart because I know how many of my students go home to parents who are missing in action. And what does someone like you have to do? Show up at the office in all-black clothing and care solely for yourself."

Although I knew Stephanie was spewing all this while reeling from what happened to Rob, I had never before heard what she truly thought about me. She considered my life a piece of cake. Not just cake. The best cake—red velvet cake. I had to care solely for myself. Well, maybe I was a hard person to take care of.

Stephanie turned the dial back to Margo.

"And you, showing up here once a century! Not giving a hoot about Mom or Dad. They're old. They could die. That's right. The next time you decide to visit could well be too late."

"Okay, Stephanie. You can stop now," Margo said softly, trying to avoid a showdown.

"You like to shovel it out, but you can't take it when it comes your way," Stephanie said.

I put my hands up, apart, as though I were separating my sisters. "Stop now. This is not a house divided. We're your sisters. We're with you, Stephanie. We're here to help."

Stephanie cleared her throat, took a deep breath.

"Feeling better?" Margo asked.

"I'm shocked. I'm scared."

"Sure you are," Margo said to Stephanie while looking at me.

"I have to take this out on someone," Stephanie said. "Might as well be you."

I wiped a tear from her face. "I knew there was a reason we stopped by."

Chapter 20

The next day, we found out that Rob had actually robbed. But only people he knew. And that included me. Over the years, I had invested with Rob, socking away a tiny percentage of my income. I was out a piddling compared to my parents. They lost a great deal, including all the money from the reverse mortgage. Fortunately, my parents had funds invested elsewhere—not every dime was tied up with Rob. But there was other damage. Rob had pilfered accounts belonging to teachers and counselors at Stephanie's school. But why did Rob need the money, and what had he done with it?

I asked Margo to speculate as she lay strewn on my couch.

"Why did he need what?" she said.

"More money. He's rich, the house in Connecticut, the one on Cape Cod. And they may be in the one percent, but Stephanie is not a blatant spender. I mean, how much money does one person need?"

"Oh, come on. There are people who can never have enough. Greed is the creed. And I blame this on Mom."

"Naturally you do. Do you blame her for World War I or only World War II?"

"All those years of painting Rob as perfect. Obviously, there's something very imperfect about him."

"Call me a fool. I thought Stephanie's marriage was flawless. I wanted to emulate her."

"You never know what's happening in someone else's house."

The truth. "I look at Stephanie, blindsided after years of marriage, and I realize I got away easy. Sadly, it took Stephanie's misery—and Kate's situation—to make me see all I had in comparison was a scraped knee."

"It was more than a scraped knee. Give yourself some credit."

Stephanie called and asked me to come by and invite the girls somewhere, anywhere. I went to Connecticut thinking I would bring my nieces to the movies, surprised to find Rob sitting in the kitchen barefoot in an old gray T-shirt and pajama pants. He had a bowl of thick oatmeal in his hands, and I wanted to throw it in his face, but I controlled myself.

"Where's Stephanie?" I asked roughly.

"No idea. She left with the girls," he said.

I stood a yard away with my hands folded at my chest as though if I stood any closer to him, I would catch his airborne disease, which appeared to me to be greed. "But I came to spend time with the kids."

"We had an argument. She stormed out."

I leaned back against the counter. "Rob, what is going on?"

"Stephanie didn't tell you?"

"No," I said, because I knew so little and I wanted to prod him on.

"Do you want a drink? Some coffee? There's more oatmeal."

He had to be kidding.

"I want answers," I replied, standing and waiting.

"No one understands."

Poor Rob.

"Try me."

"I had debts. I needed to pay the debts."

"So you stole?"

"I borrowed. I had every intention of putting the money back—with interest."

"But why did you borrow from my parents? Why didn't you ask for a loan? You could have asked me too. I would have lent you money."

"Thanks for the offer, Lauren, but I needed serious money."

"Why? What happened?"

He stalled.

I waited.

He spooned some oatmeal. He wiped his lip with his knuckle. Not a Rob thing to do.

I sat down at the table, hoping he would feel closer to me. "Rob?"

"Gambling. I was gambling."

"What?"

"You heard me." Back to the oatmeal.

I was astonished. He was a gambler? Perfect Rob? Quickly, my thoughts pivoted from him to my sister. How had Stephanie not known this? Yes, Rob handled their finances—after all, wealth management was what he did for a living—but my sister was astute. Did they have separate bank accounts? Did he use cash only?

Maybe Stephanie knew about his addiction and worried about it every day but never told us a word because she didn't want to obliterate the edifice we had built to Rob. It turned out Rob was just a person. He had foibles.

Maybe Stephanie thought gambling was his sport—like a man heads to a bar on Sunday to watch a football game or joins a community softball team or takes up jogging. In any case, how would she know what occurred in his office, a private domain? Why would Stephanie be acquainted with his business dealings? Her priorities were her family, her students, a full-time job. She had no reason to distrust Rob—how much could she look out for?

I had been jealous of my little sister since the day we met—I was three and she was about to be born. I was shuttled to my aunt's house in Howard Beach while my mother was in the hospital. I felt abandoned no matter how wonderful Aunt Roz was to me, abandoned although my uncle Marty came from work with a Hershey bar each night. When I got home, my mother was coo-cooing to Stephanie as though she had no other children, as though Stephanie were her first. I no longer had my own room in our three-bedroom house. I shared a room with Margo. I was so jealous of Stephanie, from then until now, I never considered how hard she worked to achieve her goals. I thought the good stuff just happened to her.

"I never knew you were a gambler," I said to my brother-in-law the thief.

He shrugged.

"Did Stephanie know?"

"No. And I could never let on. I could never tell her. I thought I would pay off my debts and return the money to the accounts. One day, the principal from Stephanie's school called my office. He needed to tap into his funds for a down payment on a new house. I wasn't around. The managing partner took the call. When he went to move the money, he saw the account was drained."

"I can't believe Stephanie is letting you stay here," I said in disbelief as I moved around the kitchen. There were cereal bowls, coffee cups in the sink—in Stephanie's house—unheard of. I turned on the faucet, washed the dishes.

"It is my house—and I have nowhere to go," Rob said.

"You deserve nowhere to go," I said. "Nowhere is too nice for you."

"Even my brother won't talk to me, and he never invested a dime with my firm."

"I guess he knows you better than we do."

"You're here to beat up on me too? Everyone is piling on! A man thinks he has a family, people he can count on no matter what; then this

208

happens—and poof, they're gone. I've been very good to you, Lauren. From the get-go, I've treated you like a sister."

"Well, then I guess you would rip off your sister. You stole from me. You tricked my retired parents. You've ruined Stephanie's life. And how could you do this to the girls? They will never forget what happened at the Seder."

"It's an addiction," he said.

"Right." Give me a break.

"I can't help myself."

I dried the plates and glasses. Stephanie did not deserve this mess.

"You of all people must understand."

Had he lost his mind? What was he talking about?

"Excuse me?"

"You understand addiction because you're addicted," he said in an accusatory tone.

I hurled the towel to the floor. "What the heck, Rob? I don't gamble."

"No, but you are addicted to food."

I hated that he called me out to prove his point.

"Okay. Bingeing is an addiction, but how can you compare it to robbery? You are a thief. I am not hurting anyone but myself."

I had never flat-out admitted this—that I was hurting myself, that I was a masochist when it came to my body. But there it was. Straight out of my own mouth. I put it away, I didn't want to consider it, so I stayed on Rob. "The most I have ever taken behind someone's back is a donut."

"I couldn't stop gambling. I don't belong in jail. I am not well. I need Gamblers Anonymous or some kind of rehabilitation place. It's a mental illness," he said, licking the tablespoon from the oatmeal.

I wondered if that was his excuse to get off without paying anyone back. I didn't think it was going to work. If he had just stolen from my parents or me, maybe we wouldn't have called the FBI, but those affected by his misdeed numbered dozens of people. Even if he got off with a slap on the wrist, the cost of lawyering up was going to drain their savings, drive my sister to the poorhouse. She earned a teacher's salary.

"Do you know what I have learned here, Rob? People are often different from what they seem. Eric was different. You're different. I plan on remembering that."

Stephanie and the girls entered the kitchen. Quickly, I shut down the conversation with Rob.

Stephanie was bleary-eyed, wearing yoga pants and a T-shirt she had probably slept in. She hugged me hello. I didn't want to let go. Could she age a decade in a few days?

The girls and I fist-bumped.

"Are you here to get us out of the house so Mom and Dad can fight?" Olivia said.

Exactly. Child genius.

"Where's Aunt Margo?" Liza asked.

"Aunt Margo is resting up for her audition later today." When I left the apartment, Margo was "in couch," napping with an issue of *Variety* on her face. She was in a leopard-, zebra-, tiger-striped something or other, with her hair in a wrap with a bow. She didn't respond when I asked if she wanted to go to Connecticut. It occurred to me I could have amused my nieces with that description.

Stephanie looked at me as if to say, "Go. Take the girls."

Olivia was right, of course. My sister was planning a blow-by-blow with Rob. My bet: she was telling Rob to move out. But would he? I felt torn between taking the girls to a movie and remaining to defend my sister. But Stephanie had invited me for a reason.

"Hey, favorite nieces—and also, only nieces," I called out. "Movie time. Let's buy the popcorn in the bucket. Refills are free."

Olivia said, "You don't have to be extra cheerful. We know our lives are coming to an end."

Chapter 21

When I returned from Stephanie's house, Margo was on my armchair, twisted into a knot, examining her toe. I could see how damaged it was before I approached. "That looks horrible. Have you seen a doctor yet?" I knew the answer was no.

"Everyone always tells everyone else to go to the doctor."

"No. Sometimes I say maybe you need an aspirin, but you are way beyond aspirin."

"It's fine," she said as she put her foot down. "What happened at Stephanie's?"

"Rob was there. Let me see your toe," I insisted, doubting she would let me take a peek.

"I said, it's fine," she contended. "What did he say?"

"He's a gambler. He had debts to pay."

"Who would have guessed?"

"Let me see your toe," I insisted.

To divert my attention, she went to the kitchen for a frozen fruit bar.

"This bar is only one hundred calories," she said.

"Not when I eat the box of eight. Your toe needs medical attention. There's a doc-in-the-box around the block. Let's walk over—before you can't walk at all."

"No way," she said, annoyed.

"Then let me see your toe," I demanded.

She sat on a dining chair. I took hold of her right leg. Her third toe was enlarged, red and black.

"Are you kidding?" I asked.

"Let go. It's not that bad."

"Margo, it's swollen and probably infected."

I typed "black toe" on my laptop. I saw a photo of a rotting toe. Margo's was in worse shape. How could that be? That was not good. On the web, every medical condition appeared sorrier than anything anyone would have in real life. I read aloud from the site. What it came down to was my sister could lose her toe, and if she lost her toe, she could lose her foot, and if she lost her foot, she could forfeit her leg. I imagined, horrified, that it was all happening. Margo without a toe, a foot, a calf. Margo without a leg. Me without my sister.

That was it. "Come on," I said. "We're going to a doctor."

She was done with the pop, sucking the stick. "Look, my fortune is on the stick."

"Does it say you're going to die soon? How could you let things go like this?"

"No matter about my toe; it will be fine when I lose weight."

"Maybe you need insulin."

"No way. I am not sticking myself with a needle. Ugh. I'd rather die."

Well, you might die.

I pulled her off the couch. "Now, now, you don't care about dying—just when we're close again? Let's take care of your toe before it's too late."

We entered the clinic to find a woman in scrubs behind the glass enclosure and a room full of people waiting to be seen.

"Can I help you?" she asked.

"Yes. Hi. My sister needs to see someone about her foot."

"Name?"

"Margo Leo," I said on my sister's behalf.

"It's Lamour," Margo corrected me.

I turned to Margo. "Give her your health insurance card."

"You didn't tell me to bring it," Margo said, disinterested.

"No card. No appointment," the woman said.

"Her toe is black," I pleaded.

"I can schedule an appointment for a time when she can bring the card."

"How much is it if I pay now?"

"A deposit of three hundred dollars."

The chances of Margo going home to retrieve her card, then returning to the clinic were slim. I passed a credit card to the receptionist. Then wondered, would Margo wait her turn?

"By the way, my sister has a heart problem."

"Follow me," the receptionist said.

I could feel waiting patients staring us down. Nothing worse than being a line cutter in New York City, but my sister was my sister. I turned to the audience. "She has a cardiac condition," I said, clutching my chest.

I wasn't sure if the first person we saw was a doctor, because technicians wear white coats in walk-in centers. He escorted us to a room with putty walls, a replica of a skeleton, a picture of a rowboat. He took Margo's blood pressure and asked her to stand on the upright scale.

She shook her head. Now what?

"I only weigh before my morning coffee in the nude," she said to the technician or nurse or—who knew. "If you want to weigh me, you'll have to come to my sister's place."

213

Smart man—he left without Margo's weight.

"Take off your shoe," I said.

"I will when the real physician gets here," she said.

"Take it off."

She kicked off her flats. I sat on a chair with wheels, next to a tin desk. There were pamphlets. I browsed the brochure about a foot affliction known as Pearson's Problem. Pearson's Problem was a rash.

Two doctors appeared.

"I'm Dr. Walter Sanchez, and this is Dr. Sara Glassman, who is here to learn. I hope that's okay."

"Of course," I said as Margo lolled on the examination table as though none of this had anything to do with her.

I noticed young Dr. Glassman gaping at Margo's foot. The black toe might as well be speaking in tongues.

"Are you diabetic?" Dr. Sanchez inquired as he examined my sister's toe.

"I don't take medication if that is what you're asking."

"Well, let's check it out," he said. "Extend your index finger, please."

He dabbed her fingertip with an antiseptic wipe. Margo winced at the prick as the doctor tested her sugar. I had never seen this done before.

"Your blood sugar is 405," Sanchez said as he dropped the needle into a disposal on the counter.

Margo was without emotion. She had taken her brain and gone to la-la land.

"What's normal?" I asked.

"Under one hundred," he said. "You need medication, and you need a program, young lady."

"Don't call me 'young lady,'" Margo said to be ornery.

Okay, old lady. I looked at my sister in wonder. Did she not understand she was a raging diabetic?

"Normally, we x-ray, but there's no point. Your next stop is the hospital. You need antibiotics. An antibiotic drip will save your toe."

"Save?" Margo was stunned.

Dr. Sanchez continued. "It's common to deny type two diabetes, but you must address your disease. Do you understand type two leads to the loss of sight, neuropathy—which is loss of nerve function—kidney failure, memory loss, heart disease?"

Margo replied, "If it's about losing weight, I plan to lose fifty pounds, maybe more."

Dr. Sanchez grimaced as though he had heard that a thousand times from people with toes bigger and blacker than Margo's. "Do you want to go by ambulance?" he said.

"Because of a toe?" Margo said. "A whole ambulance for one toe."

⌒ා

Margo was admitted. An MRI, this test and that, all day.

I called Stephanie. Stephanie hit speakerphone, as my mom was there.

"Don't get upset. It's no big deal," I said, because I didn't want her to think Margo was at death's door. "Margo is in the hospital."

"My Margo," Mom said.

Your Margo? I mimicked Mom in my head. *My Margo. My Stephanie. My What's-her-name?*

"Lauren, what happened?" Stephanie asked.

"Her middle toe is infected, and at minimum, she will require an antibiotic drip."

"On her right foot?" Mom said.

What difference what foot? What if she had two left feet?

"We're coming now. Dad will drive," Mom said.

"There's nothing you can do," I said.

"You're there," my mother said. "We'll be there too."

"She's having tests all day."

"We're coming," Stephanie said. "She would do it for me."

Maybe. Maybe not. She certainly wouldn't have done it for Stephanie a few months ago.

To distract myself from worrying about Margo, I checked to see if George had contacted me. But no. How could I decide anything until I knew what the deal was?

I went to the coffee shop in the lobby, sat on a swiveling stool at the counter, ordered iced tea, and thought about Rudy. I hadn't seen or spoken to him since before the Seder. I needed more out-of-town appointments, for sure.

I decided to give Rudy a call. I told him about Margo, that I was waiting at the hospital hoping everything would turn out all right.

"How was your Passover?" he asked.

"Well, let's see. The FBI arrested my brother-in-law, Rob."

"In the house at the Seder?"

"Yes."

"Anti-Semitic."

"That's what my mother said. Right before she noted how slender the agents were."

He howled. I had never met anyone who was better to share a story with.

∽

I checked my sister's room, but she was still gone. A nurse told me Margo had been taken for some kind of scan. I settled into the throw-up-green recliner. I worried until I nodded off. I woke to a tap on my shoulder.

It was Stephanie. Alone. Drawn. Sallow.

"Where are the parental units?"

"I told Mom we should visit when Margo is settled. She went home to Dad. Here I am."

I was surprised she would tell a white lie. "You ran a circle around Mom?"

"I tricked her." She winked.

"I can't believe you did that. It's so not you."

"Lauren, you always think Mom and I are in cahoots. We're not. She just feels more in sync with me than with you. She always has. And by the way, it's not a privilege to be the favorite. In fact, it's work. Growing up, I walked the line to make her proud. I still want her to think the best of me. I make the holidays because I want her to know I will carry on her traditions. And I speak to her almost every day. I depend on her, but she also depends on me. Margo and Mom? Let's just say, opposites do not attract. By the way, where is she?"

"She's getting a test. To see if she has a brain," I said.

"I'm the one who needed that test."

I raised my feet in the recliner. A pause. "Did you know he gambled?"

She sat on the edge of the hospital bed. "Of course. However, I had no idea he was Bernie Madoff. His brother is letting him move in."

"Family," I said. "You can't live with them until you have to live with them."

"There's a chance he winds up behind bars." Stephane's tone was despondent.

"What about the girls?"

"I found a child psychologist. They'll start sessions next week."

"Does she take insurance?" If she needed help, I was on it.

"Yes, I couldn't do it any other way."

"What about you?" I asked.

She shook her head as though I had asked a ridiculous question. "Haven't you learned? You can't control another person's behavior."

Eric. Glenn. Rob.

217

And Margo, I thought as she was wheeled back into the room. She glared at me. "I told you not to tell Stephanie unless I died."

"Well then, Margo, this must be it," I retorted.

"We'll miss you," Stephanie said.

"How do you like my new attire?" Margo displayed her pathetic hospital gown as though she were a one-name rock star at halftime at the Super Bowl.

A chatty young nurse tucked Margo into bed. She flicked the IV, offered Margo fresh water, asked for Margo's autograph because she watched *As the Hospital Turns* all through high school and that's why she decided to go into medicine. I could see why it would be inspiring. After all, my sister had come back from death three times.

"Do we have any paper, Lauren?" Margo asked as though I were her personal assistant.

I ripped a page from a notebook I kept in my bag.

"Oh, it's lined. I prefer blank."

Stephanie and I smiled at one another, stifling laughter.

"Do we have a pen, Lauren?"

"Ta-da." I handed one over with a flourish.

"Oh no, it's black ink. I like to sign in colors."

Tough life. But I was glad she was enjoying her Hollywood moment.

The nurse was delighted. On her way out, she promised to bring Margo extra diet gelatin.

"How's your toe?" Stephanie asked Margo.

"Don't listen to a word Lauren says. I'm fine."

"She has type two diabetes," I said. "Her blood sugar is a rodeo."

"Must you reveal all my secrets?"

I took in Margo, in the raised bed, and Stephanie, who had settled into the ugliest vinyl chair in America. I was glad I had sisters.

"What are you thinking?" Stephanie asked.

"Despite our problems, it's great to be together. I'm happy we are getting along."

Margo straightened her pillow. "Oh, Lauren, you sap, turn it off."

"Margo, when you're well, you should visit us in Connecticut. The girls had a great time watching *Sex and the City* with you. Unfortunately, they still remember that their father was arrested."

Margo smiled as though she had saved the day.

Were my sisters going to be friends?

"Just one thing," Stephanie continued. "Please, Margo, take it easy with Mom."

"Okay, golden girl," Margo replied.

"Three-way hug," I said. And we gathered around Margo in the hospital bed.

That evening, I didn't have the wherewithal to prepare or order dinner. I went to my freezer—three flavors of ice cream were on the top shelf. Thank you, Margo. I reached for my favorite pint.

Suddenly I stopped, stepping back as though I had seen a live animal looking at me from one of the bins. I slammed the door shut. Had I learned zero from the doctor's impassioned speech about the dangers of diabetes? What was I going to do? Wind up with my very own ugly, infected, big black toe? I opened the freezer again. I tossed the ice cream into the garbage can. I pitched frozen fruit bars, Sara Lee pound cake, waffles, and pancakes. A madwoman, I divested everything but broccoli florets and Lean Cuisines. I took on my nemesis, the fridge—the fridge versus me, clearing the shelves. I purged for me but also for Margo. When my sister was released from the hospital, she would have a clean start.

I wept for Margo. For Stephanie. For Kate. I sat on the couch next to Tuesday. She eyed me sadly, as though to say, "Does this health-kick routine include me, because I hope not." I cried because I knew I would miss eating night and day. Forfeiting the food was akin to losing a friend.

I made a decision. I wouldn't starve this time. I would not be as black and white as the half-and-half cookie the size of my face from the bodega on the corner. I would take it slow, journal what I ate, walk to and from the office, and reach a grand total of ten thousand steps a day. I considered a health club, but I didn't get carried away. My history with gym membership was the equivalent of my pathetic experience with Pound People. I wouldn't last long, and I would gain back whatever I lost. In my twenties, I had prepaid a gym for a year with the hope the expenditure would encourage me to keep going. It did—for a month. Then I snagged a note from my internist—I had to quit for medical reasons. Full refund.

I wondered if my sister would consider the residential weight-loss program she had mentioned. It was in southern New Jersey. I googled it. The website said attendees flew in from all over the world. There were lectures by physicians and nutritionists, three squares a day, two snacks. Group classes included aquatics, Zumba, spinning, and chair aerobics. Chair aerobics? Did they sit on the chairs or lift the chairs? Convincing Margo to attend would be thorny—even if I dwelled on the two snacks. But maybe I could offer to go with her for a while. It might give me the jolt I wanted as well.

I searched for my athletic shoes in my closet. Then I remembered. I had donated the Nikes to Goodwill. I went online. I ordered a pair for me. Another for Margo.

I called her in the hospital.

"What's up?" I asked when she answered.

"I'm eating my gelatin. With a fork."

"A fork?"

"They didn't bring a spoon."

"Buzz them," I said.

"I did."

"So?"

"They sent the nurse."

"The nurse who wanted the autograph?"

"Another nurse," Margo said.

"And . . ."

"She didn't have a spoon."

"Green or red?" I asked.

"Orange."

"Have a good night, Margo. I love you," I said.

Chapter 22

A day later, I waited for Rudy in front of the Max. We were scheduled to travel to Dara Casey's place on Long Island. I had to admit that I missed conversing with him, especially while so much had happened in my family. As soon as I got in the car, he asked me about the FBI joining my family for the Seder. I told him the story.

"How's Stephanie?" he said as we crossed town to the bridge.

"Down and disillusioned. This will make you sick. Her two girls were at the table when the FBI arrested Rob."

"How old?"

"Four and eight," I said.

"It must have been difficult to explain."

"That's where Margo came in. In fact, ask me about Margo."

"Is she with the FBI too?"

"No, she's still in the hospital."

I explained about Margo's toe.

"My dad had type two diabetes," he said. "He wouldn't take care of it either."

"Oh, she's going to take care of it," I said.

"Don't be so sure."

"Why?"

"By sixty-five, my dad was almost blind, suffered two heart attacks due to clogged arteries. Pain in his legs, neuropathy, kept him awake at night. On his last day, on our way to the hospice, he insisted we stop for ice cream—butter crunch."

"Did you?"

"Of course. It was his dying wish."

Maybe Rudy was joking. "Wow. Is that true?"

"Everything but the butter crunch. That's actually my favorite flavor."

"Well, my sister has failed many times, but suddenly there's no choice but to succeed. We have to become fit."

He seemed surprised. "We?"

I couldn't believe I was talking to Rudy about my health. What was next? Would I discuss my sleeping habits?

"Yes, we. I'm dieting with her."

He rolled his neck. "Then I hope you don't get angry when you're hungry."

~

When I emerged from To Die For, with a gold-and-black shopping bag containing two tops Dara had sold me—at a whopping 5 percent discount, of course—I found Rudy tense on the sidewalk. He slipped his cell into the pocket of his pants.

"What's up?" I asked.

"I need a favor," he said.

"Name it."

"Stacy, my neighbor, Aidan's babysitter, called. She has to drop him at home earlier than usual. I know it's asking a lot, but do you mind if I stop at my place before I drive you into Manhattan?"

"That's fine." I was happy to help out.

"We're practically passing by," Rudy said.

"No need to sell past the close," I said. "Let's go."

I was up for the detour. I understood Rudy's situation. Parenting was juggling. One reason I thought I would prefer working on my own when I had children. That after having a baby, I might set up my own shop, run by a woman who put family first. I had learned a lot about single parenting when I worked for Sage Martindale. She'd catch a game or a school play, return to work afterward. Sage did not have a spouse, a partner. Neither did Rudy. I wondered how they found time for themselves, how I would do having a child on my own.

"Thank you," he said, adjusting his sunglasses, about to start the engine.

I looked in the rearview mirror. "Nice Ray-Bans," I said. "Tell me about Aidan's mom."

He turned around, held up the phone to show a picture of a woman cuddling an infant. She had long, curly blond hair, wore a flannel shirt. The baby was in a blue onesie. He was a few months old and asleep.

"My sister, Libby. Libby Kandall. A techie at Google. Before the accident, she worked in the offices near Chelsea Market."

"She's very pretty." I took the cell from Rudy's hand to get a better, longer look at this woman, her fair skin, her lovely face, her blue eyes warmed by motherhood, her first child—and now? In a coma? How was that fair? I handed the phone back to Rudy.

I believed it was possible for Libby to miss Aidan, to yearn for him, although she was comatose. Loved ones hung with you. Whether you were out of it or they were long gone. My grandmother knew where

I was, what I was doing. Some nights, I looked up and there she was. Calling out to me, Lauraleh.

Curiosity got the better of me. "What about Aidan's dad?"

"Only his nose knows."

"I don't understand," I said.

"Coke."

Okay, so I thought I had problems?

"Enough," he said. "Let me tell you about the neighborhood."

Rudy lived in Brooklyn, but not the Brooklyn of hipsters or the one where young families donated ride-on toys to the playground, left the toys for others to enjoy—and the three-wheelers were still there when the family came back. Not the Brooklyn of grocery co-ops and Eric's Famous artisanal mayonnaise. Rudy's neighborhood was an auto-repair mecca.

We drove around, looking for a place to park, circling the same blocks, past an occasional empty shopping cart, people in their twenties idling on street corners, workmen entering and exiting tired buildings. We stopped at a light. To the right, there was a vacant lot, overgrown with weeds. A dilapidated mobile home on the property had a sign. The sign said, SIMON'S HAULAGE. There was a notice from the city on the rusting chain fence.

"Sad to see the old guy go," Rudy said as the light changed.

"You knew the owner?"

"Chatted with him as much as possible. Brought him black coffee whenever I stopped by. Sometimes he was here alone. Other times his brother, Sol, or his brother-in-law, Sydney, or his nephews—Howard and Michael—would be around as well."

"You were a fan."

"Enormous fan. He never finished sixth grade and had a mind like a steel trap. When he was eleven, he started driving a small truck for his immigrant father, who came here without a penny but somehow managed to get a wagon and make a living. The kid began moving people out of tenements in the middle of the night, hauled pianos, whatever it took. When he retired in his seventies, he had a slew of eighteen-wheelers, mostly Mack. Bought real estate as well. Last year, he donated this lot to the city for the sole purpose of creating a basketball court for teens."

Rudy turned toward me. "He would have liked you."

Why? I wondered.

"You are definitely his type."

"What type?"

"My type."

I fidgeted in my seat, my face flushed, my body warm, my mind telling me this was all hogwash, and I would be a two-time loser if I fell for a word of it. I reached for the sweetness of a dried apricot, thought of Margo, put my hand back in my lap.

"Don't tell me I embarrassed you," Rudy said.

"Try not to bullshit me," I responded. "I believed the last guy who did."

"I'm not that guy. I'm this guy."

⟳

We parked and walked to a roll-up, overhead garage door advertising a business that specialized in insurance appraisals for anything that moved, was metal, and got hit. The building was rampant with the worst spray graffiti.

"Right here," Rudy said, pointing to the graffiti that said "Make my day."

Did he live in a garage—with his nephew, a six-year-old? I hoped not.

"Just kidding," he said as he removed a key from his pocket and walked to an ordinary red door next to the insurance business. We entered a tight corridor. "Sorry, but the doorman has the day off, and the elevator is broken."

I laughed.

Four flights later, including my intermittent stops, we were in front of 9B.

"How can this be 9B?" I asked, taking a breath. "We walked up four flights, not nine."

"But it felt like nine, right?"

"Oh, if that's how we're counting, I would change the sign on your apartment to 15B."

"Sense of accomplishment? Come on, I'll show you my penthouse."

I was hoping his so-called penthouse would not be a scrap heap. As much as I was keeping my distance, I didn't want an excuse not to like him—such as his stovetop was home base to cockroaches dispersing when he switched on the light. I didn't want to trip on his inside-out boxers.

The place was spotless, pristine. The dark, wide-wood floors shone. The walls were so white, they could have been painted that morning. There was a brown leather couch along the living room wall and a pine-wood coffee table. Facing the couch was a lovely oak dining table. There were framed photos of people I assumed were family. Also, paintings signed by Aidan. I walked toward his loaded bookcase. A guitar leaning against the wall caught my eye.

In one glance, I knew he loved and cared for where he lived.

"Welcome," he said.

"I love it," I blurted.

"Really?"

"It's welcoming, embracing, a good home. Your nephew must be happy here." I zeroed in on the guitar by the bookcase. It had an old hippie tapestry type of strap. "You never mentioned you were George Harrison."

"I wish."

A key turned in the door, and a woman let herself in. She had a Western look—long gray hair in a ponytail, rugged jeans, a checked shirt, cowgirl boots. She waved hello, and a boy ran under her arm into the apartment. He looked nothing like Rudy.

Aidan was small for a six-year-old with straight blond hair and round blue glasses. His faded jeans were big, falling. His T-shirt featured a picture of Albert Einstein with hair full of static, as though Einstein had been electrocuted. He seemed to be a lively, quirky kid.

"Didn't know if you would be here yet," the woman said to Rudy, who returned the guitar to the wall.

"Does this mean I don't get snacks?" the boy said.

"We were going to have cookies while we waited for you. Aidan told me you made some last night," the woman said as she looked me over.

Rudy held his nephew by the shoulders. "Stacy and Aidan, this is Lauren."

I leaned in, put out my hand. "Great to meet you," I said. "What kind of cookies?"

"Chocolate chip," Aidan said. "We baked last night."

"Everything is in his backpack," Stacy said to Rudy. "We finished the homework, but maybe you should check the math." She looked at me. "I'm a graphic designer. Not a mathematician."

When Stacy took off, Rudy placed cookies on a paper plate. The cookies were different shapes, round, triangle, and square. The round ones were enormous, the size of pancakes.

I thought how normal everything seemed. Simple. Pleasant. Treat yourself. Have a cookie—not a whole calorie count of a scene like the one in my apartment the day my family stopped by. "Pass the brownies," I had said. "Are you sure?" Mom asked. "Pass the brownies. Or die, Mom."

This is what I'd wanted with Eric, but Rudy was accomplishing it on his own. I had never considered going solo, but then neither had he, I guessed. Until it became necessary.

I chose the smallest triangle cookie. Rudy poured low-fat milk into glasses that had been jelly jars.

"This triangle is delicious," I said to Aidan, aware this cookie would have to go into my calorie count.

I felt comfortable, more at home than I did in my own sister's house, but it was exactly this level of soothing contentment, the feeling that Rudy's place was a mirror of the home I imagined one day for me, that was making me squirm.

I had lingered long enough. I didn't need Rudy to drive me home. I could call a Lyft. I was about to suggest that when Rudy asked if I wanted to stay for dinner. I weighed whether to stay. I was enjoying myself, but the problem was I was enjoying myself.

"Please stay," Aidan said.

I didn't have it in me to say no to a six-year-old, and as much as I had been keeping his uncle at arm's length, my arm was getting shorter. *Not every man is Eric*, I thought. *You're going to have to trust someone sometime.*

When I said yes, Rudy told Aidan to wash and change into his Star Wars pajamas. I asked Rudy if I could help in the kitchen. He pointed to a cabinet. I set the table.

"These are nice dishes," I said.

"They belonged to my aunt," he said. "She gave them to me when she moved to Florida."

"That's right. People in Florida don't use dishes."

"She said she didn't need them, but I think she wanted me to eat off better plates. That's why it's English bone china around here every night."

He placed two brass candlesticks in the center of the table. "My sister's," he said.

I was surprised by the candles, not long, tapered, and decorative but the stubby white variety lit by Jewish people on Friday nights. He added a braided challah, a silver kiddush cup, kosher grape wine. He said he had been to the store for rotisserie chicken, spring vegetables, and mushroom risotto.

"You're religious?" I said, assuming he was because—the accoutrements.

"No—not at all. I observe Shabbat on Friday nights because Libby did before the accident. I would stop by her loft for dinner if I didn't have something else going on. So I thought I should continue her tradition for Aidan."

I nodded and smiled. He was a good man. But I had thought Eric was a good man.

"One more religious thing. You will be happy to hear I give Chanukah presents," Rudy said.

"I need a driver until Chanukah, then." I said "driver" to keep things professional.

I realized we were about the same when it came to the practice of Judaism, except of course, I had Stephanie to invite me to celebrations. I wondered whether she would still do the holidays, considering the turbulence with Rob. Maybe I could give it a try at my apartment.

Aidan returned in his Star Wars pajamas. We encircled the table. Aidan said the prayer over the candles, tripping over Hebrew words. After Rudy blessed the wine, he looked at me, expecting my participation. I touched the challah, covered with a cloth napkin, and said the prayer over the bread. We shouted "amen," and I added a pumped-up song I had learned at camp. Soon all three of us were singing. As we ate dinner, Aidan asked if I had really liked the cookie.

Was there something I liked better? I bit my lip and thought—*your uncle.*

But did I want Rudy, or did I want what he represented? I couldn't plunge in. I couldn't make the same mistake again. I was about to tell Rudy I had to leave when he asked me to wait while he tucked Aidan into bed. I glimpsed into Aidan's room, saw the Star Wars motif. Rudy read a Mo Willems picture book, *Let's Go for a Drive!* My nieces loved that story. Page by page, Piggy and Elephant gather the important things required for their road trip in a car. Except at the end of the book, they realize—oops—they don't have a car.

I needed to keep busy. I cleared the dining table except for the candlesticks. I beheld the peaceful apartment, friendly, warm, inviting. Rudy returned from Aidan's room, the door about an inch ajar. He turned to me, silent, finger at his lips. I placed a finger on mine. We both said, "Shh," giggling too loud. And there it was—my lifelong domestic fantasy come true. Here I finally was, connected, part of something bigger than myself, but Aidan was asleep, and I was alone with Rudy, and he was approaching the couch where I was sitting with two goblets of wine.

I wasn't going to fall into this. It was too flawless. And I had learned that perfection did not exist.

"Oh, I'm sorry," I said. "I called a Lyft while you were putting Aidan to bed."

"That's easy. Cancel it."

"I have to go," I said, hoping he wouldn't say another word about staying.

He hesitated. Crestfallen. "Is something wrong?"

I shifted into autocorrect. "The opposite. This was marvelous. Thank you."

"So you leave when everything is marvelous?"

"Before it can become un-marvelous."

He nodded, handed me my blazer. "How about a cookie for the road?"

"You're killing me."

"Nah, I just know your vices."

Once on the street, I ordered a Lyft.

A car came in minutes.

Chapter 23

I was itching to tell Margo about Rudy in person, so I went to the hospital early in the morning. A curtain was around her bed. I could hear a physician's voice. I stood waiting in the corridor, checking for an e-mail—a proposal from New England Can.

Nothing. Anxious, I tapped my fingers in the air. Come on, Lauren. George said at the cemetery he needed time to pull it together. Would I jump at the deal? One thing I knew for sure. Whether I accepted the job or not, I could make use of the proposition to show Steinbach my worth—oh what happy leverage it would be. Steinbach respected George—and George wanted me.

A grandfatherly doctor opened the curtain.

I waved to Margo. She introduced me to the physician.

"How's the toe?" I asked.

"She'll have to stay off it and wear a surgical sandal, but it's healing."

"What's a surgical sandal?"

"A soft, open shoe—black, with Velcro straps."

"I escaped insulin," Margo said. "I'll be taking a pill that I have seen advertised on television. In the commercial, everyone who takes it has green grass and someone to love."

"A nutritionist will be in to review our program for diabetics." The doctor did a half nod and left.

I was relieved she didn't have to stick herself. "No insulin. Great news. I'm sure you'll get your blood sugar in control."

She patted the edge of her bed.

I sat. "News flash. I was at Rudy's apartment for dinner last night."

"What?"

"Shabbat shalom." I raised a make-believe glass of wine.

"Get out!"

"I did get out—as soon as I felt as though I could move right in. He bakes cookies. He lit Shabbat candles. He served roast chicken dinner."

"You're making this up."

"Truth is stranger than fiction. He nestled on his nephew's bed—and read to him." I had begun to overenunciate.

"Too much, too soon, huh?"

"I had a dream—and it is in Rudy's apartment."

She went sarcastic on me. "I'd hate for you to have your dream."

Ahh! Advice from the woman who had three husbands.

"I can't jump in. I can't make the same mistake twice."

She took a sip of diet ginger ale. "Maybe it's not a mistake."

I waved her off the subject.

A nurse popped in. "I have good news. You'll be released tomorrow."

"What time tomorrow?" I asked.

"It's a hospital," Margo said. "They say you're going to be released in an hour; then it takes all day. I'll call you when freedom is imminent. And we'll have to celebrate in the apartment at Grandma's bar cabinet."

Could a diabetic drink liquor? A shot of vodka was one hundred calories. I knew the calorie count in cardboard. And thin people thought overweight people were unaware. There were two thousand calories in a family-size Sara Lee all-butter pound cake.

❧

When I arrived to take her home, Margo and the nurse who was practically president of her fan club were watching Margo's first episode of *As the Hospital Turns*. In other words, my sister was fine. Once on the sidewalk, we walked deliberately. Even so, I wondered whether my concept of slow was too fast for my sister. "Should I hail a taxi?" I asked her.

"I'd love a cab or a two-hump camel, but I might as well begin my workout today."

In my head, I heard my mom say, *Exercise. Good idea. Should have thought of it sooner.*

Margo slid a look my way. "If I said that to Mom, do you know what she would say?"

"What?" I said to my sister as though I had no clue.

"Good idea . . . maybe you should have thought of that fifteen pounds ago."

Fifteen? Margo was in major denial about her weight.

"Who am I kidding?" she said. "I'm up eighty. Already I had gained half of it when the writers bludgeoned my character instead of watching me eat myself to death. When I couldn't scare up another role, not even for a pharmaceutical commercial looping in the middle of the night, I binged. I had no choice. I had to leave California or be listed in the *Guinness Book of World Records* as the biggest woman in Santa Monica."

"Oh, come on," I offered, attempting to make her feel better even though I had visited her neck of Santa Monica. No woman weighed more than a thin slice of gluten-free bread. No one said "bread." Margo grimaced. She stood still, leaned against a parked SUV with Pennsylvania plates, a ticket on the front window.

"Lucky not to be towed," I said about the car.

235

"I wish I was towed."

"Stop with the gloom and doom." I put on a sad face, trying to cheer her up.

Confession time. "I didn't come here because I was worried about you."

Surprise, I thought sardonically. What a shocker.

"I had to escape California," she said as though she had been in captivity.

"But not in time to be a bridesmaid?" Once upon a time, I let a sleeping dog lie, but he was dead.

"Forgive and forget. Besides, I hate teal."

I was annoyed she wasn't taking me seriously. "I would've picked another color."

"At your next wedding, I will wear white." She stepped around a cellar door in front of a sushi place, and I moved farther to the curb.

"The bride wears white," I said gruffly.

"That's your problem, Lauren. You think everything has to be a certain way. Who says the bride wears white?"

"Everyone."

"You really have to loosen up. The entire Eric deal happened because you were trying to meet other people's expectations."

She wasn't wrong, but I came back at her anyway. "Look who's giving advice. You weren't talking to your own family."

She shrugged.

"Remember it any way you want, Margo. But after you left home, Mom sent me to California to see if you were okay. She wanted to go herself—or with Dad—and I persuaded her it would be better if I checked up on you."

"Free trip to LA. Free motel. With their AmEx."

"Not what I was thinking when I missed my first week as a junior counselor at camp, which I had been looking forward to all year. Because I showed up late, I got last pick of a group and wound up in a bunk with tweens from a wild kingdom and a cocounselor who faked fatal menstrual cramps so she could slack off all summer."

She cupped her head in hand, indicating I was the greatest problem she had ever come across. "I tolerated camp, but you were always a fangirl."

"So?"

"You know the reason, don't you?"

"Here she goes . . ."

"You were on your own there. You made your own decisions. You were bowled over by your sudden self-empowerment. Of course, your initial summer was no picnic. What a Mom move—writing to the camp doctor to say you had to be on a diet. I couldn't believe the nutritionist came to your table, told you in front of everyone, including that cute waiter serving Dutch apple pie, whipped cream, ice cream, or both."

It was a horror story. Mortified, I had rushed off to find Margo. I had needed her desperately because she loved me, and she would understand. There were seven weeks left at camp, and I didn't know how I would show my face again. What did Margo do? She gave me a candy bar. And sick as it sounds, I felt a little better.

Thirty-one years later, I preferred not to relive it, to hide it in a murky place I couldn't reach in my head. I appreciated Margo's show of sympathy on our walk home from the hospital, but now the degradation I felt that summer was as crushing as it had been that afternoon at camp. For the rest of my first summer, Kate was my only friend.

Margo rambled on. "By the way, for the record, I was happy you came to California to rescue me. I liked that we stayed in the blue hotel with the bean-shaped pool. I remember those guys we met."

"I remember when I informed Mom and Dad you were couch surfing with very strange strangers, they offered to cover rent for months to show they believed in you and to help you get started. Dad kept repeating, 'Who does Margo think she is—Meryl Streep?' His favorite line was, 'Who paid Julie Andrews's rent?'"

As I dug up these archaic stories and transgressions, I actually felt closer to her. Who in the world did I have this kind of history with? Only Margo—and Stephanie.

We passed a vacant city bench.

"Do you want to rest for a while?" I said, concerned we had been moving too quickly.

"I'm good," she said, stopping in her tracks.

"Okay."

"But if you slow down for a minute, I will tell you I love you."

I took Margo's hand in mine. "I know you do. When I was three, you gave me your baby doll, the one that peed and no longer had a head."

"What happened to her head?" Margo said.

"What happened to yours?" I said, kidding.

"Lauren, while I was in the hospital, I decided to stay in New York."

"But why?" She was staying, and I was thinking of going.

"Because you're my sister. I would be crazy to leave you."

<hr/>

At my building, Allie was on her way to retrieve her mail. She was in a scoop-necked, sky-blue leotard that said "I'm pregnant" about a thousand ways. The tight leotard was short an arrow pointing to where a baby would be.

"Hi, Allie," I said.

Margo did a little wave.

"Margo, are you still on the soap? Lauren and I watched your show years ago in my apartment. We applauded when we saw your credit."

"No, I'm not on the soap. They killed my character. They intended to bring her back, but I couldn't lose weight."

Allie stood silent. No idea what to say.

Margo air-kissed Allie Hollywood-style, then told me to get the door.

"You have a key." Her laziness was maddening.

"It's at the bottom of my bag." Her bag was maddening.

Annoyed, I shook my head and found my key.

The minute we were in the apartment, Margo headed to the refrigerator. The one I had cleared out.

"What? Who the heck emptied the fridge?"

"I did."

"You tossed everything?" Was she squeaking?

"I'm desperate to cut back," I said, as though I were the only one in need of a new lifestyle.

"Oh, so this has nothing to do with your diabetic sister?"

I measured my words. "I want to help you too."

"Thanks, Mom."

"Oh, come on. You're facing a daunting assignment."

She relented. "Thank you. You're spot-on. You did the right thing."

"I was thinking . . ."

"Please don't. And let's get out of this kitchen."

I followed her to the dining room table. She slouched at one end. I sat at another.

I treaded lightly. "Maybe you could try that place in New Jersey to get yourself started."

"Not happening," she said. "I hate New Jersey."

"If you want, I'd drive there and check in for a few days." I had too much going on career-wise to stay any longer.

"First of all, I looked it up online—the minimum stay is a month. And if I go, I'll starve there, come back, and binge."

"You don't know that."

She looked at me cockeyed. "Any other suggestions, Dr. Lauren? Or should I call you Mom?"

I deliberated for a moment. "Maybe we can help each other, at home in the apartment."

"Oh, no. No way. Next thing I know, you'll want to weigh me."

I rolled my eyes. "I don't want to weigh you. And it's not about you. I need help too."

"You did pretty well on your own."

"I know, but I don't want to gain it back."

She stood with her hands on her hips.

"Honestly," I said.

She thought for a few moments; then she paced. "Okay. Maybe. But first some rules. I weigh myself first thing in the morning. I do it after I go to the bathroom. Before coffee. Every little bit helps. And I shower before I get on the scale."

A light went on. "Of course—you weigh less because drying causes your skin to flake."

"Whatever. I weigh three times and I go with the best number." She sat back down at the table as though a diplomat in negotiation.

"Margo, we won't check up on each other. You can buy your own scale."

"No, I like your scale. It's two pounds lower than it should be."

"Did you have to tell me that?"

"Lauren, the nutritionist at the hospital suggested a food plan. It's basically no food and all plan, but we could follow it together. However, if I share the diet, you can't be on top of me about it. Can you hand me my shoulder bag?"

"Get your own bag. It's good exercise," I said, weary of being her gofer.

"You see—that's what I mean. Next I know you will be tracking my miles."

"Don't you mean inches?"

"Ha-ha," she responded sarcastically.

Margo unearthed the yellow paper with the plan on it. She handed it to me. "Maybe you could make a copy."

"Do you want me to go to the program at the hospital with you?"

"No, no. If I go on my own, maybe I'll meet a man. I've always been a sucker for a guy with a medical problem."

"I prefer men who are healthy."

"And drive you around."

"Do you think I'm being ridiculous about Rudy?"

"Ridiculous how?"

"My fear that he's a mirage."

"He's not a mirage. He's an endless supply of water in the desert."

Chapter 24

On Mother's Day, the well-tended gardens surrounding Stephanie's home were in bloom. Crimson, violet, and yellow daffodils danced in the breeze on her stone walk. The lilacs were heaven-sent, and even the ground cover was worth admiring.

Sadly, there was a FOR SALE sign in front of the house with a picture of the number-one Realtor in the area. My sister wasn't messing around. She hadn't bothered to have the house staged or curated or evacuated of family treasures that might remind potential buyers this was someone else's house. I imagined the number-one Realtor saying the kitchen was the kitchen, the dining room was the dining room. The people were getting divorced. A lot of discourse. Make an offer. Depressing.

The Securities and Exchange Commission had revoked Rob's right to practice his profession. His assets were frozen. Stephanie was left with what was in her name alone: the house, her car, her pay and pension. Settling Rob's case could take years. He could go to prison. As I lay in bed at night, I gauged the impact this would have on my sister and my nieces. In comparison, what had happened to me was small. I was changing my perspective. The jilt was a jolt. That's all.

I was proud of my sister, the way she was handling everything. She wasn't hiding in a dark room under a blanket. She was doing what she had to do—and more. She was the one who had invited us over. I'd call that pulling it together.

Despite the delightful weather, my family gathered upstairs in the media room. They were the Great Indoors Women. Our idea of a big hike was one end of the shopping mall to the other.

"Where's Dad?" I asked.

Dad was off with his brothers at their biannual cemetery run to visit their mother, the grandmother I adored. Afterward, there was an important ritual—they reminisced at a diner over breakfast.

"I haven't visited Grandma at the cemetery in a long time. I want to go again."

"She has enough visitors," my mom said.

Margo threw me a look.

My mother referred to Grandma as her smother-in-law. Every time Grandma rang, she let the call go to the answering machine. If we picked up and Grandma asked for her, we were supposed to say Mom was in the shower. My mother took so many showers back then, her skin dried up.

Stephanie's media room included four oversize reclining leather chairs—dark brown, beige, tan, ecru—facing the flat-screen that ate New York. The girls were fiddling with iPads. The cable news was on the television. Mom was puttering about, pointing to the screen, remarking how nice it was to see young women broadcasters and how thin the blonde in the V-neck dress appeared after having twins two weeks before. Stephanie left the room to go to the kitchen for coffee. She returned, with hazelnut in a mug that said Awesome Dad. I would have smashed that mug by now, but I figured one of the girls had given the cup to Rob.

Suddenly Stephanie shrieked, scaring us, waving the hand that wasn't holding the cup. "Get over here. Quick! What is the name of the cruise ship you booked for your honeymoon?"

"The *Courageous*," I said, wondering why she was asking.

"This week, right?"

"Don't remind me," I said.

"I don't believe it," she said. "The *Courageous* has been docked in Barcelona for three days. There's been an outbreak of food poisoning so awful that the boat is on lockdown, in the harbor, until the passengers recover and the staff can sanitize the entire boat."

I walked to the television as though standing directly in front of it might be more informative. The blond newscaster who had had twins said they had traced the poisoning to chicken on a midnight buffet.

"Eric is on the ship," I said. "He always liked his chicken wings sort of raw."

Margo laughed.

The girls peeked up from the iPads—an infrequent occurrence—and inspected the screen as though they might spot Eric on the ship. My mother and sisters were aglow.

"When Eric stopped by my place, the last thing he said was how wonderful it would be for him to go on our honeymoon alone."

"Who goes on a honeymoon alone?" my mother said.

"Eric," Margo, Stephanie, and I answered at once.

The girls returned to the iPads.

"That's enough with the iPad," Stephanie said dourly. I always wondered how she knew when it was "enough with the iPad." Olivia could recite whole scenarios from the hot series that featured the offspring of superheroes at a high school.

"Eric should only be sick and dizzy and puking all over himself," Mom said.

"Well, we certainly don't wish anyone an illness," Stephanie said, clearly for the benefit of her daughters, who were listening and no longer in possession of the iPads.

"We don't?" Margo said.

"We certainly do not," Stephanie said, cocking her head to her children, as in, "I don't want them to hear you talking that way."

But of course Mom, being Mom, continued. "An eye for an eye. A tooth for a tooth. He should only drop dead."

I realized I didn't care if Eric was crapping on a cruise ship or dead in a dinghy, whether he stayed in Barcelona until he could speak Spanish backward. I didn't wish him ill; I just didn't care where he was or what he was doing. I knew that the right way, the Christian way, was to forgive Eric. But I wasn't Christian.

I glanced around the spotless media room with the citations, plaques, and pictures on the walls and thought how Rob as well as Glenn had adored family life. Yet they took a sledgehammer to it. One moment my sister resembled her well-tended gardens. Who wouldn't want to be her? She had a caring husband, two wonderful daughters, a career she enjoyed, a home. Next day, there were two FBI agents at her Seder.

There's no way to manage, to control, what another person will do in a marriage. You could love, commit, vow, compromise, but a forever marriage was a matter of chance. Eric didn't take that chance. For a moment, I reconsidered the healing power of forgiveness. Then I did something courageous.

I decided to forgive Eric—but it was fine with me if he never got off the boat.

Chapter 25

When we returned to the city, Margo went to the movies. I hit Siena Ristorante for dinner. I said "one person in the courtyard" to the host. She checked her list and told me a table was being cleared. I waited in the foyer, where there were dark vintage pictures of vineyards in Italy. An older woman entered, brushing past me.

"Delilah Dugan—we have a reservation in the courtyard," the woman said to the host.

"I'm sorry. We don't hold tables in the courtyard, all reservations are for inside the restaurant."

"But we have a reservation," Dugan insisted, her voice irritating as a bugbite. From a horsefly.

"That was for inside. In our courtyard, there is one table for two available now, but the woman behind you is next." The host flicked her long hair and pointed to me.

"*She* is only one. One person."

For heaven's sake. Get me out of here. No. Get her out of here.

The accusations continued. "And did *she* have a reservation?"

"No, but *she* is next."

"But we had a reservation. *We* should be seated before *her*."

Mr. Dugan arrived. His wife repeated her diatribe for his benefit.

I let them bicker it out with the host. I heard a beep on my phone, an e-mail coming through—a message from George Moore at New England Can. As I opened the message, I felt as I did on a stormy day in January, many years before, when I went to the snow-caked mailbox on the side of our house in Connecticut and tore into a letter from BU. I had gotten in.

> Dear Lauren,
>
> I am pleased to offer you the position of senior vice president of communications at New England Can. As CEO, I recognize your astute knowledge of advertising as well as our business, and therefore, a generous package is outlined below. I appreciate your response within ten days.

I scanned down. Talk about enticing. It was the offer to end all offers.

Moving expenses, a company car, a down payment on a house, a signing bonus, medical and dental insurance, a four-week vacation each year, plus 20 percent more than what I earned at the agency. I would be senior vice president of communications, eligible for partnership in two years. Who cared if Far Acres was a one-horse town? I could buy stallions.

I punched Margo's number. I wanted to share the news, but before she picked up, I decided to savor the moment by myself—and hung up. Not long ago, I'd sat in an all-night diner in a battered wedding gown, and . . . well, look at me. It was heady to receive such an offer. Now that I knew details, should I snatch the position at New England Can?

"We're never coming back here," Mrs. Dugan snapped at the hostess.

"Awful," said her husband.

"This way, please," the hostess said to me.

At a table in the lush garden with tea lights, I said, "Please bring on the champagne."

I e-mailed George to let him know I had received his offer. I decided not to tell a soul about it until I knew what I wanted to do.

Chapter 26

In the morning, Rudy and I traveled to a Steinbach client in Central Jersey. There was a crowded reception in honor of their latest acquisition. On the way back, glad-handing behind me, I was dragging.

"I could use coffee," I said.

Rudy pointed to a billboard for a truck stop. I was in. We squeezed beside a Toyota wagon with a Great Pyrenees sniffing out the window. The dog's collar and the plates on the Toyota said SAMSON.

"What kind of human leaves a dog in a car?" Rudy said. "Aidan and I are getting a puppy. That sweetheart will never be stranded."

"Maybe they were running an errand."

"That dog is old. I don't like it when people are unkind to senior citizens."

We headed in. Most of the customers were in T-shirts and jeans. The truck stop boasted a Dunkin' Donuts, a Burger King, a place to shower, refreshments, pharmaceuticals, clothing, magazines, novels, stuffed animals to bring home for the kids. In the far back, there was a loopy arrow studded with bulbs pointing to a restaurant, circa the era of malt shoppes. We found a table, pulled up two metal chairs. A waitress came by. Rudy and I both said "coffee" at the same time.

I felt so comfortable with Rudy, it worried me, but I concentrated on what Margo had said. He was not a mirage. He would not disappear if I became involved with him. Margo believed Rudy was good for me. But was I brave enough to take a chance again?

We looked out the window, surveying and discussing the trucks entering and leaving the lot, until the waitress delivered coffee, placing a good-size old-fashioned carafe on the table.

"An entire pot!" I hadn't seen an entire pot of coffee on a table in years.

"You're not in Starbucks anymore, Dorothy."

He made me smile. Despite my decision to keep the opportunity to myself, I was burning to tell Rudy my news.

I lowered my voice. "This is super confidential."

"Does anyone else know?"

"No one. Well, Margo knows some, but not the details."

"And you are telling me?"

"Yes."

"I won't repeat it to anyone—unless tortured."

"How badly?" I dived in. "I have an offer from George Moore, the CEO of New England Can. He would like me to replace Arthur. George took me aside to mention it at Arthur's funeral."

Rudy chuckled. "Weren't they cousins?"

"You won't catch me saying it was appropriate."

"Tell me about the offer."

"It's a mindblower."

"Congratulations!"

I smiled big, sipped some coffee.

"You would telecommute?" Rudy asked.

"Oh, of course not. I would move to Far Acres."

He put down his coffee cup. His face deflated.

"Rudy?"

"No way. Is it worth it? Here I thought you were a Manhattan girl."

He was popping my bubble, and I wasn't taking it well. "Do you want to hear about it or not?"

"Sure, definitely." He waved me on, but the fraught look on his face was evidence he was not on Team Can. I decided to give him another chance to be happy for me. I'm generous about giving people chances to be happy for me.

I summed up the positives quietly, not in the joyful voice I had reveled in minutes before.

"I would never live anywhere but New York City, specifically Brooklyn," he said.

He adored the city. Rightly so. Where else could you decide to do something at a moment's notice and have the choice of a Broadway play, Lincoln Center, walking through Soho, or the Museum of Modern Art? Where else could I come home from a tough day at the office and feel like a lazy bum because I wasn't going out again?

I said, "You are a hundred percent Big Apple—the poster boy for that famous magazine cover illustrating the way New Yorkers envision the planet—mostly Manhattan and California."

"It's called *View of the World from 9th Avenue* by Saul Steinberg."

"Of course. You even know the illustrator."

"Everyone in the city knows the illustrator."

I sipped my coffee.

"Think about it, Lauren. For Far Acres to be a one-horse town, I would have to ride through it on a horse."

I chuckled. It was true.

He continued, sickly enjoying himself. "Far Acres is so small, the only stop sign is out of town."

"Are you having fun?"

He leaned over the table toward me. "Here's the truth. You should stay in Manhattan. What if you take the job and it doesn't work out, then what? You're parked in Far Acres? I don't think you should do it. Besides, it's a toilet company."

He was out of line. And I was out of there.

I regretted revealing the offer. I hated that he had anything but something nice to say. I wanted to tell him and be congratulated. That was it. No man-size opinions. I slammed the cow filled with cream on the table and looked at him. "Where do you get off telling me what to do? What, are you a career counselor now? If you are, maybe you should look at your own career first."

He pretended to stab his heart with his fist. "Low blow."

"Not low enough."

I stood, indicating it was time to leave. He didn't ask for a check. He reached for his wallet, tossed a Hamilton on the table.

We walked, a few feet between us, like strangers, to the Escalade.

"Can I ask you a question?" he said.

We stopped, glared at each other.

"If you must," I replied, burning up because I was angry with myself that I had shared news that was none of his business and he had reacted like he was the manager of my life. I wanted to stamp my feet and say, "You are not in charge. I am in charge." But I was way too old for that.

"It's been a while. Months. Why are you still wearing that thing-amajig on your wrist?"

Now my hand was his business too?

"When I rescued you after the crash, you said you needed to wear it a few weeks."

"You *rescued* me? What? Do you think you're a knight in shining armor?"

"Yes. My Escalade is a stallion."

"You gave me a ride. It's your job. That's it."

"Maybe you need an X-ray to determine whether your wrist is mended."

"It's not healed!"

He pointed, his finger wagging. "You're wearing that for one reason."

"Am I, Dr. Cohen?" Why didn't he mind his own business?

He moved closer. I felt his breath. His scent blended with the coffee we had been drinking. A quiver darted up my spine.

"Confess," he whispered. "You're wearing it to be with me."

The truth smacked me hard. I had trusted myself not to repeat the mistakes I made with Eric. And here I was revolving around a man. "That's ridiculous."

"Is it?"

For effect, I tilted my chin, raised my eyes as though to say, "You are out of your mind." But I knew it was accurate. I didn't want to give him up. Without Rudy, I would dwell on my aborted wedding, my vacant womb, my body-shaming mother, Margo's toe, Kate on Tinder, Stephanie's problems, my devastated nieces—probably have another accident. Maybe not be so blessed next time. He was correct. He had rescued me—from myself.

I was dependent on him. And I had to stop.

In the car, I buckled in.

He waited to start the engine. He turned back to me. "Look, Lauren, what do I know? I transport advertising people. I'm not in the business."

I didn't respond, opened my laptop, stuck my head in.

"How about those Yankees," he shouted to grab my attention.

While I was busy not talking to Rudy, I e-mailed Steinbach, short and sweet:

> Good news from Lauren. Happy to report shoulder cured. Driver no longer necessary. As always, thank you for all you have done. You are the best.

I laid my head back, pretended I was asleep.

When we reached the Max, Rudy said, "That's the longest we've gone without talking."

"There's nothing to say."

I had a lucrative offer, and whether I leaped at it or not, I wasn't allowing anyone else to decide anything for me. I would not permit a man—whether I liked him or not—to rain on this opportunity. On the street, I unwrapped the wristband. I pitched it, as I had tossed my bridal bouquet into the road, my damn wedding dress onto the floor. I overshot the public trash bin. I marched over and deposited the support in the can. On top of a shoe without laces, a pair of busted dentures, and somebody's leftover lunch.

Chapter 27

That evening, I came upon the salt-and-pepper shakers Rudy and I had ridiculed the night we opened the wedding gifts. I held the shakers in my hand, remembering how he had offered to take me to the synagogue, transforming what might have been a psychological tsunami for any woman into downright fun. I meditated on the Friday night dinner at his house.

Maybe I had overreacted to Rudy's advice in the truck stop. Maybe Rudy was correct but for the wrong reasons. The more I thought about George's offer, the more I realized it was not for me. I didn't want to leave Steinbach without a stab at becoming a partner. It would be premature, giving up with the finish line in sight. Account-wise, I preferred an array of products—the variety kept me hopping. I had the know-how, the wherewithal to sell anything, and mixing it up was invigorating. And if I stayed at Steinbach, perhaps George would keep his account at the agency. I could be a hero and hang on to the account.

Beyond business, there were personal reasons. I could live in the country; the area around Far Acres was stunning four seasons a year. I loved country stores and country fairs, rolling farms, stands selling fresh fruit, pick-your-own vegetables, and the idea of eggs from the organic chickens down the road. The new car of my choice would make life easier than it was in Manhattan. A house with room for visitors was better than my one-bedroom apartment. I dreamed of a kitchen I could sit in. I imagined myself joining this group and that—and soon I would be the "mayor" of Far Acres. But what about my sisters? We had grown close, warmer than we had ever been. Margo was settling in Manhattan and—hopefully—she would rent her own place. If her career took off, I wanted to see it. Stephanie needed me, as did the girls. And she might require financial assistance. Yes, the lucrative position at New England Can would enable that, but I could make things work with my current salary at Steinbach, more so if I became the first woman on the board.

I strategized a plan—employ the New England Can offer to ascertain my worth, as leverage with Steinbach. I would mention the impending deal to Steinbach, taking a chance a light would go off in his head, he wouldn't want to lose me, and the play I made would work in my favor. It was a shot. If it didn't work, I could reconsider the offer from New England Can.

A few days later, I gave it a go. I stopped in Steinbach's office and invited him to lunch. I chose the restaurant he preferred. One, Two, Three Fish was a popular place, a few blocks from my office. There was nothing Steinbach enjoyed more than oysters. Nothing I liked less than to watch him slowly lift a shell from the ice display, add vinegar, cocktail sauce, three tiny crackers to the top as though he were performing a scientific experiment—then slurp it down. But I knew that would happen.

"Try the oysters," he said the second we sat down.

I looked around the nautical dining room. The place was gleaming with brass fixtures, depleted of patrons before noon. Steinbach always ate lunch at eleven, creature of habit. When I ate lunch at eleven, I was ready for a second lunch at two.

"The oysters are phenomenal. I order the oysters every time I'm here."

I know.

"You must have the oysters."

Snot. "Not today," I said politely as I picked up the menu, which was the size of a submarine. Had this been a job interview, I would have ordered the oysters and whatever Steinbach was drinking. But I was years into my job. I had no need to mirror him.

"I'm glad your shoulder is better. Bet you'll miss Rudy Cohen. He's more than a driver; he's a great guy."

I nodded. Of course I would miss Rudy, but I wasn't going back there. It would be too easy to be sucked into my fantasy, the one that led me to the fiasco with Eric.

The waiter appeared. He wore a red beret, a neckerchief, a French fisherman's T-shirt. The stripes were navy and white. Nothing enhanced a fisherman's T-shirt more than a handsome, body-building, most-likely-actor/waiter. I ordered blackened Chilean sea bass—although I had read all fish is actually tilapia. Apparently, fish was a scam. Judiciously, I decided on asparagus instead of lyonnaise potatoes.

"I was wondering how you've been doing," Steinbach said with fatherly concern. He was pensive, serious, in a navy blazer with brass buttons and an open-collar blue shirt.

"I'm doing well," I said because Steinbach was my boss. And why would he want to hear anything else?

He nodded.

"See, I knew you would get over it."

Oh, of course. So easy, a cinch.

"Did you ever pick up those gifts?" he asked.

"I did," I said, remembering that day with Rudy.

"Good girl," Steinbach said.

If he called me "girl" one more time, I was throwing over the table. "Please don't call me 'girl.' It's sexist. Would you tell a man who worked for you that he was a good boy? Besides, Steinbach, it dates you. No one says that anymore."

"You're right. I stand corrected. Old habits die hard. But I'm trying to change for the better. In fact, the partners are working on a women's issues initiative."

He had provided the ideal opening for me. "The partners? The partners are all men. You're meeting about women's issues with a group of men. The agency can do better than that. Please don't exclude women from the discussion."

"We hired a diversity and inclusion training coach."

"A female coach?"

"No. No. The coach is a man."

I wondered if the coach was at least married to a woman.

"I'm happy to hear this," I said, "but don't you think it might be useful to have a woman's point of view, the feminine perspective?"

He leaned back. "I see your point."

"Maybe it's time you did," I said.

"You have mentioned it before."

"Yes. I approached you when a group of women at the agency came forward with a survey that showed Steinbach Kraus was the only midsize agency in the state without a woman partner. I never spoke up on my own behalf. So here it is. I want to be the first woman partner at Steinbach Kraus."

I forced myself to look him straight in the eyes. I needed a breath, but I didn't want him to catch me breathing. Next, I would detonate the New England Can news. I had another offer in my pocket, and I had nothing to lose.

"Partner? I heard you're considering leaving the agency." Steinbach gloated, impressed with himself.

I was rattled. I hid my hands in my lap so he couldn't see my fingers pulsating. How did he know about the offer?

"George called me."

"I see," I said.

"About replacing Arthur—with you."

258

Take it easy, Lauren. "Yes, of course."

Could this be any more awkward? I was a fool for not thinking George would talk to Steinbach. What should I say? What words would save this? I decided to go with the truth. "He approached me at the cemetery."

"I guess his grief got to him," Steinbach said.

"Well, Arthur was out of earshot."

Steinbach laughed. "George and I have been friends since high school, and he wanted me to know he was poaching. Him hiring you. A brilliant move."

Was that a compliment, praise, directed at me? I considered the theme of the restaurant and decided to fish for flattering remarks. "Because?" I said, then sipped my water to appear calm and to buy time waiting for a response.

"George wants you for the same reasons I hope to keep you."

Yes, I thought, *yes. Keep me! But make me a partner.*

"You know your stuff. You're a terrific team player, you don't ruffle feathers, yet you have a mind of your own. People like you. Most of all, he's pleased with your output, there's steady growth and an upswing in sales—so why not hire you to work for him directly?"

Well, thanks, Steinbach. Go ahead and build my confidence. I like you too.

"George Moore would not be the first client to poach a key player from my agency. But, Lauren, I don't want you to leave. In fact, I need you to stay." He pointed at me like I was a diamond in a store window.

I couldn't wait to hear more of what he had to say. Terrible timing— the waiter brought the oysters on a silver platter to Steinbach. I moved my glass so the waiter could position my sea bass.

Steinbach started decorating an oyster. It could take months. Vinegar. Cocktail sauce. Crackers.

"This is not the time to go. This is the time for you to remain at Steinbach Kraus. Take it from me, we are dedicated to positioning ourselves for the future. Substantial change, impressive and unforeseen opportunity awaits."

Did he mean for me specifically or for women in general? I was as high up as a woman had ever been at Steinbach Kraus, but I hadn't made it to the boardroom. No matter how hard I worked, I wasn't a man. But I wasn't alone. There was Joanna, the media master, as well as Sydney Leanne, the creative director. We received raises and bonuses annually but weren't invited to the inner circle.

"I can't talk about it now, but times are changing. And I want Steinbach Kraus to change. That's why I installed the vegan vending machine."

A giant step for humankind.

"No one knows the business as well as you do. I want you as the face of Steinbach Kraus."

"I'm intrigued," I said instead of what I was thinking, which was that this was terrific. I don't know why I said a word, interrupting him like a buffoon, when I knew I wasn't hearing another word until his oysters were history. For the first time in my life, I wasn't hungry, but I tried my fish to refrain from talking.

Finally, he spoke.

"If you stay at the agency, I'll raise your salary significantly. When George hires someone else to take Arthur's place, your responsibility will be to make certain New England Can sticks with us. Pull that off and you'll benefit some more."

Steinbach was concerned the new director would change agencies. That's how it worked. New people wanted their own people.

I tried not to smile. Never jump at an offer. Besides, I knew what I wanted, and it was not what he was proposing. I wanted partnership. I deserved it. *Say it, Lauren. Don't think it. Say it. You can only win. You don't have a thing to lose.*

"I want to be a partner, a principal, at Steinbach Kraus." I arched my spine, moving forward in my seat, staring Steinbach square in the face so his eyes had nowhere to go. "I've waited a long time to say this to you: at this stage, I will only consider an offer with partnership."

He slurped his oyster, licked his lips, lifted a brow from under his glasses.

I felt strong, on a roll. I continued with the facts. "Proven dedication to the agency, demonstrated ability to develop substantial business, superior relations with partners and peers, lucrative long-term clients the size of New England Can."

"Partner?" He smiled, which I took as a good sign.

"Bottom line."

"You would be our first woman partner."

"Hmm."

"Hmm?" he repeated.

"Hmm."

The talk with Steinbach had me reeling. I had no idea what he would say next, but I was proud of myself for setting my requirements out there, for judiciously spitting it out. It was something new for me—expressing what I needed.

Steinbach asked the waiter for key lime pie, the only dessert I didn't like. I would've had chocolate cheesecake, but I said "just coffee" because I was committed to my food plan with Margo.

"I can't promise."

I was aware the decision would be made by the board.

"I will raise the issue. The current partners will decide."

"Absolutely."

"Atta girl," he said.

I stared. He had to be kidding.

He corrected himself. "Atta woman!"

Chapter 28

After my positive conversation with Steinbach, I floated home and told the entire story to Margo. She was sure I would become a partner, started talking about throwing a party for me to which she would invite all her theater friends.

Over the weekend, I was in such a jolly mood, I considered weighing myself. With my right foot, I moved the scale to a spot on the floor that appeared to be sloped, thereby, I believed, causing weight to read lower. Then I thought, if I stand on the scale and I weigh less than the days before, I might eat because I have room to gain. If the numbers are higher, I might binge out of frustration. Damned if I do. Damned if I don't. The story of my life. It had to stop. I leaned over the tub. I turned on the faucet. Full force. I waited until the water was steamy. When the tub was half-full, I added the Mr. Bubble I kept for my nieces.

I lifted the scale from my black-and-white subway-tile floor.

I dropped it into the tub.

It turns out, scales don't float.

Margo heard the noise, hurried to the bathroom in her pajamas. "Nice of you to get a bath going for me."

"It isn't for you."

"Of course. I was kidding." She rubbed her eyes to wake herself.

I pointed to the scale in the tub. Proudly.

"You didn't."

"It's in there."

"Oh no. The scale doesn't know how to swim."

I snorted. "There's always the doggy paddle."

"What are you doing today?" she asked.

"I'm not weighing myself. That's for sure." I was delighted, fulfilled by my deed.

"This afternoon, I'm going to see Stephanie."

"That's nice," I said.

"I'm a sucker for drama."

"What if Mom is there?" I asked. "Tell me you won't start up."

"If Mom is there, I'll say we should take the girls to the zoo."

"And . . ."

"Feed Mom to the tigers . . ."

Margo called Stephanie on speakerphone and asked what time she should come.

"I—I need you right now!" Stephanie stammered. "Now. Come now."

I stopped folding laundry, held a towel in midair.

"What's going on?" Margo said.

Stephanie wailed. "What do you think is going on? I can't handle my life is what's going on."

"We'll be on the next train," I shouted.

Margo scrambled out of her pajamas.

❧

We ran for the train, then snagged a Lyft driven by a woman who didn't say a word.

263

Stephanie dragged herself into the kitchen in a sports bra and pink paisley pajama pants. Her hair was disheveled. She had worn contact lenses since high school, but now her tortoiseshell glasses were crooked on her face. Her eyes were irritated and red. It was painful to witness her condition.

"What? What?" I said as I followed her in.

She stopped and turned. "Sit down. Or stand up. I don't care."

I slung my arm around her, depleted at the sight of my sister falling apart.

She chewed her knuckle. "Dad intends to add his name to the actions against Rob."

No good, I thought. *Big mistake.*

I motioned to Margo to follow us into the kitchen.

We convened at the kitchen table, where our family always conferred.

"Are you sure it's Dad's idea and not Mom's?" Margo asked.

"You can't blame everything on Mom," Stephanie said. "Dad is the one who takes care of finances. Mom thinks she's in charge, but she also thinks she's out of money when she runs out of checks."

"True," Margo agreed. I had never heard Margo agree with Stephanie.

Stephanie bit her bottom lip so hard, I thought she might separate her chin. She picked up speed as she spoke. Her grievances became a rant. "I dread going into school. Some of the teachers had accounts with Rob. It was the principal, Mr. Wexler, who discovered Rob was a thief! The poor man wanted to buy a new house. He had every right to buy a new house." She cried as she continued. "He has five kids. Five. And his wife is a friend of mine. He called the firm. Rob was out. Wexler spoke to someone else. There wasn't a cent in the Wexler account. There wasn't a cent left in the principal's account. When will this nightmare end? I go into school and people act nice. They're okay. Maybe they're even better than I would be if I were in their situation or knew what Rob had done. The guidance counselor took me aside to say she didn't blame me, and I shouldn't be excommunicated. In the yard, the reading specialist put her arms around me. But then neither one had invested with my husband. Besides, none of it matters. I feel guilt-ridden, blameworthy, as though I were the one who stole their savings. I don't know how much longer I can keep going to school. On the other hand, this is no time to quit. I need the salary, the health insurance. I need to wake up with a place to go."

She caught her breath, blew in, blew out. "My psychologist suggested looking for another job."

Margo glanced at me, encouraged to hear Stephanie was seeking advice.

"A psychologist? That's good. Has it helped?" I asked.

Stephanie shrugged. "What good is her advice? Look for another job? No chance I will be hired in this state of mind. And if this brew of misery isn't enough, my own dad wants to pile on."

"Well, Dad is hurt. He trusted Rob," I said. We all trusted Rob. Ex-perfect Rob.

Stephanie reached into her pocket for a tissue, sopped up her running nose, dabbed her eyes. I hated seeing her in pain.

"For what it's worth," I said, "I don't think Dad should do it. I won't. The government and all the people who were affected are after Rob. If he's guilty, he'll be punished. Dad would be piling on, and while he was piling on, he might ruin, even obliterate, his awesome relationship with Olivia and Liza forever. They're small now, but one day they would know that Grandpa and Grandma joined in."

"Yes, that's the point. My kids are everything."

"Look, Stephanie," I said, "I think you need to get out of the house, breathe some fresh air."

"Take a lesson from me," Margo piped in. "I left the entire city of Los Angeles."

"But that was to visit Lauren," Stephanie said.

"Partly."

"How can I go out? I look terrible. I haven't washed my hair since Passover."

"Come upstairs. I'll dunk you in a soothing bath. I'll wash your hair," Margo offered.

Stephanie and I gazed at each other as though a growling mama bear with four cubs to protect had joined us at the table.

I had to laugh. "You know you have to bend to do that, Margo."

"Okay, I got carried away. How about I make an appointment for a cut and a blow job?"

"Blowout," I said.

Stephanie broke half a smile. "I'm so glad you're here. Both of you."

∽

My sisters were on the second level. I remained in the kitchen brewing a soothing herbal tea for Stephanie.

Kate called me. Her husband was living next door and she had decided to go on with her life as best as she could.

"Lauren, did you register for the camp reunion?" Kate said. "I hear everyone will be there."

And there was the rub—everyone being there.

"Okay, I'll be honest. I don't want to run into Eric."

"Give me a break. No one is looking. Besides, what kind of friend do you think I am? I made a call. Eric is not coming."

"That's good."

"I invited my new boyfriend," Kate said. "Come—and bring a bathing suit this time."

"I don't wear a bathing suit in front of people I know."

"But you wear it in front of strangers?"

"Yes, because I will never see them again."

As I hung up, Margo came into the kitchen for Stephanie's tea. I mentioned the reunion. I said I wanted to face my friends, show everyone I was doing well, and I would probably go.

"I haven't seen camp since I was the lead in the musical the counselors wrote that year."

"There was no lead in that play," I said.

"I always think of myself as the lead."

She grabbed the tea and went back upstairs.

My mother rapped on the kitchen door, peering at me. "Oh, you're here," she said.

Sorry to disappoint.

"Where's my Stephanie?"

"Upstairs with Margo."

She checked the hall to be sure Stephanie was not in earshot. "That Rob had to steal from the family. He couldn't take enough from strangers?"

"Lower your voice. Stephanie might hear you."

My mother threw up her hands. "She takes pills. I don't know how many."

Not half as many as I would take in the same situation.

"She's doing the best she can," I said.

"I'm worried sick about your sister. My Stephanie can't eat, and her two sisters can't stop eating."

I marched to the refrigerator, so enormous the Green Giant could stand frozen in the freezer. I jerked the handle, opening and slamming the door. Ten repetitions. My mother watched, her mouth the shape of an O, as in "open." Dead silence. Except for the clack of ice cubes, falling one by one into the automatic bin.

I took my time. I glowered at my mom. I looked her up. I looked her down—her close-cropped hair, the green eyes, the gray-and-white pearls around her neck, the matching earrings, her fitted top and navy pants, the sensible color-coordinated heels. What came to mind was

Rudy, what Rudy had told me on one of our first rides. That I had to speak up, put a cork in my mother, halt her shaming forever.

"You know, Mom, you have a terrible habit." I slammed the fridge door again.

She waved me off. Like a fly, a gnat, a mosquito. I was livid.

"No, Mom. I think it's time to discuss whatever I feel like discussing."

"Open season on mothers. Well, go ahead, then."

"Your terrible habit is that you turn every damn incident that occurs in this family into an opportunity to shame me."

All color drained from my mother's face. I was sure I was crimson.

"You criticize and disapprove of me, commenting constantly about my weight, referring to my size at every turn. I am no better or worse a daughter, a sister, an aunt, a person up the scale thirty pounds or down thirty pounds. My physical size is not your concern. And you know what? Listen up, Mom. I never want to hear you say another word about my body, my weight, or my food intake again. Don't as much as face me when I chew. And the next time I ask for a brownie—start baking."

My mother barked, "I have only been trying to help you."

"Help me?" She was outrageous.

She aimed both index fingers at me. Worse, she enunciated. "Yes, help you."

"That's a lie. You have used my weight to differentiate me from my sister, to make me feel worthless. I wore a size-twelve gown at the wedding. And what did you say?"

"What did I say?"

It occurred to me she had no idea. No understanding of how she battered me. "You said, 'That's a good start.'"

"I can't help it if you don't appreciate the way I look after you. Even while you were at camp."

"You watched out for me at camp? You wrote to the camp doctor and told her I needed to be on a diet all summer. The nutritionist came into the dining room during lunch. In front of the entire bunk, with my group overhearing as well, she told me I had to watch what I was eating. She lifted the piece of pie in front of me and returned it to the waiter's tray. Who do you think spoke to me after that?"

"That's ridiculous. That never happened."

I was too stunned to speak.

She continued unabated. "And even if it did happen, I didn't tell the nutritionist to announce it."

"Go ahead—incriminate yourself." There was no going back now. At last. The blowup that should have happened when I was a kid.

"Lauren, it was true in my day and whether you like it or not, it's true now—no man wants to date an overweight woman."

Blood rushed to my brain. "What the hell, Mom? Eric dated me."

"But did he marry you?"

Could I plead temporary insanity if I bludgeoned her?

I heard sound emanating from the staircase. A muffled cough. I walked over. I glanced up. Margo was on the third step. Behind her was Stephanie in a thick bath towel, green eyes wet, hair in need of a color soaking wet. It rang a bell back to when we were kids, eavesdropping on adult conversations in the dining room from the hall. Always, Stephanie would give us away with a cough or a sneeze or by forgetting to remain silent. If we thought my parents had heard us, we would race to our rooms. But now we were all adults, and my sisters came down the carpeted steps.

"Zip the lip, Mom." Stephanie pulled up her towel to cover her chest. "I don't want my girls to come home and overhear this. There's enough agony and sorrow in life. We're a family. We don't need to create more."

"I'm not creating anything," my mother huffed.

Margo chimed in. "No, Mom. It's never about you."

"Not another word—stop now," Stephanie said as though taking control of a rowdy classroom. "Mom, apologize to Lauren."

Stephanie backing me up. Now I wanted to cry.

"What should I apologize for? Should I apologize for being the best mother I knew how to be?"

What was left to say? I had made my position clear. There wasn't any point in beating up on my mom, three to one.

I turned and left, to go home to Manhattan.

I walked two miles to the train station. Now that I had finally told my mother how I felt, I berated myself for the delay. There were so many times I should've blocked her hurtful rhetoric. Maybe she wouldn't have changed. But I would have spoken up for myself. And that would have made me a stronger, more demanding woman, a woman who would have approached Steinbach years before. I considered my relationship with my mother going forward. All I could hope was that she would guard her tongue. If not, I would have to call her out again. And again. I prayed she wouldn't force me to walk away.

I had no clue of the train schedule to New York City. I needed a ticket. I'd get one on board. I crumpled onto an outdoor bench in the intense, glimmering afternoon sun, my bag in my lap, my head in my hands.

I heard my phone. Not a ring but a text: "I'm still your mother."

That's the problem.

A Volvo SUV pulled up at the train station. Stephanie driving. She leaned toward the passenger window, rolled it down.

"Mom went home. Margo said she would stay over a few days. Me? I plan to drive my sister back to Manhattan."

"Are you sure you're okay to drive?"

"No. What's it to you?" Stephanie kidded.

"Okay, I'll drive in. You drive out."

Once I was home, I collapsed on my couch with a cold Dr. Brown's diet cream, thinking of what I had said to my mother, what she had said to me. A few hours later, my father's phone number popped up. I was about to get a speech. I could hear the familiar words before I answered the phone, before he said them.

"How long are you going to carry on like this?" He said this as though I hadn't spoken to my mother in years.

"I figured at least a day." Actually, I was going to carry on like this until she apologized and changed her ways.

"She's your mother. You have to talk to her."

"Dad, I'm done."

"She doesn't mean anything."

I paused. "Of course she does."

"So don't listen."

"I can't do that anymore."

"What do you want?" he asked.

"She has to clam up. Completely. No more derogatory comments. Oh, and that goes for any wise words she may be storing up for Margo."

"I'll talk to her."

"Sometimes I wonder how you've stayed married all these years."

"When it's necessary, I look the other way."

I was delighted I wasn't his neck.

"We're in the car. Talk to your mom."

She was there. Next to Dad? Listening in?

"Hi, Mom," I said flatly.

"We need to have coffee."

"Maybe in a few weeks."

"I'm downstairs. You can see us from the window. Dad drove me. He schlepped to the city so of course, he's shvitzing. Here's a tissue, Phil."

I had blasted her. But I should've guessed she'd show up.

"He can turn on the air-conditioning."

271

"He won't touch the air-conditioning."

"Why not?"

"He doesn't put on the air-conditioning until Father's Day."

"Is Dad joining us for coffee?"

"No. I'll make it quick."

I met my mother on the sidewalk. I waved to my dad in the car. After all the years I held my tongue, I had told her off and she was acting like nothing had happened. Was she impenetrable? I was amazed. We went to Robertson's, the first place we hit. The café had an odd cachet: Robertson's made a huge deal about the fact that they didn't offer any cream or milk for coffee because their coffee is so superb, it yearns to be black. I know. I never got it either. We didn't care about coffee anyway. We settled in two twill chairs, big backs, rolled arms, facing each other. We had no need for actual coffee. Coffee is always a ruse.

"I'm here to apologize," she said, straight-out.

Whoa. Was this my mom or someone else's mom?

I sucked her words in.

She was impatient. "So?"

I looked up at the ceiling—heaven help me—wishing she had given me a day or two to recover. "Mom, I had to tell you. You have to stop. You lead your life. And I will lead mine."

"I only want the best for you." The last words of every verbal abuser.

"I understand. But you don't know what the best is. And neither do I."

"What does that mean?" She tapped on the table and actually sounded annoyed. Apparently, she wanted to apologize as long as I accepted without a response. *Stop analyzing. You know her like she is your own mother.*

Lightly, I grasped her tapping fingers. "I thought Eric was the best. But he wasn't. I thought closing myself off was best. But it isn't. I have to allow life to come at me."

"Margo lets life come at her," Mom commented.

"Right. And Stephanie planned everything."

"I know. I kick myself every day because I thought Rob could do no wrong."

"No one is perfect, Mom. Even Rob had a rub."

She sniffled. "I will try. Although they say you can't teach an old dog new tricks."

"You're not an old dog."

"I'm not a young dog. When will I see you?" she asked.

I stood up and took a bow. "You're seeing me now."

She clapped her hands together. "You're right."

My new congenial mom. The last time she agreed with me, she was lactating, and I was bawling with hunger from the crib.

My father was asleep in the driver's seat, snoring loud as reveille. He shook himself into consciousness when Mom slid in.

He looked at me and grumbled, "Everything okay now?"

I didn't want to disappoint him. "Wonderful."

As long as you buy a clamp for Mom's mouth.

Chapter 29

As I passed by his office on the first Monday in June, Steinbach waved me in while on the phone. His silver glasses were low on his nose, and he was dressed casually in a short-sleeve solid shirt. I sat across from him, peering out the window at the New Jersey skyline. I had been the ultimate welcome mat, but that had changed, and never more so than when Steinbach would end his call and offer me what I deserved.

"How are you?" he said to me as he hung up.

"Great."

"I would like your opinion."

Good start.

He handed me a white business card. I assumed it belonged to a prospective client—as in "Here's his card, Lauren. I think we can land him."

I flipped the card over. Unexpectedly, it was a Steinbach Kraus card.

Dead center, it said, Lauren Leo, Executive Vice President/ Account Service.

I ran my thumb over the card. I didn't understand. I was vice president. Now I was executive vice president. What did that mean?

What happened to partner? No longer shy about what I needed, I asked directly. "What does this mean?"

"Congratulations. We've never had a woman in this position before. Your achievement is a first. What's more, the board intends to bring your name up for partnership at the weeklong retreat next spring."

He rose to shake my hand. I crossed my arms and remained seated. Did he think he could slither off? If I were a man, I would have made partner. It was that simple. And Steinbach? Full of it. The whole seafood lunch was a fraud. He should croak on an oyster cracker and sleep with the fishes. I maintained my calm, my pleasant facial expression. I thought before I spoke. "I wonder—will there be any new partners this year?"

"Yes."

I tried to think of someone worthy of the honor. Duh?

"Matt Hutchins." Steinbach said the name the way someone roots for a team at a game. Go Matt Hutchins.

Steinbach had to be kidding. Hutchins a partner—that blowhard. My billings were higher. I was the one Steinbach relied on. I had built New England Can into one of the most profitable clients. Even my less significant accounts were gangbusters. No point in mentioning that to Steinbach now. I was fuming, angry enough to scream it, but the news was not going to change the outcome.

Hutchins. Hutchins was gifted International Tool (how appropriate) when Steinbach realized he had played lacrosse at Yale with the chief executive officer of the company. What did Hutchins have that I didn't have? A lacrosse stick and a penis.

Had this same abominable scenario occurred months before, I would have said thank you, hid my sourpuss, gone back to my desk, a good girl as Steinbach liked to say, to plot my next move. But back then, I wouldn't have asked for partnership in the first place.

I looked directly at him, almost into him. "This won't do."

"You know how I feel about you, Lauren. I tried. It's out of my hands."

I wanted to cram the card he had given me down his throat, but I thought that was overdramatic. Not overreacting—just overdramatic.

"Steinbach. I have been here eighteen years, and you just asked for another twelve months."

"We're giving you a raise."

I smiled. "And I'm giving you a little something as well."

He pushed his glasses up his nose. "What would that be?"

I stood. "A discrimination case."

"You wouldn't."

I tore the card, dropped the pieces. "I was passed over for partner because I'm a woman."

He pointed at me. "Lauren, you came on to me."

True. But I was no longer embarrassed by my posttraumatic actions.

"You sue for discrimination, and I'll sue for sexual harassment. You unbuttoned your top, button by button."

I made my voice sound like smoke. "I had no choice. Your heat was too high."

He played with the narrow collar on his shirt. He knew everyone would believe me. Corey Steinbach had a track record. Maybe not in the office specifically, but generally around the world.

"I quit," I said.

∽

I aimed for the street. I wanted to eat, to chew, to reduce the tension. I lingered in front of the window at DeLorenzo's, an Italian bakery, admiring the cannoli. I could have one, I thought. But I knew I would order many. I pictured myself mentioning I had friends coming over. Why did I care what the person behind the counter thought? She was happy to make the sale. I wasn't going to do it. I walked on.

Margo was at home, sweeping the kitchen. How did she know which side of the broom to use?

"I was passed over for partner." I was sullen, sulking.

She struck the wall with the broom. "Oh. That piece of rubbish."

"I deserve partnership. If I were a man, I would be a partner."

She propped me up. "If you were a man, you would own the place."

Maybe not that place, I thought, *but a place.* I liked that she had faith in me.

"What did you do?"

"Ahh. I quit." And that's when it sank in.

Margo leaned on the broom. "Who quits without another job lined up?"

What, was she channeling my parents? I knew that was what they would say.

"Far Acres, here I come," I shouted. "New England Can is a great opportunity."

She didn't say a word. Not good.

"Margo, help me here."

"I'll drive up on weekends—if I don't have a show and Stephanie lends me a car?"

I poured a Doctor Zhivago—vodka and diet Dr Pepper—at Grandma's bar cabinet, picked up my phone, called George Moore, and scheduled an appointment for the next day at eight thirty a.m. Maybe I had been brash quitting on the spot. I should have taken time to consider what I wanted to do, but I knew I had the Can in my back pocket.

Margo poured chardonnay over ice so it would be fewer calories. "When you were going to get married, you considered starting your own agency—like that woman you worked for in college."

"That was so I could manage my life the way I wanted. Besides, my boss way back then was a whirlwind, began with one retail account, wound up with divisions of Procter and Gamble. We called her Sage M. because she moved up so fast, there wasn't time to say her whole name."

"You are a whirlwind."

"Not really." I was no Sage.

"Clink my glass."

We clinked.

"You went back to work the day after you were left at the altar. Your biggest client offered you a job when your boss is his friend. Which, you have to admit, is a moral failing you might want to think about."

"Business is business. Steinbach would play the game the same way as George."

"Really? Then how do you know George wouldn't pull a Steinbach? How many women are in executive positions at New England Can?"

"He's offering partnership."

"When? When I win the Tony, the Oscar, and the Emmy? Promises, promises. Seems there are a lot of roadblocks on the way to becoming a partner."

"What would you have me do?"

She clinked my glass again. "Start your own agency. I promise to be in all the commercials."

Easy for her to say. She was a dreamer. She didn't have a clue what was involved and the investment it would take.

Chapter 30

I rented a Zipcar, a blue Honda Accord, and headed north. At first, it felt good to drive. There was a difference between driving and being driven, a sense of self-empowerment and self-control. I tuned in to a news channel on Sirius. An actress I never heard of was leaving a reality star I never heard of for his twin brother. Now in the car alone, without Rudy to chat with, the trip was monotonous and stretched like putty. I felt as though I were pushing the car—uphill. When I first met Rudy, he jabbered too much. But conversing with him became my survival skill, and I looked forward to it. I reviewed all that had happened. If a palm reader had predicted the future, I would've told her she was out of her mind. I certainly never dreamed of Rudy. I wanted him back in my life. I had to reach out.

I pulled over at Best Bakery Ever. I phoned Rudy, anxious he would see my number and ignore the call, more panicked he would pick up and say he had nothing to discuss with me. I left a message asking him to call. A haggard woman bent over a walker stepped slowly, carefully out of the shop. At the end of the ramp, she stopped to catch her breath, then reached into a small paper bag for a donut. I talked to myself.

There but for the grace. You will not go in that bakery. It is not your place. You will remain in the car. You will drive straight to Far Acres. And that's what I did. One bakery down. One bakery at a time.

At New England Can, a prepped-out assistant led me to George's office. George, sporting his company polo shirt, was at his conference table.

He smiled. "Glad you're here, Lauren. Take a seat. What's the verdict?"

I stalled for a moment, reassuring myself.

"Good to see you, George. I was truly moved by your generous offer." Nice speech, Lauren. Now what? As I paused, I heard Margo in my head. "I came here because I was planning to accept the position, but I've decided to remain in New York."

"I sweetened the pot as much as I could."

His offer had given me the courage to ask for what I deserved. And when I was denied it, I knew where I stood, realized I had the power to grow elsewhere, to build my career into whatever I wanted it to be. Where I wanted it to be.

I felt like I had let down a friend. "I appreciate your confidence in me."

"You're a New York woman. You don't want to leave the city behind."

"Honestly, it's not the city. It's my family."

"So we will continue as client and agency," he said warmly.

"You haven't spoken to Steinbach?" I was surprised.

"I have a phone meeting with him later this morning."

What? Steinbach had missed the opportunity to spin my departure before I did?

"I've left the agency."

"Well, where are you going? Which agency? Perhaps I'll go with you."

What? The business relationship between Steinbach and George had existed since the day Steinbach hung a sign on the door.

I heard Margo's voice. *You're a whirlwind.*

"I'm launching my own agency." I thought of all I had to do. I needed a desk. And an office to put it in. Most of all, I needed a client.

He smiled. "Good for you."

"Thank you, George."

"Nothing like your own place."

I smiled. He smiled. I spoke in the language of sports, because George enjoyed that: "Here's to meeting around the track."

He tilted back in his chair. I had jumped the gun. He wasn't finished with our discussion.

"I'd like to switch agencies—from Steinbach Kraus to you."

My eyes popped as George spoke. Had I heard wrong? No, he'd said it. He wanted his business to go to me. But what should I say next? Accept and then tell the truth, Lauren.

I stood, walked over to him, and put out my hand. "Well, George, no one will work harder for you than me."

"I know that. That's why I am giving you the account."

"George, I have to be honest. You would be my first client."

"I like coming in first. If I can't hire you to work here for me directly, why not hire your firm?"

Exactly. Why not?

He smirked. "Of course you lose the car, the down payment on a house . . ."

"The dental coverage too?" I joked.

"Poor you," he said sarcastically. "All you get is your agency fee."

My teeth could rot.

⌒⌒

I was triumphant. I blasted the radio. I sang every song super loud. I tapped on the steering wheel. When I got to New York, I was surprised there wasn't a ticker-tape parade for me down Fifth Avenue. I checked my phone to see if Rudy had called. Nothing.

In my apartment, Margo was at Grandma's bar cabinet with a joint.

"I got a part." Margo Lamour sang a few rounds of "Hallelujah" by Leonard Cohen.

"In what? In a play?" Amazing. On the same day, we both had success that would change our lives.

"In a drama, Off-Broadway. The piece I did the reading for. Remember the night I had my theater friends over? The director Robinson Mulvaney? The play is being produced."

"I thought Mulvaney only wanted you for the reading, and he needed a bigger name for the actual play."

She howled, like a wolf at the moon. "He said it, but he didn't mean it."

"You were that good."

"I was that good. I have other news," Margo said, unable to stop talking. "My blood sugar is way down. Between the medications, the exercise, and the food plan, my count is normal. I hope that doesn't mean I have to become a normal person too."

"I don't think you'll ever have to worry about that. But the blood sugar is terrific."

"I get a lot of support at the program. Would you like to tag along with me?"

"I thought you didn't want company because you're attracted to men with heart stents. Or some preexisting condition."

"You can come to the meeting at the hospital with me," she said.

"Okay, I will. Are you ready for my announcement?"

She went downcast. "Not really. When are you moving?"

I yelped, "I'm staying in the city."

She went full wattage. "When did you decide?"

"In George's office. You pushed all the right buttons last night."

"That's what sisters are for."

"And I knew I could do it."

She hugged me. The joint fell on the floor, but she actually picked it up and snuffed it in a cereal bowl she was using as an ashtray.

I jiggled my sister with both arms. "Margo, I'm starting my own agency."

She shook me back. She shrieked.

"And sit down." I pushed her onto the couch. "I have my first client!"

Her eyes went wide. "It's New England Can!"

"Yes! Here's to porta potties!" If I shouted any louder, I would be evicted. But I was so excited, I probably wouldn't notice.

Margo flipped her head dramatically. "To my first role in a commercial for porta potties!"

"To my first client—and my next and my next."

~❧~

I reached Kate in Chicago. She was waiting for a massage at a day spa, so I guess she was doing well. Kate was concerned Steinbach would sue me for nabbing his account. I told her I had an ace in my pocket.

"I'll sue for discrimination. I have a case—and he knows it. I'd like to see him explain why after eighteen years I'm not a partner, but lo and behold, Matt Hutchins is suddenly a principal in a company led exclusively by men."

"Are you going to pitch any more of his accounts?"

"First of all, I didn't pitch New England Can. George Moore pitched me. I'm not initiating calls to former clients. But I am eager to see who gets in touch."

"Congratulations, Madwoman. My masseuse is beckoning. I better see you at the reunion. You can start working hard after that."

"Call Stephanie next," Margo said. "She was praying you wouldn't take the job, but she refused to butt in."

"She told you that?"

"Stephanie and I are sisters."

Stephanie was in the car, returning from karate with Olivia and Liza. A shout went up.

"Thanks, fans," I said. "By the way, what did you learn at karate?"

"Nothing," Olivia said.

Stephanie said, "That's not true. We learned a yellow belt costs Mommy thirty dollars."

"That yellow belt is on me. All belts—even seat belts—are on me!"

I stood on my terrace. My mind wandered to Rudy. His absence in my life made me want to fill out a missing person's report. I checked my phone. No sign of him. I thought of reaching out again.

No. Rudy knew my number.

Chapter 31

Buzzing with thoughts about my new business venture, I pulled on my prehistoric straight-leg jeans. I added a well-worn camp shirt tattered at the neckline, the logo—a pine tree—cracking. It had been two days since I had decided to launch my own agency, and despite everything I had to do, I was going to the camp reunion. I was gung ho for seeing my longtime friends, joining Kate and her guy, the periodontist. She said he had nice teeth.

I missed Rudy, especially at a time when I had so much to share. I became obsessive, visualizing how awesome it would be if Rudy and I had patched things up and he was attending the reunion with me. The long trip to Stormville, New York, would have slipped by as though the length of a television commercial. Without a doubt, I would want to drive. As I opened Rudy's passenger door, I would ask if he preferred flat or sparkling water. Once we got off the highway, we'd stop at a store to stock up on liquor. Immediately after Frieda's Famous Hot Dogs, there would be a weathered sign on rusty hinges—WELCOME TO CAMP RABBI YITZHAK CHAIM. A solid American name for a sleepaway camp. I would bear right, onto a gravel road, sheltered from sun by foliage, abundant oaks and maples. We would pass the crystal lake, fronted by a crescent beach, scented with pine. I would steer up a verdant hill to the center of camp, point out the green bunks, their porches where I'd told my secrets to Kate. We'd park in a field near the recreation hall. I would introduce Rudy to my friends. We would unload our weekend luggage, the bottomless stash of scotch, vodka, and wine.

Enough daydreaming. In my living room, Margo was pacing as she rehearsed her lines. She paused long enough to give me a sister bear hug, wish me a good time. I rolled my travel case to the sidewalk, stopping to search for the Metro-North train ticket, buried in my straw bag. I caught sight of a black Escalade cruising toward me. Rudy? I became warm, flushed with excitement. Until I saw the woman driver.

I fished out my phone. I had to try calling him again.

"It's me," I said.

"Hello, you."

"Do you think we could talk?"

Rudy was nonchalant. "Matter of fact, I was on my way over."

"You were?" He was?

"Can you wait fifteen minutes?"

I could wait fifteen days.

I stared at the time passing on my phone as though counting down before a space launch. Rudy pulled to the curb. His wavy hair was slicked back. Was that how he wore it in warmer weather? He climbed out of the car in a white textured golf shirt, black jeans, no socks, loafers. I liked his sunglasses, but I wished I could see his eyes. We ambled toward each other. I was delighted he had shown up. I prayed it wasn't because Steinbach's assistant had emptied my office before I had the chance and had asked Rudy to drop off my belongings.

"I'm glad to see you. Relieved you answered my call."

Rudy stroked his chin. "Honestly, I was about to call you. I'm wondering if we could speak?"

I soaked him in. I had a lot to say. The first words being, "I'm sorry."

Just then, Allie, eight months pregnant, exited the Max, button-holing us at exactly the wrong time. Allie was wearing an army-green maternity tent instead of her usual body-sharing leotard, her long brown hair scrunched and frizzy. I'd never seen her like this. She always straightened her hair. Allie glanced at her tummy several times to make sure the baby was still there.

"What's going on?" I knew she was not herself. Something was askew.

"I don't feel well. At all. I reached the doctor. She told me to go to the hospital."

I was alarmed. "Is Marc around?"

"At a convention. I left him a message. He's on his way back to the city."

I was dying to know why Rudy had shown up. No matter the reason, this was my chance to explain myself, to make up with him. Except there was no way I was allowing Allie to grab a taxi to the hospital alone. "I'll go with you, Allie."

"Really?" She was surprised—and relieved.

I turned to Rudy. "I'm sorry I can't talk right now. I really want to, but . . ."

"Climb in—I'm driving," Rudy said, pointing to the Escalade.

His offer warmed me all over. Allie and I followed him to the car without a question.

I suggested Allie sit in front because I felt it would be comfortable. Rudy took her hand and helped her in. I'd been a fool—dashing off after that Friday night dinner, stalking out of the truck stop, fighting off affection for fear of being hurt again. Who knew what he thought now or what he had come to say to me? I wasn't inquiring in front of Allie.

From the rear, I offered Allie a bottle of water, but she declined. Blocks down, the traffic light was green, but cars were bumper to bumper, in a standstill. No reason to be worked up. We were tried-and-true New Yorkers. As we waited, I thought how miraculous it felt to be back in the Escalade with Rudy—but then I noticed drivers stepping out of cars to see what was causing the delay. We'd been idling for a half hour. I monitored Allie, perspiration dripping on the back of her neck. I removed my seat belt. I massaged her shoulders.

"I wonder what's happening?" Allie stared forward.

I imagined the standstill traffic dividing somehow to let us through. "New York is happening."

"Not much to do," Rudy said calmly. "The president is in town. Who knows what else?"

Some time passed. Allie began to moan, softly, as though trying to keep it to herself.

"Allie?" Don't tell me she's in labor.

Allie shrieked. "Please, please. Get me to the hospital."

"Okay, okay." I was frightened for her, startled. I shook my head to calm down.

Rudy surveyed the situation, craning forward, figuring a way out of the jam. He cut the wheel to the left so we would be near the sidewalk in order to pull over if necessary. Horns blew—bad, long honks; hoots; beeps emanating behind us. Allie glued both hands on her mouth. She never turned to look. She stared ahead. We were wedged in. I pictured the only way out— soaring over the hoods of the other cars, landing where the traffic cleared.

I was sweating and had no idea what to do. I panicked about delivering Allie's baby in the car. I had never seen an emergency birth, except in movies where the women always knew what to do and menfolk paced in another room.

"I'll call an ambulance," Rudy said. "911. That's the only way."

"Lauren, can you reach Marc?" Allie said. "He's on his way from Philadelphia."

Answer the phone. Answer the phone, Marc. I left a terse message.

Allie was huffing, puffing. I assumed it was Lamaze. I leaned toward her seat, blew in and out, following her rhythm, hoping my accompaniment might help. We heard sirens. I could see an ambulance way behind us. A Lincoln Town Car crept onto the sidewalk. A Jeep

followed. Motorists turned their vehicles, making room for the respond-
ers. I steeled myself, remaining calm.

I moved to the seat behind Rudy. "I have faith in you."

"No pressure there," he said and laughed.

Rudy stepped out of the Escalade. Where was he going? He climbed
onto the front hood, waving his hands high to direct the oncoming
ambulance our way.

I shifted into the driver's seat in order to comfort Allie. "It's going
to be okay."

"Everyone always says that."

"What? What do they say?"

"It's going to be okay. We don't know it's going to be okay."

I insisted, "Allie, it's going to be okay."

I rubbed her hand in my palm.

"We're calling him Karson. K-A-R-S-O-N."

"Great idea," I said. "You'll save money. He'll never find a souvenir
with his name on it."

Allie blubbered as she said, "Lauren, consider your cat fed forever."

At long last, the ambulance arrived. Rudy stepped off the hood.
I hustled out of the car, rushing toward the EMT. Her badge said
Sophia Gomez.

"She's in labor." I had been somewhat calm, but now that help had
arrived, I was shaking.

Another EMT. Tall, lanky, in his forties.

"Which hospital?" I asked. "I have to leave a message for her
husband."

Someone said the name of some obscure hospital as Allie was lifted
onto the gurney.

"I never heard of that place. Can't we take her to Presbyterian? I
think that's where her doctor is." I'd lived in New York long enough to
recognize that if I didn't know the name of a hospital, I didn't want my
friend giving birth there.

I held my breath.

Gomez agreed.

Relieved but needing to reassure myself, I said, "Okay, Presbyterian it is. All right if I ride to Presbyterian with her?"

Gomez had a sense of humor. "Yes. And what was the name of the hospital again?"

Once Allie was in the ambulance, I turned to Rudy, touching his arm, "Thank you. I want to talk as soon as we can."

He nodded. "We will."

In the ambulance, I was on a bench with a seat belt across me. "Should I call your mother, Allie?"

"Yes." She rattled off the number.

When Allie's mom answered, I spoke rapid-fire. She said, "Tell my little girl I'm on the way."

Allie gritted her teeth. I held her hand, attempting to soothe her. A siren blared, the loudest I had ever heard. We moved a bit, a bit more, then picked up speed, so I knew we were in the clear. I kept repeating, "We're almost there. You're doing fine. Everything will be okay."

We bolted through emergency. Not long after, Allie's mom rushed toward us. She was wearing a suit, heels. Black mascara ran down her cheeks.

"Allie, your mom's here," I told her.

There was a visitors' room on the maternity floor. I settled in a chair. Marc rang. He was making good time on the Garden State Parkway. I paced. I paced some more. There was a man with a little boy popping a colorful rubber toy in and out, an older woman in a sari.

Rudy appeared, his eyes darting around the drab room.

"Rudy," I shouted as though blocks away. I dashed to him. He caught me in his arms.

"I had to find out how she was," he said.

"I'm waiting."

"Do you want anything?"

He was asking, and I was speaking up this time. "To be here with you—and to wait."

He grinned and took my hand. *Have my hand,* I thought. *Keep it. It's yours.*

I clued him in. "Her mom is with her."

"She got here fast. Did Marc call?"

"Yes, he's on his way."

"It's beyond my imagination how devastated he must feel to miss the birth of his first child."

I love you, I thought.

Time crept. At last, an older physician in blue scrubs appeared at the door, scanned the room. I poked Rudy. I could feel this doctor was looking for us. We shot over.

Before we could introduce ourselves, he said, "Congratulations. Allie had a boy."

"It's a boy," I shouted as though Allie hadn't told us the baby's name in the car.

"Mom is doing well in the recovery room." The doctor spoke quickly, sprinting off as though he had a flight to catch.

Rudy reached out and held me close. I hugged him thinking I would never let go. After all, I'd had a baby with this man.

"Let's get some air," he said, clasping my hand.

Without another word, we were outside, on the street. I couldn't wait any longer. I pulled Rudy aside, away from passing people, less than an inch between us.

"I'm sorry about the truck stop," I said.

He whispered in my ear. "No need to rehash."

So I rehashed. "I was afraid to become involved after . . ."

"Experiencing my meat sweats?"

We smiled at one another.

"Exactly."

"Rudy, what did you want to say this morning?"

"This morning? That seems like days ago."

"It was only this morning."

"I drove Steinbach and Hutchins to the airport. A lot of chatter about your resignation. As I listened in, I realized I had to see you. I had to tell you why I overreacted when we had coffee."

"I'm the one who—"

"When you told me about the offer in Massachusetts, I was disappointed. I was anxious that your sudden, inconvenient move would end our relationship. But I realized I wanted to be with you. I was willing to go with you—to Far Acres. To the farthest acres."

No clue how my heart still fit in my chest.

I wrapped myself around him. "Rudy, I'm not moving."

"You're not?" He swooped me up off the ground. He planted a kiss. Another. Another. He placed me back on earth. "But Steinbach . . ."

"I turned down the position. I'm launching my own agency. Here. In the city."

I opened my arms wide to the world like I owned the town.

He was taken aback. "That explains it. That's why Steinbach told Hutchins he would not squabble with you over clients or anything else."

"He said that?" Every so often, you're just having a good day.

"He said he couldn't risk a discrimination case."

We kissed for a long time. But not long enough.

Suddenly, Rudy asked, "Why were you carrying a suitcase?"

"This morning? I was leaving for the reunion at my summer camp."

"Are you still going?"

"Come with me," I said as I tugged on his shirt.

"Hmm. Do I get to sleep on a bunk bed?"

I played along. "Rudy Cohen, are you coming on to me?"

"One more question," he teased, "before I decide."

"Okay," I laughed.

"How's the pool?"

"I brought my swimsuit."

Acknowledgments

I have a lot of people to thank. Is it okay if the acknowledgments are longer than the novel?

First of all, hats off to you—the reader. I hope *Crazy to Leave You* lightened your day.

A standing ovation to Danielle Marshall, editorial director of Lake Union Publishing, for seeing the promise in this story and choosing to edit my work; Joelle Delbourgo, literary agent to the stars; and Tiffany Martin Yates, developmental wunderkind.

Also, author Jennifer Belle, at the helm of the workshop I attend every week, along with my fellow writers Melanie Jennings, Amy Lorowitz, Andrew Delaney, Joan Leinwoll, Angela Dorn, Erin Hussein, and Marie Pramaggiore.

Curtain calls for the advice of Sharyn Rothstein, my first-favorite playwright. Also, Lanie Robinson, my second-favorite playwright.

I am grateful to everyone at Lake Union Publishing, including Gabriella T. Dumpit, Nicole Burns-Ascue, Stacy Abrams, and Jill Schoenhaut.

Shout-outs to my buddies, the novelists at Blue Sky Book Chat, for the trumpets every time: Bette Lee Crosby, Patricia Sands, Barbara Davis, Lainey Cameron, Peggy Lampman, Alison Ragsdale, Lisa Ann Braxton, and Aimie K. Runyan-Vetter.

I am overwhelmed by the supportive and generous authors I have encountered on this journey, including Thelma Adams, Lisa Barr, Jamie

Brenner, Barbara Claypole White, Gabi Coatsworth, Jane Healey, Jan Crossen, Fiona Davis, Maddie Dawson, Mandy L. Haynes, Kristan Higgins, Kerry Anne King, Camille Di Maio, Camille Pagán, Rochelle Weinstein, Amy Poeppel, Sophfronia Scott, Meredith Schorr, Loretta Nyhan, Eldonna Edwards, Deborah Mantella, Renee Rosen, Rebecca Warner, Yona Zeldis McDonough, Meryl Ain, Judy Keim, Jacqueline Berkell Friedland, and Elaine Neil Orr.

Gratitude to the book mavens: Ann-Marie Nieves, Andrea Peskin Katz, Laura Blank Margolin, Suzanne Leopold Weinstein, Linda Levack Zagon, Susan Peterson, Barbara Bos, Kate Rock, Tonni Callan, Kate Vocke, Kristy Barrett, Annie McDonnell, Denise Birt, Sheree Janovic Kun, Jeanne Frederickson, Jennifer Gans Blankfein, and so many more.

I tip my tiara to Kathy L. Murphy, founder of the International Pulpwood Queens and Timber Guys Reading Nation. My gratitude to Lake Union Authors and the Women's Fiction Writers Association.

Shalom to the Jewish Book Council. What a delight to meet readers at Jewish Community Centers (where I enjoy speaking much more than I would exercising).

Here's to Alison Barto for ongoing neighborly advice in two states—and her son Ben Barto for placing my novel in the hands of the *Mona Lisa*. Martha Paley Francescato, you are a gift.

I thank my sisters: Debbie Simon—and her editorial assistant, Jay Johnson—for the brilliant red pencil and Sandra Simon Klein for listening to me complain or kvell (whatever the occasion calls for).

To my daughters, the aforementioned Sharyn Rothstein and the daring Marisa Rothstein: I strive to follow in your footsteps.

Jeff Lesh and Nolan Robinson—keep pouring.

Lucien Parker Lesh, Francesca Dare Lesh, and Sydney Leanne Robinson—I could write a book about how much I love you.

Honest Leo and Frieda Simon of blessed memory: I hit the jackpot to have you as parents.

And most of all—thank you, Alan Miles Rothstein.

About the Author

Marilyn Simon Rothstein is the author of *Lift and Separate*, winner of the STAR Award for Outstanding Debut presented by the Women's Fiction Writers Association, and a second novel, *Husbands and Other Sharp Objects*. She grew up in New York City, earned a degree in journalism from New York University, began her writing career at *Seventeen* magazine, married a man she met in an elevator, and owned an advertising agency for more than twenty-five years. Marilyn received an MA in liberal studies from Wesleyan University and an MA in Judaic studies from the University of Connecticut. For more information, visit www.marilynsimonrothstein.com.